DESTRUCTION

JENNIFER BENE

DESTRUCTION

A DARK ROMANCE

JENNIFER BENE

ISBN (e-book): 978-1-946722-16-4

ISBN (paperback): 978-1-946722-19-5

Cover design by Laura Hidalgo, Beyond DEF Lit.
https://www.beyonddeflit.com/

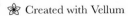 Created with Vellum

This book has dark romance in its veins. I loved the characters the first time they came into my head, in an old short story, but I knew I hadn't written their story the way I needed to. With 'Destruction' this story is right. You may recognize components of it if you've read all of my older work, but in this new book the characters come alive. They are here in all the dark and twisted glory they were meant to be, and I hope you love it, lovelies.

Chapter One

LIANNA

"What do you mean you're not coming home?" Walking towards the table, Lianna dropped her laptop bag and purse onto it, squeezing the phone tighter as his sigh brushed across the line.

"Lianna, I already explained this. I have a meeting that I cannot miss."

"That's the same thing you said the last time we planned a trip and you canceled it." Her heels echoed across the tile as she started pacing, a harried *clicking* that only seemed to file her nerves down even further.

"Business comes before fun, princess." The words were barely out of his mouth before she heard someone else talking to him, muffled and indiscernible. His answer came through loud and clear, "Yes, arrange it. No, I don't want to wait until the morning."

"Dad," she tried to interrupt him, but he didn't hear her. He'd pulled the phone away from his ear, talking to someone he valued enough to take with him, while she suffered another minute of his low muttering across the line.

This is such bullshit.

Raising her voice, she spoke again, "Dad, I'm hanging up."

"I'm here." Another of his quiet sighs. "Look, I will make this up to you. Why don't you go shopping with one of your friends this weekend? Or keep the reservations and take some of them skiing like we planned."

"Why didn't you bring me with you?" Her question came out steady, even though his words stung. He was trying to placate her with petty distractions like he always did, when all she wanted was a little time with him, a taste of how things used to be — but instead she was alone, chewing her thumbnail and destroying her manicure.

Her father stayed silent, not even a sigh this time.

More useless pacing, heel to toe. *Click. Click. Click.* Around and around the island in the kitchen as she waited him out. A negotiation tactic that *he* had taught her. Never fill silence when you want an answer.

"I'll try to be back by Sunday. We can go to dinner, just the two of us."

Lianna stopped in place, laughing bitterly as she stared up at the lights in the ceiling until her eyes watered from their brightness. *Of course he wouldn't answer her.* "I don't know why you wanted me to work for you if you're not going to trust me with anything that's actually important."

"Don't be petulant, Lianna. You've been involved in over half of our acquisitions in the past two years, worked on multi-million dollar mergers, and that's more than most people will do in a lifetime. You should be grateful—"

"Grateful?" Her fingers ached with how hard she gripped the phone, and she swallowed down the anger that swelled whenever he used his favorite phrase.

"I do not have time for this, Lianna, we need to take off."

"Fine. Then enjoy your flight." Ripping the phone away from her ear, she pressed her thumb to the end button and then tossed it onto the granite countertop. It skidded, spun, bumped into the blender and finally stopped.

It should have felt satisfying to hang up on him. Throwing the phone should have eased some of the rage inside her, but it hadn't done anything worthwhile. If anything, the bitter anger was fading into simple bitterness, tinged with sadness — which was worse.

Tears stung her eyes and this time she couldn't even blame the bright lights because she was staring at the floor, at her shiny, black Louboutins that were a stark contrast to the pale tile. She was still dressed for the office, in a form fitting skirt suit that would have worked perfectly for the dinner at Silver Den they were *supposed* to be having in an hour and a half.

She'd picked it out just in case they'd both worked late, the ivory Dior top was meant for transitioning from office to evening, but it didn't matter anymore.

"You are not going to act like some child upset because her daddy left. You are not going to fucking cry," she hissed the words to the air above, a promise already broken as she felt the damp on her cheeks.

You should be grateful.

"Damn you!" Lianna shouted, scrubbing at the tears on her cheeks as she turned to look across the quiet penthouse apartment.

To say it was beautiful was an understatement. Two floors of custom designed perfection, and room by room, item by item, she'd slowly transformed it until it no longer resembled her childhood home. Practically every piece of furniture, every piece of art, had been chosen by her. It was still her father's home though. He owned it, *hell*, he owned the entire fucking building, and she shouldn't be staying here anyway. Shouldn't have agreed to redesign the apartment. Shouldn't have agreed to get the MBA, shouldn't have agreed to work for him…

Shoulda, woulda, coulda.

Muttering to herself, she walked to the stairs, taunted by her heels echoing in the silence. So, she tore them off before she went upstairs. It only took a few minutes to trade the nice clothes for pajamas, and by the time she'd washed her face and put her hair up the anger had left her completely.

Now, she just felt a heavy weight settling over her. Standing at the top of the stairs, looking out over the dim apartment, only made it worse. She was too aware of all the empty space. It was too much room for one person. Too much for even two people, and for the millionth time she questioned why she kept staying here during the week when she had her own place. Her apartment was smaller, warmer, and it wasn't thirty-two stories up and atop her father's company.

But the commute was a hell of a lot easier from here.

The not so subtle rumble of her stomach beckoned her

back to the kitchen, and she rifled around in the freezer until she found one of the pre-packaged meals from the delivery service her father preferred. As the oven started to heat up she sat down at the table and plucked her laptop from her bag.

By the time the oven beeped to tell her it was pre-heated she was already deep in email, pulling documents from the shared drive to review them before she answered one of their department heads. It was only the insistent tug of her stomach that finally made her stand up and pop the dish in the oven so it would heat up.

Staring at the papers scattered over the rustic wooden table, she sighed in a way that reminded her of her father's trademark exasperation. No matter what she did, no matter how hard she tried — at the end of the day she still wanted to make him proud.

All of the work spread out on the table made her remember times when she'd sat in the chair in his office and played with important papers, pretended to type on his computer, legs swinging because she was too small to touch the floor. Back then she'd just wanted to be like him, that was true... but now she wanted him to *respect* her, to value the work she did for the company, the time she put in. Wanted to prove to every asshole in the company that gave her the side-eye when she held meetings or walked the halls that despite being the daughter of the CEO she was still *earning* her position.

Which was exactly why she was working at eight o'clock on a Thursday night when she was technically supposed to be on vacation already.

Not like the vacation was on anymore.

She should really call Patricia and have her cancel everything. That would be the nice thing to do since they wouldn't be arriving, and just the idea of trying to get people together to go felt exhausting. Her father had told her to hang out with friends, but if he ever paid attention he would notice she never had time for that anymore. It had been weeks since she'd even met up for a happy hour or a spa day. Two years post-grad school and she was as much of a workaholic as her father.

Success is never handed to you, princess, you have to reach out and take it.

Another snippet of her father's wisdom playing on a loop in her head, outlining the cutthroat business mind that had made him such a success. But when had he become her inner monologue? When had his ideas, his goals, overwhelmed her own?

As she sent off the email she'd been working on, she pulled up her personal email and flipped through the various correspondence she'd had with art museums and auction houses around the world. A handful had responded to her inquiries of open positions with some interest, and her fingers itched to answer one. To pursue her own dreams instead of her father's.

Guilt gnawed at her as she re-read the response from Sotheby's in Lyon, France. Her French wasn't perfect, but it had apparently been good enough to garner a response and they seemed very interested in speaking with her — which felt like an impossible dream.

Impossible because it would involve leaving her father. Not just leaving him, but leaving the country, and it had been just the two of them for too long.

He would never let you do it.

The smell of smoke jerked her out of her reveries and Lianna jumped to her feet, rushing to the oven to turn it off. Opening the door let out stinging, acrid smoke and she grabbed the potholder to rip out the ruined meal so she could slam the oven closed.

Staring at the blackened dish of what had been chicken and vegetable couscous she tossed the offensive thing into the trash and walked to the wine fridge in defeat.

It had been a shit day, and calories were calories, right?

At least she couldn't ruin wine.

Chapter Two

DAVID

Leaning forward, David stared at the monitor and wondered if she could feel his hate, his rage. At the very least her ears should be burning underneath all that blonde hair. Hell, she should burst into fucking flames.

Everything about her was so clean. Tidy. Neat.

But every pristine inch of that place was coated in blood, and so was she. It didn't matter how pretty they packaged it, rebranded it, covered it up. It still reeked of death. Corruption.

Movement on the other screen distracted him and he glanced over to see Harry walking around the cell, eyes on the ceiling like he was checking on everything one last time. As he left the room, David flicked off the first monitor and rose to meet him in the hall.

"Everything looks good. Were you able to get the wiring finished last night?"

"Yes, and I've run a few tests this morning. It's just fine.

Liam did a good job on the ceiling." David lifted his chin towards the room. "How's the door?"

"It would be easier for someone to drill through the concrete than break that door down. Same as the others." Harry shrugged his shoulders. "But as I told you before, seems a bit of overkill."

"I don't leave things to chance."

A short, barked laugh made Harry flush under his baseball cap. "If you're going after who I think you are, then you're already playing with fire, or C-4, or something equally as stupid. Those doors aren't going to matter. Whatever it is, you should let it go."

"Let it go?" David asked, a threatening edge tainting the question.

"That's my suggestion."

Lips pulling back from his teeth, he growled. "I'm not the only one who wants to—"

Harry raised a hand. "Like I said before, I don't wanna know what you've got planned." Swinging the new, thick metal door on its hinges, he shook his head slowly. "And I definitely don't wanna know why you needed this place outfitted like a fucking bunker."

David forced a slow, deep breath. "That's fine. I appreciate the help."

"Yeah, well, this was the last favor I owed your family. But... out of respect for your father I've gotta tell you that the last thing he'd want you to do is get yourself locked up, or killed." Harry brushed his nose and then braced his hands on his hips, staring into the concrete room that was finally complete.

"This is *all* about respect for my father," David answered, settling against the concrete wall in the hallway. Studying the older man's features as they pinched for a moment and then smoothed out.

"Hmm." The noncommittal grunt was the only break in the silence for a few moments, and then Harry turned away from the room and shut the door. It was a heavy, satisfying sound, the hinges screeching from the weight of it.

It was perfect for a prison.

"Is that the key for all the doors?" he asked, looking to the small silver key sticking out of the handle.

"Yep." Harry tugged it free and held the key out, but as soon as he reached for it, Harry pulled it back. "I don't wanna know what you're doing, David, but I do wanna know *when* you're gonna do it."

"I don't know. It depends. Why?" Watching the man carefully, he noted the way his fingers tightened around the key, a subtle shake to his hands betraying his nerves. He didn't want to hurt Harry McConnell, but he would if the man tried to interfere in this.

He'd been planning for too long to have it fall apart now.

"Soon?" Weathered blue eyes held his and he answered with a curt nod. "Then I think I'm gonna take me and the boys on a trip. Somewhere public, with surveillance cameras. Vegas, maybe."

"Why's that?" The ice-cold calm was creeping through his veins as he stared the old man down, everything shutting off except for his instinct for violence, the urge to protect the only thing that mattered now — the plan.

"Because if the cops come around asking about you, or this place, or whatever you're planning to do in it, I'm gonna have proof me and my boys weren't within a hundred miles of this shit." Harry offered the key again, and this time he let David take it. "Building is in your name now, so I'm out now, understand? I'm not involved. This goes south, you don't speak my name, and I won't say shit about you either."

David nodded, tucking the key away in a pocket. "Sounds good to me, Harry."

"Then I'm gonna go."

"Alright, I'll walk you out." Pushing off the wall he waited for the man to start moving before he fell into step beside him. As they approached the new double doors at the end he had to admire the craftsmanship on the thick steel doors. They were braced well, and the security system he'd installed was just extra insurance now. Harry had been the right man to call for this. Even if he'd effectively burned this bridge by involving him… he'd never hated him. He'd known him his entire life. "I meant what I said, I appreciate you helping with this. You and your boys do great work."

"Yep." Tugging off his baseball cap, Harry scratched at his thinning hair before replacing it and offering his hand so they could shake. "I'd say good luck, but I don't know if I want that on my conscience."

"Have a good time in Vegas, Harry." David took his hand, feeling the firm grip of a man who'd spent his life working with his hands as they finalized the handshake.

Nodding, Harry stepped through the door and David held it open as the man turned around and met his eyes once more. "You ever heard the saying, before you go on a journey for revenge, dig two graves?"

Something twisted in the cold inside him, but David made himself smile. "Since when did you start spouting philosophy, old man?"

"Since I became an old man, had grandkids, left the old life behind." Harry adjusted his baseball cap again, sniffing loudly as he looked towards the stairs. "It's the truth though."

David felt the cold settle inside once more, a chilling numbness that left him with only the clarity of his well-honed hate. It felt good. "Well, sometimes revenge is worth the graves we have to dig."

"Then, for your father's sake, I hope one of them isn't yours." Harry didn't even turn around this time, he just walked up the stairs.

David stood listening to his footsteps ringing out on the metal, bouncing off all the concrete until the door to the first floor opened and shut. The man's words hung around though, floating in the air, simmering... but none of it mattered. The plan was the plan, and it had been years in the making. There were too many promises, too many deaths wrapped up in the shit already, and even if one of the graves ended up being his, it wouldn't matter.

Revenge was all he had left anyway.

Chapter Three

LIANNA

"No, I'm not in Vail. Dad had to go on a trip for the company so we're going to reschedule."

"Did you want to go out with us then? Mark and Tiffany wanted to hit up this new club called The Green Spot downtown. It's supposed to be awesome." Denise sounded hopeful, but as Lianna looked down at her pajamas, she already knew her answer.

"It's okay, I'm already in for the night. You guys have fun."

"Come on, Li, you never go out anymore. Just come party with us, get drunk, do something stupid and irresponsible for a change."

"Tempting…" She laughed and took another sip of her wine. "But I'm already halfway through a bottle of chardonnay so I think I should just hang out here tonight."

"Are you working?"

"Not anymore, I promise." Lianna found herself smiling as she leaned against the counter, cheek pressed to the phone to hold it against her shoulder so she could scrape the last of the food off her plate and into the trash.

"Then fuck it, just come out with us. Call a car and meet us there, I can give you the address and—"

"Denise..." Dropping her plate in the sink, Lianna groaned and headed back to the table.

"Just do it, Li! If he's out of town there's no reason for you to be sitting at home alone. I can swing by and grab you if I have to!"

"I'm at my dad's place tonight and, really, it's okay. You guys go have fun."

"You're supposed to be my wingman, remember? Tiffany and Mark are always all over each other. I'll basically be alone. I might even go home with some loser, *all* because you're at home drinking wine and secretly working."

"Am not." Lianna pulled back from the email on her laptop and clapped the thing shut like she'd been caught red-handed.

"Liar," Denise hissed, a clear laugh in her voice. "Whatever, if you want to be lame, go ahead and be lame. I'm going out. If you want to join in then text me later and I'll tell you where we are. Mark has a yacht and you could be waking up on the ocean tomorrow morning instead of *alone* in your father's house."

"Don't be a bitch."

"Not being a bitch, just being honest." Her friend let out a breath and then sounded a little more serious. "Did I mention Mark has a full staff on his yacht? A personal chef and a butler and everything?"

"That sounds over the top."

"Your dad owns a private plane *and* a yacht."

Actually, two yachts, but that's not the point. "I'm still not going out tonight, Denise. I've got wine, and television, and pajamas. I'm just going to relax after working all week, okay?"

"Like you need to work," she muttered.

"You should try it sometime."

"Why?" Denise laughed, and Lianna just shook her head.

"Remind me again why you went to NYU with me?"

"Because the guys were cute and I could shop when I wasn't in class?" Another loud laugh from Denise. "Oh! That's Tiffany calling on the other line, if you decide not to suck later text me so I can order you to get your ass out of pajamas and join us."

"Sure, have fun." The call cut off before she even had the chance to pull the phone away to look at it. On the screen the little red notification dot glared, taunting her with the voicemail her father had left when she'd refused his call.

Part of her craved to hear what it said, and the other part wanted to ignore him like he had ignored her, but after a moment she opened it anyway. His voice came over the line just as she took another sip of wine.

"Hi, princess. I know I've upset you by not bringing you with me for this meeting and I never meant to. This is just a different side of the business and it needed to be handled quickly. I would much rather be skiing with you this weekend than dealing with this, and I promise I will make it up to you, but I do hope you made some plans to replace ours. I've got some good news, I received confirmation that our

acquisition of the company in Argentina may be progressing which means our next trip could be down there. Business before fun, but the country is beautiful and we could find something to do. I have to go now, princess, but I will be home soon."

She'd started smiling before the voicemail was even half over, and she chided herself for already thinking about forgiving him — but the fact that he'd called and understood why she'd been upset was nice. The fact that he was already planning to bring her with him on his next work trip was even better. Maybe he was *finally* starting to get it... which meant he might actually fix it.

And *that* meant that her France based escape hatch wasn't necessary. Yet.

The Sotheby's job shouldn't even be tempting her at all, she'd worked too hard to be where she was in the company. Too many hours invested to throw it all away. She just needed to get a better balance in her life so that the company wasn't *everything*. Her whole vacation day had been wasted working, but tomorrow she could go to her apartment and relax. If she left her laptop here she wouldn't even be *able* to work — and maybe Denise and some others would meet her for brunch. Or she could see if any of her old art history friends would like to visit the MOMA or the Met. There were options to fill her time that didn't involve working constantly, or abandoning everything to move to Lyon.

A happy median.

A social life *and* the job at her father's company.

Both of them could be happy, and the world wouldn't end.

Lianna stretched as she walked back to the living room, the

buzzing voices of the television keeping her company in the empty apartment as she settled onto the couch. The shining white tile reflected the images moving across the screen where some sappy sweet romance movie had started while she'd been finishing dinner.

No thanks.

Click. Cooking show. *Click.* Reality show. *Click.* Commercial. *Click.* Dad?

The volume was too low to understand the chipper looking woman on the screen, but she turned it up fast. "...to attend. Corporate magnate Robert Mercier is showing his softer side this week as he opens the Mercier Shelter for Women. While Mr. Mercier is well known for his contributions in the business world, he's not often caught in the public eye, but he appeared today with his daughter Lianna as they cut the ribbon to open this..." The voice on the screen faded in her ears as she watched the flashes of images. Her father cutting the ribbon, smiling and waving at the cameras, all blond hair and dimples — the perfect CEO. Then they were both waving, his arm around her waist — a picture perfect father and daughter.

Her voice came over the surround sound speakers and she cringed, hating herself for agreeing to that damn interview. "My father just wanted to do something to honor my mother's legacy. I'm really just, um, glad to be here for it. It's nice."

Nice? You're such a fucking idiot.

The news mercifully switched back to her father, his vibrant voice filling the room for a minute as he walked the camera crew through a tour. The one and only Robert Mercier, practically perfect in every way.

Perfectly poised, perfectly dressed, and perfectly happy as a workaholic.

And she was turning out just like him, minus the poise.

As Lianna sulked, promising herself she'd do something fun tomorrow, the reporter appeared in the frame again. "The facility is set to open in the next few weeks, and according to Mr. Mercier's representatives they are already in active communication with support organizations throughout the city. We can only hope others follow in his footsteps. Back to you, Tom!"

When the news anchors took over she slid the volume down a little and sighed. Waking her phone, the display revealed 9:17 in bright numbers, and she contemplated calling him back — but if he was in Europe it would be the middle of the night. And, regardless, she wasn't quite sure what she wanted to say yet. He was a good man, a great businessman, someone who gave back to the world in so many ways, and it still felt selfish to want him all to herself just because he was her dad.

But she did, at least for one fucking weekend.

Lying back on the couch, she tilted the wine glass back and forth, watching the pale chardonnay blur the skyline outside the floor to ceiling windows. The night sky was a black hole above the city, not a star in sight with all the light pollution.

There are probably stars visible above Lyon.

Muttering under her breath, she didn't understand why she kept thinking about the job. It wasn't like they'd even offered it to her; they'd just been open to a conversation.

Sotheby's hadn't even mentioned an interview in the email — but the idea wouldn't go away.

Being the daughter, and thus the charmed employee, of the head of Mercier Systems had a lot of benefits, a lot of benefits that she couldn't just ignore to pursue some random dream she'd had in college. But everything about working for her father came with a lot of strings. Threads of obligation, of responsibility, of being *grateful* that were hard to explain to other people.

Fuck, it was hard to explain to herself, much less her dad, which was another good reason to wait to call him back. Lianna groaned and lifted the wineglass. Empty. With a sigh, she pushed herself off the couch and wandered back into the kitchen to refill. The stack of papers she'd laid out lurked underneath her laptop on the dining table, tempting her to just bury herself in work again.

Damn it all.

"Let's just drink until we fall asleep. How does that sound, Lianna?" Talking to herself, she grabbed the whole bottle of wine and headed back to the couch. Glass refilled, cold and biting as she swallowed, she zoned out on the newscast. Something about a shooting, police investigating, blah blah blah. So much chaos in the world, so many angry people, and she was complaining about being wealthy with a six-figure salary working in one of the largest companies on the East Coast?

"Fuck. Enough. We need something mindless. No more working, no more thinking tonight."

Leaning forward she set her wine down and grabbed the remote, flipping through until she found a movie and turned up the volume. It was a horror movie, complete with a soundtrack of taut strings that gave an atmosphere of tension to the scantily clad woman walking across the lawn in front of a house. As if anyone wore strategically attractive lingerie to bed? It was stupid, but mindlessly entertaining.

Perfect.

Smiling to herself, Lianna leaned back and watched the stereotypical chase scene. Slow-moving killer, co-ed running at full speed who somehow still got caught. None of it even remotely made sense, which made it more funny than scary. Still, a shiver rushed over her, sending goose bumps across her skin as the murderer leapt out and the music peaked.

Turning to reach for the throw on the back of the couch, she caught a dark shape in her vision, too close, and then the sharp pull of someone's fist in her hair made her gasp. Panic flooded her with an overdose of adrenaline and she kicked out, her foot colliding painfully with the coffee table, just as screams echoed across the surround sound. Her struggles sent her wine crashing to the floor, and an instant later she was hauled over the back of the couch. Lianna landed hard on the tile, but with the adrenaline rushing through her veins she made it up onto her knees, planning to run like the stupid girl in the movie, when the hand returned to her hair. Air hissed between her teeth, a whimper rising up as the man tightened his grip and then forced her flat. A knee between her shoulder blades pinned her painfully against the cold tile.

"Let me go!" she shouted as soon as she caught a breath, her voice breaking, but there was no one to hear her in the empty building. It was a Friday night and the murder playing out on the speakers was louder than she was.

No one is coming. Fight.

Reaching back, she dug her nails into gloved hands, trying in vain to tear his grip free. A growl rumbled above her just before he cracked her forehead against the floor. Pain flashed like a firework behind her eyes, turning her stomach while she tried to protect her face. Her ears were ringing, and for a moment she was so stunned that she didn't notice the jerking motions at her waist until she felt the cool tile on her lower belly.

Oh God, he was taking off her pants.

"NO!" Lianna tried to push up, but he moved and dropped his knee into her back again, crushing her until her ribs creaked. He was so heavy, too strong, and her fingers slid over the smooth tile finding no traction. Tears blurred her eyes as she whimpered, the sensation of his gloves brushing her thighs as he pushed the soft pajamas down making his motives all too clear. When he grabbed for her ankle to pull off the pants, she kicked her legs, and his knee dug harder into her back, pain radiating up her spine as it became almost impossible to breathe.

"You want to fight me?" The rough voice preceded a hard spank across her ass, and then there was another, and another. Merciless, hot, and stinging. "Go on then. Let's see what you can do. Try and run, whore."

With a sharp tug, her pants were removed, and then she was free. Lianna ripped air into her lungs, her ribs aching as she eased up onto her elbows. When he didn't grab for her again, she lunged forward, scrambling to her feet to run for the security system by the front door.

Panic button.

She needed to hit the panic button so someone would come. So someone would know what was happening. Two minutes for building security, six-minute response time for police. She could survive two minutes.

Wait, why hadn't it gone off?

The red light was blinking on the front of the security panel, glowing confidently as if it were still armed, and she was barely five feet away when the full weight of the man slammed into her from behind. The hard hit sent them both to the floor, bruising her knees as she caught herself on her hands.

No!

His arm wrapped across her throat, blood pounding behind her eyes as he began dragging her backwards — away from the panic button, away from the front door, away from escape. "That was pathetic," he hissed against her ear. "Spoiled little cunt."

She couldn't breathe, her lungs burning as she tried to claw at him, but his long sleeves were tucked into the gloves. *Fight, dammit!* She had to fight. She wasn't going to die like the idiot girl in the movie. Reaching behind out of desperation, she went for his eyes. Stiff cloth. A mask. Before she could find the eyeholes he yanked his head back, and his grip on her throat tightened further, an oppressive blackness creeping in from the edges of her vision, her hearing fading like she was moving down a long tunnel.

No. No. No. No.

He twisted her suddenly and she found herself bent over the back of the couch. For a moment she didn't even care as air returned to her once again, her lungs starving for it, but then his knees were spreading her thighs. Lianna choked on her first attempt to speak, reaching back to try and push him away. "Stop! Don't! Please, don't," she begged hoarsely as she tried to bring her legs together.

"Shut up, or I'm going to cut you." The harsh voice came again, and she froze as she felt the sharp metal of a knife trace over her waist. Shivers made her muscles jump involuntarily, fear plucking away inside as the slow scratch of the blade kept her still. With a nudge, he spread her further.

"I—"

"I said shut up." There was a tug at the edge of her underwear, his fingers stretching the fabric, and then the tension gave way as he cut them off her. Tears burned her eyes, her heart still racing as she tried to catch her breath.

"Don't do this, you don't have to do this." A hard jerk on her hair silenced her, and then she heard the sound of his zipper. "*Please*," she whimpered the word, body shaking as he shuffled clothing behind her. Light from the television played across the floor, and she lifted her eyes to the new scene. Bright sunlight, a group of beautiful young characters talking with concerned looks on their faces, but she couldn't focus on the dialogue filtering through the surround sound.

He was behind her, between her legs, holding her in place, and she knew what was coming.

The first swipe of his fingers along her pussy made her buck against the couch, fingers digging into the cushions. Somehow, the worst part of it wasn't the all too intimate stroke at the juncture of her thighs — it was his low

23

chuckle behind her as he spoke. "Wet little whore, aren't you?"

"No!" The shout tore from her throat as she tried to lift up, but he shoved her back down, toying as he slid a single gloved digit deep inside. Lianna whined, clenching as if she could force him out, but he continued until she could feel the wetness he'd mocked her for.

Why? Why? Why?

"Tell me…" His cock brushed her next, the slick latex of a condom the only tiny comfort before he leaned over her, his voice growling, "What would your father think if he saw you now?"

Heat bled into her cheeks and she grew desperate, scrambling for leverage, but her toes were barely touching the floor. "Let me go, please, don't—"

"Shut the fuck up and listen." His hand stroked her cheek, reaching forward to grasp her chin and rub his glove roughly over her lips. "I'm going to take everything from him. I'm going to tear down everything he cares for, and I'm going to start with *you*. His sweet, little, *princess*." The man snapped her head back, the nickname sending a cold shiver down her spine as the light from the television painted the ceiling in flickering waves. Fear pulsed through her veins when he brushed her pussy once more. She opened her mouth to plead, to beg, to barter, but he slammed inside her in one brutal thrust.

She screamed through clenched teeth, fingers digging into the soft cushions of the couch, but there was no avoiding this. It was a sharp, sudden stretch, and he bottomed out, longer and thicker than she'd expected.

Groaning low behind her, he withdrew and forced himself back in, sending a shudder through her insides as her body stretched to accommodate him.

"Don't," she hissed as he began to viciously fuck her, his grip on her face releasing when he increased his pace with low grunts of effort. The invasion was inescapable, because no matter how she struggled there was no fighting the power of him. His hand wound tightly in her hair, bowing her painfully, while his other hand pressed at the small of her back. It was only her fists clenched into the cushions that let her breathe as the ache inside started to pulse, her body gripping him involuntarily. "Stop..." she whispered.

"You want me to stop?" He almost purred the words behind her, just before delivering another hard, deep thrust that opened her up further. "Say it."

"I want you to stop!" The cry was lost as he laughed low and craned her neck back harder. Pain spread through her back as she strained to lift herself up enough to ease it, a sob catching in her throat from the effort. He wasn't going to stop. The realization settled inside her, worming its way through her conscious, infecting it and tearing her to shreds.

Under the disbelief that it was happening, the raw dread of what would happen when he finished... she could feel the impossible, horrible, tingling beginnings of an orgasm. It was as if she had tumbled into her own personal hell, her body turning traitorous. Reaching back she tried to stop the hard thrusts, to halt the rising rush, but he simply caught her wrist and used it as further leverage to pull her against him.

"Take it, princess. By the end of this you're going to be my little whore." Each brutal movement had her whimpering, her hips bruising against the back of the couch, and she tried to focus on that. To focus on the pain, the ache in her shoulder from how hard he pulled on her wrist, the pain in her neck and the fierce sting as he twisted his fist in her hair, anything *but* the heat coiling in her lower belly as his cock slammed against that bundle of nerves deep inside her over and over.

Her pussy clenched tight, gripping him for a moment, and he growled behind her as she struggled to hold back, precariously walking a fine line of pleasure and pain. "Please," she begged against the strain in her throat, another plea obliterated by his harsh breaths.

"Shut it! I'm going to destroy you, and I'm going to make your bastard of a father watch."

Watch? She fought harder against his hold on her, his fingers tightening painfully until her wrist sent sharp, white-hot pain up her arm and she stopped. Went limp. Let the tears go.

He released her hair and she dropped forward in relief, but then he grabbed for her other arm. The ratcheting sound of handcuffs gave her a surge of energy to fight again, and she managed to rip one of her hands free from his grip. His low growl was a warning, but she ignored it and tucked her free arm underneath her, shielding it as best she could. Pinning her hips against the couch, cock buried deep, he locked the first cuff a notch too tight. "Wrist. Now."

"Just let me go, please." She kept her arm tucked protectively, mindlessly focused on keeping some pathetic semblance of freedom, but he leaned back and spanked her ass hard. Again, and again, and again, making his cock rock in and out of her. "PLEASE!" The fiery heat should have been only pain as she begged, but somehow it was merging with the thrumming pulse between her thighs and making it all worse. Making it all the more intense as he moved his hips against her.

With a grunt, he reached forward, his fingers digging into the tender flesh of her upper arm, ripping it back like her fight didn't mean a thing to his strength. The cuff locked fast, and then he held onto the chain between them as he started to fuck her again.

"No, no, no... Please!" she screamed and started to sob as the metal dug into her skin, his merciless thrusts growing rough until she was strung taut between the awful pain and unforgiving pleasure. She wasn't sure which of them she was pleading with, him to stop, or her to hold back the orgasm she knew was floating just beyond some terrible horizon. The buzzing waves of heat inside took on a razor sharp quality, obliterating the fear until there were only her short pants of breath, her pulse racing in her ears as he pushed in. Thoughts swirled, nerve-endings sparked, delirium blending with hell — and then she came. Body on automatic. Flashes of light behind her eyes as she clenched them tight, her arms pulling at the cuffs, her body tensing under the assault of pleasure, and he laughed as he continued to slam into her.

"Little whore," he snarled, and then she felt his cock kick as he thrust deep, the waves of her orgasm still squeezing him against her will. It was a cacophony of emotion, pain and fear and shame and hate, and as each tried to take control of her brain, they all faded into white noise. He stayed buried inside her, his gloved hand brushing over her ass and up the curve of her waist, but her body only twitched.

Too much.

The chemical cocktail of terror and orgasm was fading, nothing else rushing in to fill it. Numbness was washing through her instead, neurons misfiring in a confused pattern, the white noise building to a steady hum just inside her ears. When he finally slid from her, she stayed where she was, obscenely displayed over the couch, wrists burning, not budging an inch even when she heard him walk away across the tile.

There was something wrong with her.

She shouldn't have come.

She should be screaming.

She should have fought harder.

Turning her face against the cushions, she felt the tears on her cheeks cooling in the air, but she couldn't think straight. All she had were broken, unfinished thoughts.

As his footsteps returned, heavy thumps of boots on tile, she didn't even flinch. She barely twitched when he slid two fingers inside her, pumping them slowly. Then a third finger forced its way in, the sore ache of her pussy a quiet flash in her mind, and then the sharp stick of a needle in her ass made her jump a little. "That's right, princess. You're going to do everything I say."

"Why me?" she whispered, her wrists twisting in the cuffs.

"Why?" he mocked as he stroked her, his fingers playing with her for a long minute in silence before he withdrew. Then he lifted her effortlessly, tossing her over his shoulder to carry her through the dim apartment. "Because."

It was a blithe answer that made her brows pull together as she bounced on his shoulder. When he set her down by the front door, she slumped against the wall and her mind focused on the word.

Because?

She wanted to scream at him, rage that she'd done nothing to deserve this — but there was *definitely* something wrong with her, a fuzzy feeling in her head like it had been stuffed with cotton. A languidness in her muscles that made them feel weighted and strange. A shaft of light from the hallway poured across the tile when he opened the front door. His large body briefly outlined by the pale gold, all dark clothes, broad chest and shoulders — and that mask over his face. So dark. All darkness.

Run, her mind urged her. She should be running, but her body wasn't responding except with stilted shivers.

The rattling sound of a cart wheeling in made her lift her head. She hadn't even realized she'd closed her eyes. Hadn't realized that in her efforts to move, she'd only slid to the side.

You've been drugged. Stay awake. A tiny, urgent voice in the white noise of her head.

Stay awake, Lianna!

With more effort than it had taken in her entire life, she forced her eyes open again and sat up to look. The thing looked like a janitor's cart. A trash bag on one end, and a larger section by him with drawers for cleaning supplies. Without a word he pressed something and the whole set of drawers opened like a single piece — because they weren't drawers, it was a door. Dread pooled in her stomach, far below the emptiness of her thoughts. There was an empty space on the inside. An empty place meant for her.

"Please?" Her voice came out slurred, her brain and body lethargic. There would be no more running, no more fighting — but somewhere deep down there was a spark of survival instinct, that tiny voice asking if she were going to die. Begging her to satisfy it with a comforting word.

But she didn't have an answer.

"Time to leave, *princess*." The man knelt down by her, lifting her into the space as if she weighed nothing. Folding her legs against her chest, he looked at her and she finally saw the fierce, tawny brown eyes behind the mask. There was no mercy in that gaze, only hate, and then they disappeared as he shut the door.

Darkness surrounded her like a suffocating blanket.

She tried to shift but her muscles wouldn't respond at all as the cart started to move. Her wrists were pinpoints of pain in the dark, and she tried to hold on to them, to consciousness — but then the black behind her eyes swallowed her whole. Like some ancient sea monster, sending her down deep where no thoughts, no pain, no panic could reach her.

Chapter Four

DAVID

He'd done it. He had Lianna Mercier in the cell, and everything had gone exactly to plan.

Well, not *exactly* to plan.

Fucking her in the apartment hadn't been a part of the plan, but as soon as he'd seen the blonde halo of her hair lit by the light from the television — everything had gone red. The cold rage had taken over him, and all he'd wanted to do was make her scream. To hurt her in *his* house.

It had felt good to ruin the fake perfection of that fucking apartment. Her shattered wine glass on the floor, the coffee table askew. Hell, he'd fucked her so hard against the couch that it had moved across the floor, and he'd left it angled on the tile with the shredded scrap of her underwear and those pale pink pajama pants behind it.

Listening to her beg had been better than all of it though.

Spoiled little cunt, daddy's little corrupt princess,

screaming and crying before she'd come on his cock like the whore he already knew she was. It had been so much better than just drugging her and taking her out of there.

His dick was getting hard again just thinking about everything he'd do to her before this was all over — but from now on he'd stick to the plan.

No more surprises.

He still needed to verify the building security cameras had kept his loop going, and then he had to revert them before some half-assed security guard noticed it. So much to do before the girl woke up and he got to move to the next phase of the plan.

Ruin. Suffering. Destruction.

David smiled as he turned up the audio for the cell. Harry had been wrong, completely and totally wrong. This was *exactly* what he should be doing. Revenge felt fucking amazing.

<hr />

Lianna

Everything came back online slowly.

First her mind, head pounding like she'd had too much to drink, and then her body lit up in sections. Pain pinged reminders across her skin, echoing confused memories of terror through her battered veins, forcing her out of the comforting daze of sleep.

After a few minutes, Lianna knew she was awake, knew her eyes were open, but the room was pitch black. No difference whether they were open or closed. Blinking, she tried to lift her hands and heard metal clatter as cuffs dug into her already aching wrists.

"Shit," she hissed between her teeth as the twinge spiked and ebbed.

Oh God.

She *had* been taken. It wasn't some horrible nightmare fueled by the stupid horror movie.

Her heart started to race, beating too loud in her ears as the panic threatened to take over, but she pushed it down and tried to breathe, to evaluate her surroundings. *Think,* her mind urged through the haze. *Survive.*

There was a hard chair under her, her arms run through slats in the back so she couldn't sit up all the way, and something was holding her legs wide to the outsides of the chair. Not more cuffs, rope? No. It felt smoother than that, sharper on the edges. It didn't matter.

Worst of all she was completely naked. She could feel the absence of cloth over her breasts and the brush of cool air across her skin. She was naked, tied-up, and trapped with *him.* The memory of the man sent a chill down her spine, but there was nothing left to do but call out.

You can't break handcuffs, just get it over with.

Swallowing against the dryness in her throat, Lianna raised her voice into the black, "Hello?"

Instead of light, a huge television suddenly blinked to life in front of her. For a moment it only showed a blank screen behind the plastic shield that surrounded it — then a video started. It was her, in a black and white image from a high angle, sitting on the couch in the apartment. She watched as her mouth moved, but no sound could be heard. She watched as she set the wine down and started to mess with the remote. Then the dark figure of the man walked into the frame from the right, standing just behind her as she flipped through the channels.

No, no, no... he'd recorded it?

It was eerie the way he stood completely still while she leaned over the remote, fidgeting with it before she leaned back, only feet from him. Watching the movie, unaware of the real danger. When the figure on the screen suddenly grabbed her and yanked her over the back of the couch, she clenched her eyes tight.

"STOP! I don't want to watch this!" Shouting into the emptiness, she tried to forget the sensation of his hands on her skin, of the things he'd done. Even unable to see the video her mind was filling in the blanks, tracing the aches across her body like a transcript. Dropping her chin to her chest, she shook her head, her hair falling like a curtain against her cheeks as if she could shut off the movie inside her own brain. But her eyes snapped open again when the sound of her father's voice bled through speakers into the room.

Dad?

Snippets of interviews from over the years started to play. Robert Mercier, always smiling and well dressed, dimples punching into his cheeks when he laughed. It flashed through clips of him at public events, recordings of him discussing business on what *should* have been private virtual stockholder calls, and too many others. Then they grew shorter.

Quick, abbreviated snippets of his voice over, and over, and over.

His smile, his laugh, and just as the videos started to speed up to a dizzying rate — they started to zoom in on her. Always sitting just to his left or right, in a variety of designer clothes, her dad's voice running over the top of it. It should have been soothing to hear him, but the videos were all of her and too strange. Slowed down clips of her half-smiling during events, her staring down at her hands in her lap, her standing in elegant heels to clap. Just her, over and over, and it only made her panic worse. "STOP!"

The last image of her clapping and smiling in a dress froze. Hands almost touching, she looked like she might have been praying.

Finally, the television went black for a moment, and then a single scene played on the screen at normal speed. It was her father standing outside the Mercier building, speaking to a gathering of reporters. "My inspiration for what I do with Mercier Systems?" He chuckled, all charm and wit, blue eyes sparkling as he nodded at the microphones. "Well, I want a better world for my daughter. She's my everything. Without her—" He lifted his hands. "I'd have nothing."

The television clicked off and bright lights instantly flared to life from either side of the television, effectively blinding her. "Dammit!" She flinched, closing her eyes tight as she heard a door open somewhere to her left. It shut again, the sound heavy and metal. Lianna tried to look, but the bright lights were impossible to see through.

"Did you hear that, princess? You're his *everything*." The low voice was slowly moving behind her, and then a large hand wrapped around her throat and squeezed just enough to make her heart stumble over itself. "Tell me, how do you think he's going to feel when he gets that first video?"

"Go to hell," she spat, and he yanked her head back, tilting her chin up so she could see the mask again.

"You're the one in hell, princess, you just don't know it yet."

Fear squirmed in her belly and she tried to struggle, but only rewarded herself with pain as the cuffs tore at her skin and his grip tightened further around her throat. "What do you want from me?" she croaked through the strain.

"What do I want? I want your father to suffer. I want to see him ruined like he's ruined the lives of so many others." He grabbed her chin and forced her head back further, making her back arch painfully as her arms pressed into the chair. "And you're going to help me destroy him, *princess*."

"My name is Lianna," she hissed.

"Oh, but daddy dearest always calls you princess, doesn't he?" It sent a shudder through her that he knew that fact. How long had he been watching them? Watching *her*?

"I don't know what you're talking about."

"Don't lie to me. I know *everything*, slut. Remember that. Now, you have a task to perform." He let her go and she rolled her neck to ease the ache as tiny red dots sprang to life in the ceiling. One directly in front of her, two in the corners, and as she turned her head she saw they went around the room.

The man stepped behind her again, leaning down to speak

directly into her ear, "Go on, talk to him. Tell Daddy how much you want to come home. *Beg.*"

She pressed her lips together, clenching her jaw tight, and he sighed.

"Now," he hissed, a large hand gripping the back of her neck.

"No." She pushed the word through gritted teeth, and he dug his fingers into her skin for a moment before he released her with a shove. His footsteps were heavy across the floor, still in boots, but she wasn't playing into the kidnapping game. Uncle Mike had taught her better than that.

The door creaked open, and then slammed hard.

Swallowing, her eyes blurring against the fiercely bright lights, she tried her best to twist and see the rest of the room. Concrete, empty concrete everywhere, and corners cast into dark shadows. Pulling in a deep breath, she grabbed onto one cuff and tried to force her hand through it, but as she strained the pain became too much and she stopped with a whine.

Fuck, fuck, fuck.

The man returned too quickly, anger radiating off him even as he stayed silent. Her eyes had adjusted enough to identify his outline as he moved closer — still wearing dark clothes, still masked. Smooth leather caressed her bare shoulder, sliding forward until she could see the dull black loop of a belt. She swallowed hard as he slowly slid it between her breasts, inching it down her body, leaving shivers in its wake.

Forcing herself to stillness, she committed to not moving,

refusing to reward him with a reaction, but then he leaned forward to tap the belt between her spread thighs and she jerked against the bindings.

"Last chance, princess. Tell him to save you." The words were quiet, meant only for her.

A curt shake of her head was her only response, and then he brought the belt down hard on her thigh. She couldn't bite back the yelp of pain just as he delivered a matching line of fire to the other side. The burning marks made her whine under her breath as the heat spread, but she steeled herself.

"Do it," he hissed against her ear.

"No."

He stepped to her side, a looming shape in the light, and brought the belt down hard across the tops of her thighs — once, twice, three times and the bright red lines showed up fast even on her tanned skin. When she bit back the scream, he landed the next lash across her breasts. There was no stifling the cry then, and she found herself whimpering and yanking on the cuffs as he forced her head back so she couldn't lean forward to protect herself. He snapped the belt across each breast in fast succession. Back and forth, each new blow making her scream incomprehensible pleas, begging him to stop.

Finally, he pulled away and she slumped, desperately trying to halt her tears as the sharp ache bloomed over her skin. His fist wound into her hair, jerking her head up so she was facing the camera again, blinded by the lights. "Speak."

"Please, just let me go." Her whine was answered with a vicious slap of the belt directly between her thighs, the bright lightning strike of agony making her hips buck. "God, please!"

"Beg *him*." The command was rough, and she kept her eyes low, trying to be brave, but then the whistle of the leather lifting in the air forced pleas past her lips.

"Stop! Please, I want to go home. Just let me go home." Lianna whimpered, hating herself for caving to the pain, hating that she was so exposed to the cameras. "I don't want him to see me like this, please, just——"

The masked man stepped around her and slapped her hard, pain exploding in her cheek, her head snapping to the side as she gasped. He leaned down, his words hissed through a filter of rage, "Do you think I care what you want?"

"Please... let me go. You can still just let me go, I don't know who you are, I don't——" Another sharp slap silenced her, making the hot pain bloom across her jaw, and then he moved behind her once more. She was crying hard now, the ache in her cheeks temporarily overwhelming the other parts of her body.

His breath brushed over her hair before he spoke, "Good girl, cry for him. Tell him to do whatever it takes to bring you home." The belt snapped across her thighs again and she sobbed. "Say it," he hissed directly into her ear.

She was weak. Tired, in pain, and terrified. So, she gave in, lifting her eyes to the red dot in the ceiling. "Dad, I'm so sorry. I'm s-so sorry... Please just do what he says. I just want to come home. Please, Dad, help me. I just——"

A gloved hand covered her nose and mouth, pinching off her air so that she panicked and jerked against the bindings. "Perfect," he cooed against her ear as she struggled. "Now we get to see if he really loves you, princess."

Lianna waited for him to release her, but instead he simply dropped the belt and wrapped his other arm across her throat. Terror took hold, tearing the skin at her wrists as she struggled against the cuffs, making pathetic, muffled sounds.

"Shhh…" His voice whispered against her cheek, and then she felt a prick of pain and the black closing in again, fear warring against the inevitable. Desperate, she tried to stay conscious, to fight — but there was no fighting this.

Chapter Five

LIANNA

And all the king's horses, and all the king's men…

Memories were clashing inside her as she fought her way free from the depths of sleep. Strange and twisted flashes that surfaced and disappeared as fast as they appeared. Her father's voice reading nursery rhymes from memory as he brushed her hair as a child. Small hands turning the colorful pages of the book. The twinge when one of her strands caught in the brush as a woman's voice overwhelmed the story, crying and screaming just out of sight. His hand picking up the fallen book from the floor. Whispers. A door shutting. Another page turning as her father's baritone washed over her…

They could never put Humpty Dumpty together again.

With a groan, Lianna tore herself from the haunting dream and turned over on the cold floor, opening her eyes to dim light. Still naked, but no longer bound. The chair was gone and the room was empty now. Well, empty except for a recessed corner that held a toilet and the kind of water faucet usually found outside. Her eyes wandered up — every one of the red dots in the ceiling were glowing.

Damn him.

He was watching her.

She sat up and pulled her knees to her chest to hide her nakedness — not like it mattered — he'd seen every inch of her.

Tenderly, she touched the raw skin of her wrists, the flesh broken in places, already scabbing. Nothing to be done for them. Her ankles were reddened but otherwise okay, however the welts across her thighs and breasts were impossible to ignore. Angry and red and raised on her skin, a few spots darkened by growing bruises. She wanted to scream, to rant and rave, but there was no use. The only one who would answer was the one she didn't want to.

Lianna wrapped her arms around her shins and curled up tight, rocking slightly as she tried to make her mind work. She was smarter than this. Smarter than this damsel in distress act. Assholes always underestimated her, never looking deep enough to figure out that she might actually know something. Might actually be smart *and* blonde. It had happened in school, it happened every damn day at Mercier Systems — but unlike all of that bullshit, in this case being underestimated might just save her life.

Think. Fucking think, Lianna. What information do you have?

She made herself remember the outline of him, the rough timbre of his voice, but she had no idea who he was. His voice wasn't familiar, nothing about him drew on a memory, and he obviously knew too much about her already.

Not a good start.

He had said her father had ruined people, but what had he meant? As far as she knew, the company had never done a layoff, Mercier Systems had expanded too fast for that. In fact, the company was actively recruiting and acquiring other companies to expand reach internationally. And how the hell would a technology company ruin anyone? More bullshit. He was probably just insane. After all, sane people didn't kidnap other people, or assault them, which wasn't comforting at all.

Move on, Lianna.

She started to chew on her thumbnail, an old, nervous habit that let her focus as her eyes traced the room. The television was off and useless, especially behind the thick plastic case surrounding it. Near the door a small tray caught her eye, but she stared at the door first. Heavy, industrial, and likely locked. A guaranteed waste of time.

There had to be a way out of this. If he wanted money why didn't he just say so? Her bank accounts probably held more than enough to satisfy whatever fucking demands he had. There had been no need to hurt her, to do the things he'd done. As her stomach twisted and her mind spun in circles, her eyes drifted back to the door.

You know it's locked, her mind chided her.

"Yeah, yeah," she muttered under her breath.

Deciding it was better to know, she rolled her eyes at her own thoughts and stood. As she moved towards it, she kept one arm across her breasts, realizing the futility of the action even while she maintained what little modesty she could. Testing the handle gingerly, she sighed when it barely shifted. Not just locked, but impassable. The thing might as well be another part of the concrete.

Looking down, she wrinkled her nose at what she saw. The tray on the floor held a plastic cup of what looked like water, and a simple sandwich. Unidentifiable meat between white bread. She wanted to leave it, to be like one of those people who did hunger strikes to stand for something, but her throat was so fucking dry. The result of whatever he'd drugged her with along with all of the screaming.

Don't think about that right now.

Sliding to the floor beside it, she watched the food for a while, debating inside as to whether she should risk it, as if the disgusting little sandwich might suddenly start talking so she wasn't just going around in circles by herself. It could all be drugged, poisoned, but as terrible as he had been, he seemed to want her alive. Deciding to test it, she committed to a single taste of each, but the first sip of water undid her. As her stomach growled, she emptied the cup and hurried to refill it from the corner before she ate the sandwich in slow bites, hunkered down across the room from the door.

As the food settled, her head seemed clearer, the cobwebs fading away, but along with the clarity came the return of the panic. He had recorded what he'd done to her in the apartment, and in this room. He had made videos. Was the man really sending them to her father? Was he sending them to other people, or posting them across the internet? Had she really come underneath him as he'd forced her over the couch?

The soreness between her legs and the sudden wash of

shame verified the last part, but only time would answer the first. A sickening twist of her stomach almost brought the sandwich back up. She couldn't imagine her father seeing those videos, either one, and the worst part of it all was that she knew the man wasn't done. If he were done, she'd be out of the damn room — or she'd be dead.

That was not something she was interested in waiting for.

She needed answers. Needed more information. Needed to figure out a way out. And there was only one way to do that.

"Why are you doing this?" she asked towards the ceiling, making eye contact with one of the red dots that floated near the recessed lights that were far out of reach. When no response came after a few minutes she felt a flash of anger. "Hey! Asshole! Why the fuck are you doing this to me?!"

The dull silence that echoed back at her was infuriating. She'd always gone out of her way to be kind, to know the names of the people who worked for her father. There was never a time she left out a *please* or a *thank you*, and she was proud of that. Hell, she called her father's head of security Uncle Mike. She wasn't like her stuck up friends, so caught up in their wealth they didn't even bother to try. Yet, here she was — naked, bruised, violated, *alone*.

And you could have been on a yacht with Denise.

Rage prodded her and made her growl at the unfairness of it all.

"I don't even know who you are!" Lianna stood and screamed at a different camera. "I haven't done a fucking thing to you, so what do you want? Money? Just tell me how much you want!" Her voice was raw, the lingering ache in her throat from his rough chokeholds made her run out of steam faster than she wanted, but nothing happened. Tearing her fingers into her hair, she pulled at the roots like she could hold herself together if she could just keep her head from coming apart. Emotion roared through her as the situation settled over her. Kidnapped, assaulted, and apparently being used as a pawn against her father by a psychopath.

"Answer me, you son of a bitch!" Reaching down, she snagged the tray off the floor and threw it at one of the cameras — it missed — but the television flared to life showing a vibrant number five.

"What the fuck is that supposed to mean?" She walked over to the television and slammed her hands against the plastic case that protected it. The number ticked down to four, and then continued dropping as she started talking. "Is this the deal, you'll only talk to me when you have me pinned down or tied up? You know what? Fuck you! You're a twisted, fucking—"

The screen showed a one, turned red, and then flicked off, just before the heavy metal door opened.

Lianna turned fast and forced herself to hold her ground. His dark outline in the doorframe made her stomach flip flop, but she swallowed down the sudden nausea. Adopting the voice she used during negotiations, she tried to meet his eyes. "I want answers."

"No, *princess*, you don't." His voice was clear and threatening, but she stayed strong.

"What do you think my father did to you? Why are you doing this?"

"I don't *think* anything, I *know*, and I'm sick of listening to you shouting. Shut the fuck up, or I'll gag you." He had one large, gloved hand on the door to hold it open, and she could see a plain looking cement hallway behind him. Nothing helpful.

"Then why not just fucking tell me? Just tell me why you're doing this! Tell me what you want!"

"Don't push me."

"Why not? Are you going to kill me?" She wasn't sure where the question had come from, but it was somewhere deep inside her, somewhere underneath all of the helpful logic she'd been nursing since she'd woken up. When he laughed, a low and sinister sound, Lianna took a step backwards.

"No." His head tilted. "Not yet anyway. Now, are you going to be a good girl and keep your fucking mouth shut until I tell you to speak?"

"Go fuck yourself," she spat, and then he stepped into the room. Backing away fast, she tried to circle him, to stay out of his reach, but her back collided with the wall when he suddenly lengthened his strides. With a quick movement he caught her, his large hand wrapped around her arm to throw her to the floor like a ragdoll. Landing hard on her side, she tried to scramble away, but he was on top of her too quickly. One hand gripped her throat and squeezed as he dropped a knee between her thighs, forcing her legs apart.

"Want to repeat that?" The menacing question was punctuated with a tighter grip that threatened her airway and made her cough as she grabbed onto his wrist. "Hmm?"

"Pl—" She tried to beg but was cut off with a choking sound as his thumb dug harder into the tender column of her neck.

"I don't think you understand your place in this situation. You are nothing more than a conveniently useful tool in my plans. The fact that I can fuck you to torture your piece of shit father is just a bonus, but if you continue to piss me off I will start to *really* hurt you. Do you understand?" His low laugh returned from behind his featureless mask, those tawny eyes taunting her with his clear enjoyment of her suffering. "Nod for me, whore."

She nodded, and his crushing grip released. Her first breath was a cough, and he ran one gloved finger over her cheek.

"Now, you're going to keep your fucking mouth shut and not irritate me anymore. Isn't that right?"

With a painful swallow, she nodded again, and a shiver ran over her as his eyes wandered down her naked body. Whether he had meant it to be an unspoken threat or not, she knew there was absolutely nothing she could do against his strength. If he wanted to hurt her, he would. If he wanted to fuck her again, he would. If he wanted to kill her—

"That's a good slut. I'll be back later. We're just waiting to see what Daddy thought of your performances." He stroked down her neck, brushing her breast before he pushed himself up, one foot planted between her legs as he towered above her. "You should pray that you were convincing."

Lianna stayed on her back as he stepped over her and moved towards the door. He scooped the tray from the floor and then yanked the heavy metal open, and she waited to hear it shut and lock before she sat up slowly. Her throat was a circlet of pain as she pulled her legs tight to her chest. Wiping roughly at the tears slipping over her cheeks, she tried to stop the shaking to no avail.

Above her, the cameras winked back on one by one.

"I'm sorry, Dad..." she whispered into the emptiness, wondering if he would ever hear her apology, or if she had just made a terrible, mortal error.

Chapter Six

LIANNA

Time passed without measure, broken only by the two times he slammed his fist against the door, telling her to step back.

Always masked, he would hold the door open just long enough to set a sandwich down on the concrete, no more trays. Both times she huddled on the other side of the room, not interested in another clash. Both times he only glanced at her and then left in silence.

But at least he hadn't touched her again, and she'd spent the unknown number of hours ripping herself apart for baiting him in the first place.

So fucking stupid.

She needed to avoid his attention, to wait for her father and Uncle Mike to find her and save her. With their resources it couldn't be much longer, she just had to survive.

Since she had nothing else to do, she started to count the

strange metal half-rings that stuck out of the concrete in various spots. Some in the floors, some in the walls, but soon she knew their number by heart, and it wasn't changing — twelve. There were also eight cameras. Six lights in the ceiling, and two lights of a different style on each side of the television.

One water faucet, one toilet, with one drain in front of it.

One plastic cup that he'd left her.

One locked door, and one terrified woman.

Nothing else to count, because otherwise the room was empty, barren, the concrete strangely smooth and polished. After pacing for what felt like hours, one corner felt like the best place. The one across from the door, opposite the toilet, where she was unable to see the television if he turned it back on. Lianna sat with her back against one wall, legs against the other. It made her feel more secure, more stable. A small place as safe as she could make it that made the unending silence a little more bearable.

Then... the lights went out.

There was no stopping the scream that escaped her, but she bit down on it, cutting it short so she wouldn't draw him back. Pitch black once again, nothing to see but the eight glowing red eyes peering down at her from the ceiling. Closing her eyes tight, she started to bite at her nails, anything to distract her, but eventually not even that helped.

Was she supposed to be sleeping? Was this some twisted form of bedtime?

Her eyes roamed the ceiling, trying to ignore the imagined shapes in the dark. The shadows blacker than black. *They were imaginary, right?* Shivers passed through her as she stared up at the little red dots, silently pleading for him to turn the lights back on. Then the one she was looking at turned off.

Lianna blinked, hoping she'd imagined it, but one by one the rest of the cameras started to wink out.

No.

She crawled forward, her breathing growing rapid as panic clutched her chest tight. "Wait!" she shouted into the black.

Five left.

"Hey!" Lianna stood up and waved her arms in front of a dot, shouting, but it winked out, and she spun around.

Three left.

Two.

"PLEASE DON'T LEAVE ME IN THE DARK!" The scream was pure terror, and then there was only one dot, her eyes locked on it, praying under her breath for it to stay on.

Zero. None. Alone.

She instantly felt dizzy, claustrophobic, the perfect blackness making her mind warp. Was the ground tilting, or was that her? Was something crawling on her? In a panicked flurry she brushed at her arms and legs, winding her hair up and back, and then she stumbled towards a wall. She couldn't tell which one it was, had no idea where she was in the room, but she followed it to a corner and sat down, pressing her ribs back against the concrete so she could feel somewhat grounded.

"Please, please, please turn the lights on," she begged into the dark, breaking his rule for silence, her voice cracking as she cried. "Please…"

No response. Not even to her speaking.

There was nothing.

So much nothing.

It stayed dark for hours, for forever, or at least it seemed to… mind torturing her with imagined shadows. Each time her hair brushed her skin she jumped, whining into the empty space around her, shivering as her eyes started to play tricks. Flares of color that weren't actually there, more shadows, she *knew* they weren't there. Nothing was there, and she was losing it.

Fear of the dark wasn't irrational, it was one of mankind's oldest fears for a reason. No light meant you were vulnerable, it meant you were in danger, it gave the predators the advantage, and Lianna knew where her predator was. Outside the room, outside of the dark, waiting for *something* that she couldn't figure out.

Not like it mattered.

She was already vulnerable, already in danger, and so she started to plead aloud. She begged in hoarse whispers for him to give her back just one camera light, anything real to focus on. Apologized for speaking, apologized for shouting at him — but there was no answer.

No change. Just endless black. Endless silence.

After too much time in the false night, too much time

where she was sure she would really go crazy, she heard the door unlock. Beautiful, bright light suddenly flooded in and she wanted to run towards it, to bathe herself in the brightness, not even afraid of him for a brief moment — but then she saw the chain hanging from his bare hands. Heard it shifting as link rubbed against link.

Unconsciously she'd clambered to her feet and taken a few steps towards him, hungry for the glow in the hall, but now she was frozen. In the opposite corner of her safe spot, and he was simply staring at her from behind that damn mask. Her voice wobbled as he adjusted the chain in his grip. "Pl-please turn the lights back on?"

"What will you do for me if I do?" The question sent a chill down her spine.

"What do you want?" Lianna whispered, taking a tentative step back, and then he let the door shut. Darkness covered her again, only now it wasn't just a random fear, an imagined shape in the black, now she *knew* the danger was real.

"I want you to come here." The chain jingled in his hand as he started to walk towards her, and panic raced through her as she staggered backwards until she hit the wall. His heavy footsteps moved quickly, but she darted past him out into the open space. He growled, a hint of anger tainting his voice. "Come on, princess. Don't you want the lights back on?"

"Yes," she answered and then ran, his footfalls moving to where she'd been. A low laugh rumbled out from him when he didn't find her.

"Come to me on your own and I won't hurt you... much." He started to pace the room, a predator hunting for her, but she stayed ahead. "However, if you make me catch you…"

Lianna covered her mouth, trying to breathe as quietly as possible as she inched along the wall, taking careful steps. He was big and he made noise when he moved, and not just because of the chain he carried. Every bootfall, every breath, seemed louder in the empty black.

"Last chance." His voice was closer than she'd expected and she had to hold her mouth shut so she wouldn't make a sound as fear wound like icy fingers around her spine. A part of her mind urged her to give in, to beg him not to hurt her, to simply submit, but that was the foolish, weak part — and there was no way in hell she'd listen. His movements were too close so she sped up, but with the next step her foot landed on one of the metal pieces embedded in the floor. A painful punch to the arch of her foot made her stumble and draw in a gasp as she scrambled to right herself.

Even as she covered her mouth, she knew it was too late. His massive form slammed into her, the breath leaving her lungs in a yelp. "NO!" she screamed, but he caught her arms as she tried to shove him back. In a moment, she was pinned between his hard body and the wall, and she screamed again, desperate to escape.

Weak. Pathetic. Stupid.

This was so much worse than being alone in the dark.

"Do you like running from me, princess?" He nudged her hair out of the way as his lips ran down her neck. "Do you like it when I catch you? Is that why you shouted at me earlier? So I would come?"

"No," she whined and tried to break his grip, but he tightened his hold until the fine bones of her wrists creaked as he pulled them high above her head.

"Oh, I think you *do* like it." Adjusting until both her hands were captured in one of his, he let the chain drop loudly to the floor beside her. His touch was like a live wire over her skin, making her muscles jump as he traced a path down her neck, over the swell of her breast, and down her waist. "Does it make you wet knowing I can do anything I want with you right now?"

"NO!" she shouted, but he growled and forced a knee between her thighs, spreading her until he could press her legs wide with his.

"Really, princess? Let's see." He swiped at her slit, dragging damning moisture towards her clit just before he roughly shoved two fingers inside her. Struggling, she screamed through clenched teeth because she *was* wet. She knew it before he even started to laugh, his breath brushing over her cheek. "Desperate little whore, I know you better than you know yourself."

You are a whore.

You should be terrified, not turned on.

There's something broken in you, damaged, fucked up.

Her own mind turned against her, a vicious inner voice that was somehow worse than the steady, sharp thrusts of his fingers. No gloves this time, it was his skin on hers. Her pussy ached when he finally slid his fingers from her and caught her chin, tracing her juices blindly over her lips. "Open up."

With a violent twist, Lianna tried to break free, but his hips pinned her to the wall and he dug his nails into the skin of her wrist. The hard press of his cock behind his pants was impossible to ignore and she whined, hating him, hating her body for betraying her like this.

He slapped her, the sting making her gasp before she clamped her jaw shut as he grabbed her chin again. "I said open up, slut. I want you to taste just how wet you are. I want you to lick it from my fingers. I want you to realize that *this* is all spoiled, selfish cunts like you are good for." When she tried to shake her head, he dug his fingers into her cheeks, prying her mouth open. "You're going to obey me, princess, and if you bite me? I'll do things to your body you can't even imagine."

A shudder passed through her at his words, wishing once again that she were braver. Brave enough to bite down, to spit in his face even though she couldn't see it. But there was no mercy in him as he pushed his fingers in slowly, testing her, and she whined as he forced them to the back of her tongue, making her gag.

"Suck."

She tried to plead around the invasion, unintelligible sounds, but he didn't care. He was going to do what he wanted — and if she obeyed *maybe* he wouldn't hurt her. Maybe she'd survive this long enough for them to get to her, rescue her. Sealing her lips around his fingers, she traced them with her tongue, cringing as she tasted herself.

"You're going to have to do better than that with my cock in your throat, might as well practice now." He thrust his fingers deeper, gagging her again, and she tried to pull at his hold on her wrists without success. "Tsk, tsk. Don't fight me. Just accept it."

Soft cries started to leave her lips as she struggled not to choke, swallowing the saliva that pooled in her mouth. When he pushed them deep again, she felt the drool spill past her chin, and she was thankful for the cloak of darkness.

Ripping his fingers from her mouth, he wiped them on her cheek slowly, smearing the wetness across her face as he rubbed a thumb across her lips. "On your knees."

"Please don't do this."

He sighed and released her hands, grabbing her by the hair to force her to the floor in front of him, her knees bruising on impact. There was no point of reference in the room, but somehow she could still *feel* him towering over her, she could *feel* his eyes on her. "This wasn't what I had planned, but since daddy dearest isn't responding I need to send him some encouragement. It might as well be you deep throating my cock like the little whore you are."

Not responding? Was he still overseas? Was he on the plane on his way home?

Flinching, she swallowed hard as she listened to him opening his zipper, desperate to avoid what she knew was coming. "He may not even have your demands, he was on a trip to Europe."

"He has them." The sound of fabric moving in front of her face made her whine, eyes tracing the empty ceiling. *No cameras.*

"Wait! Your cameras aren't work—" Just as she started to speak the little lights came to life around the room, eight red eyes watching her on her knees. Clenching her fists she stared up at one of the red dots, tears blurring her gaze. "But, but it's dark. This is pointless, they can't—"

"Nightvision. Now open your mouth like a good girl. Make me happy and maybe I'll give you something to sleep on other than the floor." His fist returned to her hair and he pulled her forward, his hard cock brushing her cheek. "But, don't forget, I already told you what happens if you use your fucking teeth."

"What about the lights?" she asked anxiously as she reached up blindly to find the base of his shaft, moving her face away from it.

"If you want the lights back, you better make me *really* happy after you made me chase you." He jerked her head forward, rubbing himself against her again in an unspoken command.

Her stomach roiled, and she wanted to shout at him, to tell him that *he* was the one who controlled the fucking lights and he could have turned them on and found her in an instant if he wanted to. *He* had been the one enjoying the chase, *not* her — no matter how her damn body responded. But, instead of screaming, instead of being brave, she parted her lips and licked at the head of him. He tasted like clean, male skin, the precum coating her tongue.

So normal for such an insane situation. Too normal. She squeezed her eyes tight, a ridiculous effort since she couldn't see him anyway, but it made it easier to imagine someone else, someone kind, as she slid him deeper into her mouth. Moving her tongue along the underside, she started a steady rhythm while she stroked him with her hand, hoping he'd just get it over with.

For a few minutes he let her control it, barely shifting his hips as she worked him in and out, the only response the low groans from high above her head. Then his fist tightened and he thrust, knocking her head back against the wall. He eased back for a moment, and then on the next forward movement he pressed into her throat, choking off her air. Her hands went to his hips, trying to push him back, but he slapped one of them away and growled. "Hands behind your back. Now."

As if to make his point, he forced himself into her throat again, pinning her head to the wall so that she couldn't breathe at all, and then he held still. It took everything she had to pull her hands from him and fold them behind her back, her lungs burning, but finally he eased out of her throat and she tore air in through her nose. She had enough time for a few quick breaths, and then he was face fucking her in deep strokes, allowing her sips of air that kept her on the edge of panic, pleading wordlessly.

"You know your whimpers only make my cock harder, princess." His voice was growling, but somehow amused, and she hated that she sounded so pathetic, whimpering and choking. Every hard thrust felt bruising, each time he held himself in her throat she whined low in her chest, uselessly begging for air. She couldn't stop him, couldn't fight him, and so as her head started to grow fuzzy, she relaxed and stopped struggling. It made it easier. It hurt less as he forced himself deep again and again, and he started to moan steadily above her. "Fuck, *yes*, now swallow."

Another thrust and he held himself all the way in, her nose pressed to his skin as he came in jets. She swallowed as fast as she could, her lungs screaming for air, her nails digging into her hands so she wouldn't try to shove him away.

Finally, he pulled back and she felt drool running down her chin and chest as she gasped and coughed.

"Good girl," he crooned above her, and then the lights came up by a fraction. Enough to turn the pure black into a dull gray as she flinched and looked up at him. "Beautiful."

Heat flushed up her chest, scalding her cheeks, and she tore her eyes away from that tawny brown gaze. The lower half of his face was revealed, the mask pulled up to just above his lips. "Ple—" Her voice cracked as she tried to speak and she had to swallow. "Please leave the lights on?"

He leaned down as soon as his pants were put together, holding her chin hard as he tugged the mask back down. "You want the lights?"

With effort, she opened her eyes, meeting the furious intensity of his, and nodded against his grip.

"All right. Only because you behaved and put on such a good show." Grabbing the chain from beside her he stood and walked towards the door. As he opened it wide, he paused and turned back towards her. "You know, I expected you to go for the door when I was chasing you. It was unlocked, but…" A shrug. "I think you like being my little whore."

Standing up, she opened her mouth to shout at him, to curse him, but he lifted a remote in his hand and she froze. *Not the darkness. Not again.*

"That's right. Behave." He chuckled, a low and ominous sound. "Sleep well, princess. I've got another video to send to daddy dearest."

Chapter Seven

DAVID

The girl was awake again. Lianna Mercier, the darling daughter of the son of a bitch that deserved to die for all that he'd done.

No, not die.

Suffer.

Killing him would have been too easy.

That was the entire reason he'd changed his focus to the girl. He'd spent years gathering data on the father, but the man's heart lived in the beautiful blonde currently crying in the other room. His eyes flicked over to the monitor with the video feed, the angle changing every thirty seconds to show a new view of her curled up in the corner. He wanted her again, wanted to make her scream again, wanted to hurt her in ways that would break the man.

Not yet.

Turning back to the computer screen, he forced himself not to watch her, not to stare at the curves he could still feel under his hands, to ignore the steadily growing hardness against his fly. It had barely been five hours since the last video he'd made, but he knew it had been received. As soon as the file had started playing, David had received the alert.

Now, he just had to wait.

The first set of videos he'd put together had gone unanswered, but the fucker hadn't been stupid enough to call the police. He'd called his head of security instead, Michael Turner, but neither of them were capable of finding him.

It wouldn't matter who they called in. They wouldn't find the girl until he *wanted* them to find her. After she was broken down, crawling on her knees for him — hollowed out and empty. Destroyed.

"Let's see if you want your *princess* back when I'm done with her." The seething anger was like a toxin in his blood, slowly eating away at him, and the only balm he'd found was in her sweet screams. The way her body bowed under his, the way she fought against him only to bend to his will again and again — it was perfect.

The cell phone to his right started to ring, a chipper little sound, and he quickly verified that the routing program he'd written was still working. Picking up the headset that would distort his voice, he pressed the answer button and waited.

"Hello?" Robert Mercier's voice was exactly like it was on his television appearances, only a little... edgier. "Are you there, asshole?"

"Oh, I'm here."

"Where the *hell* is my daughter?" He was shouting now, and it made David smile slowly.

"You mean your sweet princess?" There was a series of curses on the other end of the line, a rush of muffled speech from Turner, the jackass giving him useless guidance.

"I want proof of life."

"You want another video?" David taunted and chuckled when Mercier started shouting again.

"Don't you dare touch her again! You will release her immediately!"

"That's not how this is going to go, Mercier. You're going to do some things for me. If you obey, she won't suffer... much. But if you—"

"I'm not doing a thing for you, asshole. I'm going to find you, and I'm going to—"

"You *won't* find me, and you won't find your darling daughter either, no matter what your men are telling you. Not until you've followed every last demand I have."

"What do you want? Money? Out with it!" Mercier's desperation started to leach back into his voice, and the satisfaction was almost equal to the way he'd felt holding Lianna down on the couch just before he'd fucked her in the man's fancy penthouse.

"I don't want your money. I want everything. First things first though, you own three subsidiaries based out of Hong Kong, Seoul, and Mumbai. You're going to sell them."

"Are you insane?" The fucker was shouting again.

"*Maybe*," David conceded before he continued, "but that should concern you since I've got a particularly beautiful young woman locked in a room just one door away. You have eight hours to sell them and return the documents as instructed. You'll receive the offer packet by courier within the hour. Consider the five-hundred dollars restitution for what I'm doing to her."

"I'm not selling you my companies! I'm not doing *anything* for you! You will return Lianna and—"

David laughed, cutting off the idiot's tirade. "Now you have four hours to respond."

"Just tell me how much money you want!"

"Two hours, and if you haven't sold them by then we'll see just what else your *princess* can take."

"This is not—"

"Clock is ticking, Mercier." With the press of a button, the call ended and he leaned back in the chair, swiveling side to side before double-checking the program that had bounced the signal through so many digital gateways on so many continents that they'd never find the real source. With a swipe, he navigated to the timer and started it.

Two hours and he could have her again.

Glancing at the screen, he knew he should feed her, keep her strength up — but he wasn't sure he could go in the room and not take her. When he'd turned the lights off, her fear had been palpable, and through the black and white of the infrared he'd watched her panic as he had slowly turned each camera off. She had screamed so loud, begged so prettily, but he'd held off. Waited until her whispered pleas from the microphones were their own kind of music.

Then, Mercier's first timeline had expired while the man had been busy fucking around with his men instead of calling the number he'd provided.

Not like David *minded* him missing the deadline.

The tight grip of her throat had been glorious. The wet, choking sounds in the darkness better than he'd ever imagined. He'd wanted to chain her up, to take her again, and he would. There was an endless list of things he could do to the pretty blonde, a thousand ways he could shatter her — and if Mercier's timeline ran out again he'd just have to decide what came next.

Two hours passed by so quickly.

David slammed his fist down on the desk, leaning forward to glare at the screen, grabbing the mouse in a grip hard enough to make the plastic creak. The timer had gone off over ten minutes ago, but he was still sitting in the chair watching his email and waiting for the confirmation that Mercier had sold the companies.

Are you really going to test me you son of a bitch?

With a growl, he grabbed the bottle of rum, tilting it up to take another harsh swallow. The fire burned its way into his belly, joining the cold rage that had been a constant companion for years, but not even the alcohol could calm him right now.

The bastard had wasted another two hours, and ensured his daughter's suffering in the process. Some part of him knew that he was a sick and twisted asshole to be excited by the ideas floating in his head, the possibilities of what he could do to the vulnerable woman in the other room. He just didn't care enough to stop himself.

Lianna Mercier was just as guilty as her fucking father. Still criminal. Both of them squatting in the top one-percent of wealth in this country, and her father had destroyed or bled everyone he'd ever met dry to make that true.

And she worked for the bastard. Always at his side.

He'd made himself king of a corporation, and she was his pretty little princess. The heir to his bloody kingdom. Mercier Systems was the key to destroying them both, destroying all of it... and it was clear Robert Mercier wasn't giving it up without a fight.

But this wasn't how it was supposed to go. None of this was how it was supposed to go.

David growled and tapped the bottle against his forehead. Something was *wrong*. She wasn't supposed to be so delicate, so pretty when she cried, so sweet as she pleaded — no, she was supposed to be vicious and biting. Catty and cruel. Like every one of those rich bitches who filled the rooms of the city's elite.

And Robert Mercier was supposed to be falling all over himself to get her back.

Setting the dark liquor back on the desk he flipped over to his tracking program, checking his work for the tenth time — but he hadn't made a mistake. The papers hadn't been signed, the courier had not been called to pick them up, and there was no call coming in on the cell phone.

Mercier knew exactly what he was doing to her, to his only offspring, but he wasn't responding.

Was she not the key? Did the bastard even have a weakness?

David growled and kicked the CPU under his desk as he pushed himself away from the set up. He was surrounded by evidence. Filing cabinets full of things that damned the asshole and verified that the blonde was the crux of whatever was left of Robert Mercier's soul. She had been pampered since birth, protected, given everything the man was capable of providing. The best of the fucking best.

"Spoiled little bitch."

Rage, a welcome old friend, purred in his chest. Erasing the visions of her biting down on her pretty pink lips, her blue eyes searching his for a mercy she wouldn't find. She was Mercier's heir, his pride and joy, and he was going to tear her down off her pedestal. He traced the edges of her naked body on the screen. "You're not safe anymore, princess, and *Daddy* is about to see just how serious I am."

The idea formed in his mind like oil spilling into water. Corrupting and dark.

No more hollow threats, no more countdowns, no more half-measures. Robert Mercier was going to fall in line or he was going to watch the pretty blonde break.

It only took a few minutes before he was dressed, the stifling mask over his face, and all of the tools he would need gathered together. Leaning back over the computer, he sent an encrypted email through the server, turned on the routing program, and then took another long drink of the rum. Sweet and burning, all the way down.

"Let's see how long you hold out, bastard." Spitting the words at the unresponsive screen, he left the room and walked a short way down the hall. He paused at the heavy door, taking a steadying breath so he could calm the hate rushing under his skin.

Don't kill her, just make her scream.

Turning the key, he shoved the door open and watched her long limbs contract into an even smaller ball. Pale blue eyes widened as she lifted her head, and he couldn't help but smile at the open fear on her face.

"Seems like Daddy doesn't want to save you, princess," he cooed, keeping his voice low and quiet. With careful, measured steps, he approached her. The way she shivered was beautiful, and he wondered if it was the chill or his presence that made her muscles quake like that. "I think something a little more direct will help, don't you?"

"No, *no*, wait. I'll get him to do what you want. I'll talk to him again, I swear. Just let me talk to him!" Her pleas were desperate as he paused beside her, staring down at the terrified form. It sent a thrill through his blood. That blonde hair like an actual fucking halo, as if she were some angel and not the spawn of the fucking devil.

Still, even Lucifer had been an angel once, and her hair was like spun gold on her shoulders that he had an urge to push his hands through, to pull until her lips parted so he could—

Stop. Fucking focus.

David looked her over, letting his rage blow like a cold wind through his core, hollowing out the pieces of him questioning his plan. "That's exactly what you're going to do, princess. You're going to get him to do what I want, but you're not just going to talk to him, you're going to scream for him."

Chapter Eight

LIANNA

Lianna pulled her knees closer to her chest, tucked into the corner, but as he stood over her she knew nothing could protect her. It was just the two of them, and he wanted to make her scream. "I can get him to do whatever you want, you don't need to hurt me."

"You'll have your chance." The man answered quietly as he walked toward the back wall.

"Please, just let me go. He'll do whatever it is. I swear." A fruitless plea. A useless collection of consonants and vowels strung together to no effect as he looped the chain through a steel half-circle high on the wall. The grating sound of metal on metal made her whimper.

"Come here." He pointed at the floor, but she just stared at him, at his masked face and dark clothes, and stayed still. "Do you really want me to drag you?"

Shaking her head, she tried to get her muscles to move, but she wasn't able to obey. Everything told her to escape, and she finally gathered enough strength to move. Then she ran for the door. Her fingers brushed the handle, felt it turn, felt the heavy weight of the door shift towards her — and his arm came around her waist. A band of muscle that felt like steel as he lifted her off her feet, ripping the handle from her hands, tearing her away from freedom, and she screamed as loud as she could.

"That's right, princess. Scream for him."

All of her struggles were futile as he carried her back to the wall and slammed her against it, bruised ribs aching as her arms were forced upward. The man wrapped the chain tight around her wrists and then locked a padlock through the links. He tested them first with a jerk, but even when his hands moved away she still pulled, feeling the metal dig into her aching wrists as she tried to squeeze a hand through.

"No!" she sobbed, feeling tears forming, and then he slipped something over her head. Glancing down, it looked like a pocket on cord, and she twisted to face him, confused and terrified. He tilted his head and pulled a phone from his pocket, a simple cell phone that still had all the number keys.

"I'm going to call Daddy, and let you talk to him. Like I said."

Excitement feuded with terror, because she wanted to speak with her father, wanted to know he was coming to save her. To help her… but she knew it would come at a cost. "What do you want him to do?"

"Simple. I want him to sign the paperwork I sent."

Lianna's mind whirled, trying to understand what *paperwork* could be worth doing this. "What's in the paperwork?" she asked in a whisper.

"Does it matter? You just need to beg." Holding down one of the numbers, he pressed another button, and she heard the speakerphone kick on as the ringing came out loud and clear. He tucked the phone into the pouch against her chest, and then stepped behind her.

The door opened, closed, and the click of the phone connecting made her breath catch.

"You son of a bitch, I want my—"

"Dad?" she spoke, tears almost choking off the word, but her father's voice softened instantly.

"Lianna? Are you alright, princess?" Noises came out of the phone, rapid whispers, and then he came back. "Where are you? Who is he, do you know him?"

"He took me from your place, I don't know who he is or where I am, just please help me. Please, I don't know what—"

The man was back, the loud sound of the door opening and closing stopped the words in her throat, but her father filled the silence. "Lianna? Is he there? Let her go now!"

Pain snapped across the backs of her thighs and for a moment her legs gave out, wrists straining against the bulging links of the chain, and she realized she'd screamed just like he wanted.

"DO NOT HURT HER! Let her go immediately!"

Another strike, and another, and she was crying, breaths

too short, panicked, because there was nowhere to escape as she pressed herself forward against the wall. Unfortunately, it only seemed to amplify her father's voice as the little pocket rested above her breasts.

"You son of a bitch! You won't get away with this, I'll kill you!" Her father's shouts held a rage she'd heard so few times in her life that it even made her quail, but the man behind her simply moved closer.

Brushing her hair away from her neck, he spoke quietly, "The paperwork, princess. Beg him to sign or I keep hurting you."

"Dad, please——" Cut off by another strike of pain across her ass, she whimpered, trying to coalesce her thoughts into language. "Sign the paperwork! Please!"

"I can't just sign this! You have to listen to me, the board won't approve it!"

The board?

Agony took away her thoughts again as the next strike landed across her shoulders, followed quickly by another. It was the belt again, the fierce snap of it — she knew it was the belt, and he wasn't going to stop. "DADDY PLEASE!"

"Princess, you know this is complicated. What he's asking I can't just *do*. Selling a company takes time." Robert Mercier's trademark calm and collected voice came through the phone just as another lash landed and she screamed in pain. "Lianna, listen, it takes time. I'm trying."

Trying?

Belt. Pain. Scream.

"Please sign, please…" She was sobbing so hard it was difficult to push the words out, but she could hear her father whispering, the speaker end of the phone angled towards her face so that she was forced to listen to him debating with someone in hushed tones.

Another strike, and then another. Always in a new place, a new agony, and her sobs were making her choke as she strained to keep herself upright. Reaching for the chain with one hand she held on, trying to ease it, but nothing stalled the torture.

The man pressed against her back, cock hard in his pants as he spoke quietly, "Get him to sign, or I won't stop."

Sniffling, she drew in breath and nodded as she babbled, "Just sign what he sent you! Just sign it so he'll stop, Dad, please, *please*…"

A harsh sound came through the phone. "Selling a company takes time, Lianna. You know this!"

Torment coursed through her nerves as a flurry of strikes landed on her ass, over and over, until she was keening in a high-pitched whine as the pain became too much. Legs giving out, wrists straining and threatening to snap against the unforgiving steel of the chain. "Please, please, Dad! I'm begging you, sign, please!"

The phone was dead, not even the scratch of empty air coming over the line, and after one more debilitating strike across already aching skin, the man came forward. Plucking the phone from the pouch, he growled and walked away.

A moment later she heard the door open and shut, and she leaned forward against the wall, sobbing.

Why hadn't he agreed? Why hadn't he signed?

Why wasn't her father saving her?

Chapter Nine

DAVID

David fumed, breathing hard as he stared down at the phone with equal parts rage and shock. Had the call dropped? Had the man hung up on his screaming daughter?

Stomping away from the door he entered the other room and threw the belt against the wall so he could settle in front of the computer. Just as he woke it up, the phone rang again, but he let it ring as he waited for the program to scatter the signal once more.

Picking up the headset, he answered, "Technical difficulties?"

"I won't listen to you torture her."

"Sign the documents or I start it again, and this time I'll send you a new video." David took comfort in knowing his voice was distorted, but he hoped his rage was coming through regardless.

"Look, I can sell one of them, the one in Mumbai, but I

need more time for the others. Two hours wasn't enough for this! You're asking the impossible."

"Prove it."

"I can stop all activity at our Mumbai location right now, but I'm still working on approval for Seoul and Hong Kong." Mercier had his cold, corporate voice on, not even a shred of the concern he'd shown over the phone when the girl first started screaming.

"You have four hours then. Two hours per location. If the paperwork isn't signed in four hours, you'll get another video."

"Release her now. You'll get your companies."

David laughed, smiling as he leaned back in his chair and looked at the ceiling. "You think you're in charge? Just sign the paperwork or I make her bleed. I'll rip your princess to pieces and make you watch."

"You—"

Ending the call he stood up and ripped the headset off, not wanting another word of Mercier's excuses and lies. The girl was hanging by her wrists.

Pushing his rage away he stomped back to the other room, ripping the door open to see her jolt, pressing her lithe, striped body against the wall. She was exquisite, beautiful. All feminine curves, marked by his hand, and his cock jerked in his pants.

You promised four more hours.

Clenching his jaw he moved forward, plucking the key for the padlock from his back pocket he tried his best not to touch her skin as he unlocked it. As soon as he loosed it from the chain, she collapsed, and on instinct he caught her by the arm. Easing her to the floor, he met her pretty blue eyes as she looked up at him. Tear soaked and terrified.

It shouldn't have aroused him further — but it did.

All he wanted was to push her to the floor, spread her thighs, and plunge into the silken wetness between. If he slid his hand down, through her soft pussy lips, would she be wet for him?

His fist tightened on her arm unconsciously, but her whimper woke him up to it and he let her go completely so that she crumpled to the floor. "You begged well."

A sniffle and a shuddered breath were his only responses, as he stared down at the tangled mess of her hair.

"He has another chance to save you, let's see if he takes it."

Unthreading the chain from the wall, he looped it over his arm, and then he walked away from her. *Had* to walk away from her, because if he didn't his cock was going to do all of the thinking and then he had no idea what he'd do to her.

It was better to walk away.

Smarter.

Chapter Ten

LIANNA

Pain pulsed across her backside. The ones on her shoulders she could separate into the individual marks, but her ass and thighs felt like one solid bruise. Her skin was hot, aching, and when she looked she could see where the belt had wrapped to the outside of her hip or thigh at times. Bright red rectangles, some with little purple dots where the bruises were surfacing fast.

He'd chained her up and beaten her, used the belt so many times she'd lost count, and she knew she should hate him the most, every ounce of the futile rage she felt should be aimed at him — but it wasn't.

Selling a company takes time, Lianna.

Her father had sounded so calm, so detached, and then he'd hung up while she had screamed and begged him for help. It had to have been more than a day by now, maybe two, and there were no police breaking down the doors. There was nothing except the man in the mask, and her father's voice in a tone she'd never heard him use with her.

Tears pricked at her eyes again as she curled closer to the wall, head pressed against it.

Her wrists were a wreck, darkly ringed in bruises, she seemed to hurt everywhere, and her father was lecturing her about the complications of selling companies. Didn't he remember what he'd tasked her with for the past two years?

Acquisitions.

Literally buying companies and folding them into the umbrella of Mercier Systems. She knew exactly what it took to sell a company because she'd sat in hundreds of hours of meetings listening to the fucking process. Assisting with it, supporting it, managing it.

She knew the board had power, but her father ran the company. He could sign whatever he fucking wanted to. He rarely asked permission before acting, and it was that attitude that had infuriated stakeholders in the past. In meetings and on calls where he got into shouting matches, his voice echoing through the apartment even through the closed door. *That* man wouldn't let this happen to her, would he?

Unless he was angry with her? Furious that she had let herself be taken? Did he see this as some sort of suitable punishment?

Did she deserve this?

Doubt spiraled like razor-winged butterflies through her mind. Torturing her and tormenting her. Slowly, inexorably, breaking her down.

She pulled her lip between her teeth and bit down, trying to stifle the sob that swelled in her chest. Eventually it escaped, and she focused on staying as quiet as she could until the exhaustion finally pulled her down into sleep.

Bleary eyes opened to find the room brightly lit again, no more half-gray haze, and Lianna turned over before she remembered her welted ass. It hurt, but not as much as it had before she'd slept. A dull throb instead of the sharp sting.

Beside the door was a plastic grocery bag and she stared at it for a moment before she pushed herself off the floor. As she stood over it, she wondered if he'd come back as soon as she picked it up, but then she looked inside. There was a toothbrush and that was more than enough temptation. There was also an unopened travel-sized toothpaste, a washcloth, and a protein bar. *Vanilla almond, her favorite flavor.* The little bag seemed like a trick of some kind, but she wasn't going to question the opportunity to brush her teeth or eat something other than lunchmeat and white bread.

After the food, she brushed her teeth and scrubbed herself with the frigid water from the tap, keeping her back to the cameras while standing over the little drain in the floor.

Now, she was shivering hard enough to make her teeth clatter, yet it still felt good to be somewhat clean, even if she was freezing.

Lianna filled the plastic cup, but the sudden jolt of the lock on the door made her drop it. Water splashed on her legs as the cup bounced on the floor, and then the man filled the doorway once again.

Tall, and broad, and terrifying.

His bare chest stunned her, carved muscle leading down to the same dark pants and boots. There was no question in her mind where the strength in his limbs came from, because he would have resembled a Greek statue if his skin weren't so tan. But for all the bared skin, for every shadowed curve of muscle, that damn mask was still in place leaving him an expressionless, foreboding wall of male aggression.

"Against the wall," he commanded and she pressed her back firmly to it, but he growled and snapped his fingers. Impatient. "Face the fucking wall, hands behind your back, and do *not* turn around."

With a shudder, she obeyed, turning and holding onto one wrist. There was movement, something soft and heavy dropping onto the floor and then being moved. The rattle of chain came next and she whimpered, fighting the urge to turn and see what it was. When the door slammed shut, she jumped, almost risking a glance before she heard him moving, accompanied by the metallic sound of heavy links scraping over the concrete.

Eventually, his heavy footsteps came closer, stopping just behind her, and she tried to suppress the shiver of fear. "It seems your father *still* doesn't take me seriously. Deadline is almost up, princess."

Her stomach dropped, and she shivered again. "Just give him more time, he just needs—"

He ripped her head back by her hair, a gasp of pain escaping as he pulled her away from the wall and turned her so she could see the thin, bare mattress on the floor.

No, no, no.

"Didn't I say I'd give you something to sleep on?" He shook her hard by her hair, the ache spreading across her scalp. "Say thank you."

"I don't—" Her words were cut short as he threw her to the floor, and she barely caught herself on her hands before he dug his boot into her hip and knocked her to her side.

"Say thank you, slut."

When she didn't immediately respond, he reached for her, but she scrambled backwards. "Thank you! Okay? Thank you." She faced him, trying to move back a little further as a tremor of fear raced up her back. "I said it, just please don't—" When she put her hands out to hold him off he simply grabbed a wrist and started to drag her towards the mattress.

"That didn't sound very sincere," he muttered as he hauled her behind him.

Lianna tried to stop him, tried to slow his advance, but her struggles were useless as he shoved her onto the dingy fabric. "I'm sorry! Just please—"

"I don't want to hear it, lay down."

Twisting at the waist, she caught sight of the cluster of chain at the top of the mattress and she tried to run, to throw herself off the thin, padded surface, but he caught her. His heavy body absorbed every flailing hit as she fought and scratched, ignored every screamed plea that tore at her voice.

Useless.

He overpowered her easily as he pinned her shoulders

down, his thumbs digging furrows of rage above her collarbones. "Is this how you show gratitude?"

"Let me up! Just STOP!" She recognized the impending threat in him, but she didn't want to be chained again, didn't want him to hurt her again. She *couldn't*. "Don't do this! Please!"

"You can thank Daddy for this, princess. Apparently he doesn't love you as much as his precious company." The words were like a punch to the stomach as he straddled her hips and forced her wrists down above her head. She sobbed and kicked, trying desperately to buck him off her — but all of it was pointless. A waste of precious energy.

Why wasn't her father doing everything he could to save her?

Fuck the company. Fuck the board.

He could do what he wanted and they both knew it.

The pile of chain above her head shifted and he released one of her hands to clasp the other into some kind of leather cuff. She inched her free hand down towards her chest, but he simply huffed and snagged it again, gripping it tight. "Stop fighting me, these cuffs won't fuck up your wrists as bad as handcuffs or the chain." In a matter of moments he had both of her wrists bound, tiny locks keeping the new cuffs closed despite her desperate attempts to rip them open again. That masked face stared down at her, ominous and blank. "This is where you say thank you again."

Lianna almost laughed, confused and angry. "Why would you care about my wrists *now*?"

"Because if you break them there's a ton of fucking issues that could happen that I don't want to deal with." Rage snapped in his voice and she flinched, squeezing her eyes tight, but he didn't hurt her.

His weight settled over her hips, and she clenched her jaw tight.

"Your father is a selfish bastard, you know that?"

"You don't even know him!" The urge to defend him was automatic, even when a tiny voice inside her agreed with the asshole right now.

"Apparently I know him better than you do," he growled as he leaned forward and tugged the two lengths of chain taut through the ring in the floor. He dug in a pocket, his abs stretched above her, shifting under his bronze skin. Finally he moved and she watched as he linked the sections of chain with a large padlock. When he let go she couldn't lift up at all — held down as sure as if his hands were still on her.

"Why are you doing this? What company do you want him to sell?!" She half-screamed the questions at him as he checked the lengths of chain to ensure she had no slack.

"That's not what you need to worry about, princess. You just need to worry about convincing Daddy to do it." Moving to one of her legs, he caught her foot when she tried to kick him, and the glare he gave her through the mask made her start crying. His torture from before was still fresh, and there was no way she could win against him — but she still hated herself as he wrapped the cuff around her ankle. Locking it to the chain, he ran it through another ring on the floor before he secured it in place.

And she let him.

Passive as a sacrifice, doing her best to ignore how wide he spread her legs to repeat the process on the other ankle.

The bright light of the room highlighted his toned arms as he worked, and she couldn't figure out why he had taken the shirt off. It was cool in the room, the chill making her shiver when she wasn't curled up, but there he was half-naked, hidden behind a mask, using another padlock on the last bit of chain. Closing her eyes tight, she tried to block out the feeling of his eyes on her, the quiet buzz in her skin that waited for him to touch her.

Foolish. Helpless. Weak.

"Why are you doing this? *Please*, just tell me why." Her eyes opened to find him staring at her, that tawny brown gaze losing some of the predatory gleam now that his prey was secure.

His fingers brushed over her leg almost reverently, his body stilling as he settled beside her on the thin mattress. "Because you're the only weakness he has, princess."

"Stop calling me that!" she screamed, but with a quick movement he pinched her inner thigh hard and she yelped in pain.

"You're such a brat. A spoiled fucking brat." He shook his head, looking back at the door before he turned that masked face towards her and sighed. "I would teach you a lesson right now if we weren't waiting for your father to miss another deadline."

"No, no…" There were tears in her eyes, and she tried to blink them away, to summon some internal strength again. "You have to give him more time, you have—"

"You know, princess, Daddy's nickname for you actually

fits very well. You're the pretty little heiress to his corrupt fucking kingdom, aren't you?" His voice was a rumbling murmur as he talked over her, twirling a section of her hair around one finger, white gold against his tan skin. "Do you enjoy being at the right hand of the devil?"

Lianna dropped her head back and clenched her eyes tight, refusing to answer. Refusing to entertain this bullshit. Why was he even talking to her like he thought she was a person? He'd made it more than clear what he thought of her. Nothing more than a tool to use as he pleased.

Despite her silence, he continued in that strangely calm monotone. "Is that why you got the MBA after the Bachelor's in art history? To guarantee a spot in his empire?"

"Why the fuck do you care?" she snapped.

He spanked her inner thigh, the fiery shock making her hips lift involuntarily. "You will speak respectfully or you will be gagged. Understand?"

When she stayed silent, he pinched the delicate skin again and twisted, sharpening the pain to a pinpoint of lightning. Her yelp made her gasp. "Fine! Yes!"

"Good girl." The man smoothed his hand over the sore spot, petting her like she was an animal, and she hated that some level of her found it soothing, even as he poked at the one issue she couldn't even answer for herself. "So, is it everything you ever dreamed of? Working for Daddy?"

"It's my job." Lianna forced the words through gritted teeth, and he tilted his head as he started to trace his fingers up to her lower belly, down across her waist, and then over her hip to return to her thigh.

"There are a lot of companies in the world, princess."

"What do you want me to say? That I took the job because it was handed to me? Fine. I did. I'm lazy and selfish and spoiled and all that other shit you keep shouting at me. Okay?" With a jerk at the cuffs, she muttered curses under her breath. The dull ache in her wrists reminding her that she wasn't healed, and that his calm behavior was nothing more than a fleeting respite.

Even if he was tormenting her in ways he couldn't possibly know.

"You're not lazy," he mused.

"*Thanks*," she mumbled, refusing to look at him.

"In fact, you seem to work all the time." His fingers stroked up until he brushed against the apex of her thighs, and she pulled hard at the cuffs binding her ankles in an effort to close her legs.

"*So?*" she hissed, digging her nails into her palms.

"Just like Daddy." There was an odd quality to his voice, something strange that belied the anger she'd normally heard from him.

"Why do you keep calling him that?" Lianna swallowed hard when he raised his eyes to her, the only expressive part he allowed with the rest of his features covered in that dense mask.

"Because I'm not going to say his name."

"Robert Mercier?"

"Yes, that asshole." His hand stilled on her skin, ceasing the endless circles he'd been making.

"Why do you hate him, *us*, so much?"

A low chuckle left his lips and he lifted his touch from her completely, giving her his back as he turned away. "You have no idea."

"Why? Tell me. Tell me what you want from us." She rattled the chains at her hands and feet. "It's not like I can do anything, so why not just tell me what the hell we've done to deserve this before you decide to torture me again?"

"Oh, princess..." For a moment she couldn't tell if he was just fucking with her by using the nickname, or if he didn't want to say her name either, but when he twisted to look at her again the hunger in his eyes seemed to be something else entirely. "You don't want to know what I know."

"Don't tell me what I want or don't want, because *trust me*, you don't know." Their gazes locked for a moment, and she didn't budge, didn't back down, even when he faced her and slid his palm up her leg to cup her mound.

"I think I know what you want more than you want to admit, and you have *no idea* what you're asking for, princess."

"Try me."

He shook his head slowly, one finger dipping between her lips to tease the liquid heat that her traitorous body summoned around him. "Tell me, did Daddy ever touch you, princess? Is that why you stick so close to him?"

"What?! No!" The recoil from his words was immediate, but when she struggled he just pushed inside her. Teasing her with torturously tender touches.

"Are you sure? Not once?" He shifted until he was looking down at her, his hand still buried between her thighs, a crook of his finger sending a tremor through her muscles. "He never snuck into your room to have a taste?"

"You're sick!" she screamed at him, but he just rolled his eyes and pulled away from her, leaving the stoked heat at her core untended.

"And you're apparently blind, princess, but that's why you're chained to the floor while he walks free, isn't it?" There was a poisonous edge to his tone as he stared at her. Her lips parted to respond, but her mind froze. It was something in his eyes, those tawny pools filled with some kind of knowledge, and for a flash there was no anger — just pity.

For himself? For her?

He broke their gaze then, facing the wall he'd pinned her against before. The memories were bitter fire, twisting and winding their way through her. Urging her to fight, to scream, to demand he answer her. But then, without another word, he stood and walked to the door. Leaving before she could rally her thoughts enough to respond. When the door clanged shut, she let out a frustrated scream, bucking against the chains as if they'd suddenly decide to free her.

"You don't know anything! Not about him, and not about ME! This is just some sick game you're playing, you asshole! You *bastard*!" Her throat ached with how loud she shouted the words, her vocal cords straining.

He doesn't know me. He doesn't know my father.

He's a liar, a monster, and my father will fix this. He will.

When she dropped back to the thin mattress, she hated how much warmer she felt on top of it, hated how her body seemed to urge her to sleep since, for the first time in what seemed like days, she wasn't curled up on a cold, hard floor. The lights dimmed a bit, but they didn't go out, and despite her racing heart and bubbling anger at his twisted accusations — she was grateful he kept the soft glow in the ceiling.

As much as she wanted to nurse her rage, the exhaustion was winning. It didn't care about the aches across her backside, or the pulse between her thighs, or the terrible things he'd said. There were only the eight glowing eyes blinking to life as sleep swallowed her whole.

Chapter Eleven

DAVID

Bracing his hands on the desk, he waited.

Waited longer than he should have, thumb tapping out a rhythm on the wood as he rapidly switched his gaze between the silent phone, his empty inbox, and the cameras where the girl was sleeping, spread wide and vulnerable. Tempting him. Waiting for him.

"Fuck!" Growling, David scooped up the rum and knocked some of it back. It was almost empty, but he'd brought spares. He always planned for everything — so why the fuck hadn't he planned for *this?*

For the possibility that Robert *fucking* Mercier would drag his feet?

Every piece of his timeline was off, behind, and the cold control he relied on was failing. He was the one that kept a steady head, that thought things through, no rash decisions… but it was all cracking, spider webbing… and if he wasn't careful he'd fall straight through the ice and drown.

But if he went down, he'd take her down with him.

Didn't Mercier realize that? After everything he'd done to the girl, after everything he'd sent, he had to understand that he was serious. Shaking his head, David slammed his knuckles into the desk, making the keyboard and mouse bounce, but he knew what he had to do.

Missed deadlines were missed deadlines, and that meant another lesson for *both* Merciers.

Dragging his chair back he sat down and set up the encrypted email with the correct link, and then he double and triple checked the programs so he'd know they were working properly.

A few minutes later he had what he needed, and his hand rested on the key to the door but he couldn't turn it. Something flickered in him, questioning him as he pictured the sleeping feminine form on the other side of the door. Blonde hair pooled under her head, delicate lips, sweeping curves.

She's never threatened you. Never threatened to have you killed. Nothing.

His stomach turned, tightening around nothing but alcohol because he hadn't eaten since… yesterday? Shit. He was barely sleeping, barely eating, but he'd made no progress. The bastard hadn't even officially sold one of his bullshit companies.

"Stick to the plan," he hissed, clenching his jaw and turning the key to unlock the door. Before he could think about it he yanked it open, letting it slam shut behind him so that she woke up. Her body jerked, making the chains rattle, and he had to admit it was a beautiful soundtrack to the rise and fall of her breasts and the trembling of her limbs.

Pale blue eyes found him before moving to the bag in his hands. "Whatever it is you want, I can help you get it. You don't have to do this."

"You can't," he answered, and he knew it was true. The lack of action from the asshole when she'd begged on the phone had made it clear. As long as he stopped, Mercier would continue to drag this out — which left only one option, he'd have to hurt the girl, torture her until he gave in for real. No more promises, no more time, no more deadlines.

Action or destruction.

"I can. Ju-just give me the chance." Her hands tightened into fists as he moved closer, tugging at the chains that he already knew wouldn't give her any slack.

"No more chances for you or Daddy. Either he signs, or we keep going until you're done."

"Done?" she whispered, and the tears pooling in her eyes caught the lights making them shine. *So fucking beautiful. Such a fucking waste.*

"That's right."

"Oh God!" The girl fought hard, ripping at the cuffs, making her breasts bounce, nipples hardened by the cool air in the room, and he watched for a minute as a few tears leaked out into her hair.

"Don't worry, I don't want you to talk to him this time." Lifting the ball gag in his hands, he smiled underneath the mask when she shook her head, panic making her flail harder at the chains while his cock stiffened against his leg.

"*Please!* Just let me talk to him again, please, tell me what you want him to sell and I'll convince him! I swear! I'll do it!" As she begged, he knelt down beside her, taking a moment to trace one finger over the soft skin of her arm. She felt so pure, so *good*, and how someone like her had come from someone so evil he couldn't figure out — but none of that mattered. All he needed was her suffering.

"Open up." He held the gag in front of her face, offering her the easy way, but she clenched her teeth tight just like he'd expected. Somehow the girl was simultaneously terrified of him, and still defiant. Where was her sense of self-preservation? Why wasn't she submitting to him fully in an attempt to make him lenient?

Not like it would work.

Wrapping his hand under her chin, he dug his fingers into the muscles of her jaw, slowly forcing her mouth wide as she whimpered. As soon as there was enough space, he forced the ball gag between her teeth, and then pressed his hand down to keep it there. "Tsk, tsk. I wasn't asking, princess, and when you disobey you just make me angry."

A sharp, incomprehensible shout escaped her lips, so he locked the gag a notch too tight, leaving her groaning as her jaw strained.

"You should hope he loves you as much as you think he does." Reaching for the bag, David dragged it toward him and slowly collected a handful of the vicious little clips. Lifting one in front of her face he pressed it open and let it snap closed.

Her voice climbed in volume as she whimpered, pleaded, and he couldn't help but smile as he pinched her nipple lightly between thumb and forefinger.

"All right, princess, time to scream." Cupping her breast, he positioned the teeth of the clamp around her nipple then let go. She bowed up on the mattress, her body arching prettily as she cried out in pain.

This was what he needed to calm the storm inside.

Pinching another bit of breast he attached another clip, and then another, picking up a rhythm as he moved to her ribs. Her pleas were stuttered with the earliest sobs of pain, but he just soaked it all in. There was something about the way she writhed, trying so hard to avoid the next bite of the clips even though there was nowhere to go.

Again, and again, and again.

The subtle *snick* of the little black clamp finding her skin, the yelp of pain, followed by another round of sob-filled babbling. Even through the gag her voice was soprano sweet, undulating in agony, and his cock twitched behind his zipper in response.

Moving down to her waist he placed another and then he looked between her thighs, stroking up the inside of her leg, and she tried to jerk them together, making the chains rattle. A stream of muffled curses came around the gag, nowhere near distorted enough for him to misunderstand.

The rage flickered in his chest and then returned with force.

Reaching into the bag he grabbed the last few clips he'd need for this part and then he applied them one at a time to one side of her cunt. Decorating the tender flesh of her labia with tiny clips that had her crying softly up above, back arching.

It only took a few minutes to weave the string through the little clamps. Starting at her breast, down her ribs, her waist, and then down between her thighs. Maybe twelve in all, and he knew they hurt, but this would be the best part.

"You know what they call this, princess?" He stood up, trailing the string in his hand as he stood over her, one foot braced between her legs on the thin mattress.

She shook her head slowly, but he could see her working it out, following the string that looped around each clip, all the way down her body, and then up into his hand.

"It's called a zipper. I'm going to count to five, and if Daddy hasn't called by the time I get to five, I'm going to take the clips off the hard way." He almost didn't finish speaking before she was sobbing, jerking at the bindings. "Ready?"

The girl screamed, begging through the gag, sucking in air as she whined, and he couldn't deny how painfully hard his cock felt in the confines of his pants. *Still, deadlines were deadlines.*

"One... two..." David was counting slowly on purpose, partially to give the asshole time to call, but mostly because the girl looked divine writhing on the floor.

"Three. Four."

Glancing up at the camera he'd set as the default for this little event, he waited and then sighed. "Five."

With a sharp jerk, he pulled the string hard and the little clips ripped free of her skin all the way up until the final one popped off her nipple and she screamed louder than he'd heard up to that point.

Son of a bitch.

The girl was pleading through the muffling effect of the gag, her voice bouncing off the walls as she wailed, screamed, sobbed. His cock twitched, so many red marks from the clips, from his hand, but he did his best to ignore her, reaching into his pocket to ensure he hadn't missed a call.

Nothing.

Looking at her again was a bad choice, lips stretched around the gag, skin marked, breasts rising and falling with her cries. The urge to hurt her resurfaced, to hear her scream for him, and he moved to her other side and picked up the zipper of clamps — and then he started to apply them again. Faster this time.

As the minutes passed, he watched Lianna's expression contort with a kind of detached fascination, the clamps standing out stark on her skin from nipple to cunt. Every bite was followed by a yelp or a cry or a sob, her cheeks shining with tears. Those baby blue eyes sparkled when they were open, but she was mostly keeping them clenched tight — trying her best to be strong.

So strong for such a tiny thing.

Just as she started to hiccup, the sobs making her entire body shake in ways that had his cock uncomfortably hard against the fabric of his pants, the little phone in his pocket rang and he stopped before he applied the last clip beside her cunt. It was a sweet tone that chimed and stuttered her hysterical panting, her eyes opening wide. "Looks like Daddy got the message, princess."

Pressing the button on the phone, he wrapped the string around his hand and stood, facing the active camera. He stayed silent as the arguing from the other end of the line slowed. "Are you there, asshole?"

David raised his hand a little and gave a single wave to the main camera, refusing to answer. While the video stream had a filter on the sound to distort their voices, the little cell phone did not.

"I signed your paperwork! Now let her go! Let Lianna go immediately!" The command made him want to snarl, and he looked back at the soft, shuddering form of the girl and ripped the string up, tearing the set of clamps from her skin.

Her screams were so perfect he almost came in his pants, but he managed to control himself so he could slowly crouch down beside her. Laying the phone down between her breasts, he tapped the speakerphone function.

As if on cue, Lianna started to plead wordlessly, shaking her head through a mess of unintelligible, feminine sounds.

"Lianna?" Mercier's voice flowed out of the tinny little speaker, and she started to sob and shout even louder, ripping at the cuffs that bound her wrists and ankles, likely bruising them worse than they already were. Silently, David traced the fresh welts left behind on her ribs. She whined, pleading softly through the gag, and Robert Mercier started to shout. "I signed your fucking contracts! Check with your people, it's done. Now let her go!"

David lifted his gaze to the camera and tilted his head. Mercier was trying to command him? Was he really so used to being obeyed by all the lemmings around him that he didn't even think about who was really in charge in this situation? The silence reigned between them, the anger a low boil in his blood as he slowly moved his hand between her thighs.

What the fuck?

Wet. So fucking wet.

She wasn't just wet, she was slippery as he slid two fingers between her lips, spreading her wide. Glistening, pink skin that surprised him, made his cock ache and his pants feel even tighter. Her hips bucked as he stroked, her cries increasing again as she likely begged him to stop.

"You said you would release her!"

David looked up at the camera and shook his head slowly, making sure the man saw it before he forced three fingers inside the girl. The wail that burst from behind the gag was unmistakable, and the series of curses that followed from the speaker confirmed that the king of Mercier Systems was watching every glorious moment.

Hot, silken wetness clenched around his fingers as she kicked at the chains, arching her back prettily, and before he'd thought about it, he had started to stroke that bundle of nerves deep inside. She tried to twist away, to escape his touch, but he held her in place with one hand on her hip so his other could work. His thumb found her clit, rolling until she eventually went silent, shaking her head, but he could feel the steady squeezing as she fought the pleasure. Lianna was swallowing, the beginnings of moans cut short in her throat, and he thought back to the way her body had gone rigid underneath him on the couch, her pussy milking him as she came — he wanted it again.

"Stop this. I sold the companies, what else do you want?" Robert Mercier's voice almost sounded concerned. Perhaps the splendid, squirming form under his hands *was* the man's weakness, the only chink in the bastard's armor.

David put a little more pressure on her clit, increasing the intensity, and she bowed beautifully for him. The phone slid up her chest, catching by her neck and he picked it up to rest it back between her breasts. Her eyes opened, blue eyes locking onto his, pleading wordlessly as a flush raced into her cheeks.

He knew exactly what she wanted even though she couldn't articulate it — she wanted him to hang up before she fell apart. She didn't want the son of a bitch on the other end of the line to hear her come for him.

Not a chance, princess.

With confident movements, he built her higher and higher, her hips twitching, her breaths increasing with soft murmurs of pleasure, those blue eyes clenching tight as she angled her head back to expose the tender column of her throat. It was a beautiful sight, her body stretched out and vulnerable, covered in his marks. Whether she hated it or not, her hips started to lift for him, matching each stroke of his fingers, hands balling into fists as she got closer and closer.

Then the first sweet moan slipped from around the gag. She bit down on it, her jaw muscles twitching as she sealed her lips to it, drawing in a hiss of air through her nose.

His eyes drifted to the phone screen, each second of the

call ticking away. Mercier was still listening, still watching, and David was going to make sure he understood exactly who was in charge, and what happened when he didn't meet deadlines.

Lianna started to shake her head from side to side, her hips rolling in a constant rhythm, and as much as he wanted to take her — in this moment he wanted to break her more. To break them both. Picking up the pace, David forced her to the edge, dragging her there with each devious stroke of his fingers, and before he could stop himself his other hand found its way into her hair to hold her down to the thin mattress. He hovered above her, mesmerized by the struggle painted across her face.

Mine, his mind purred and he forced his fingers deeper, stretching her.

As he tightened the grip in her blonde tresses, she suddenly came, a loud moan escaping as she arched hard off the fabric. Her hips jerked, bucked, trying to pull away from his touch but he followed her and dragged it out, ignored her whining pleas for him to stop. A moment later she screamed louder, her body shuddering into another orgasm, and there was nothing he could do in that moment but stare.

So. Fucking. Perfect.

Slowing the swirl of his thumb over her clit, he pumped his fingers, amazed by the pool of wetness forming under her. Lianna went limp, only a soft whine leaving her on an exhale, her muscles shivering. With a hint of regret, David withdrew, releasing her hair and unlocking the gag before he grabbed the little phone. The call was still going as he stood, and he looked up at the camera, grateful the mask hid his expression before he abruptly pressed the end button. Tucking it away in a pocket, he forced himself to walk out of the room. Away from the all-too-feminine form on the floor, chained open, and soaked and waiting for him.

So wet. She'd been so wet.

As David pulled the door closed, he locked it and then leaned back against the metal before he ripped off the mask. In a moment of weakness, he brought his fingers to his lips and tasted her. Even better than how she smelled, better than how she moaned — she tasted like heaven.

"Get a fucking hold of yourself," he hissed and wiped his hand off on his pants. With a quick adjustment of the bulge behind his zipper, he moved towards the office, steadily reassuring himself. "Mercier says he signed the papers. It worked. She's a means to an end. That's it. A privileged little whore."

He slammed the door, putting one more barrier between him and the girl. Plugging in the phone, he double-checked that the routing program had operated perfectly. Still hidden, still safely tucked away in the little prison he had built just for this. A quick check of his email confirmed receipt of the package. *Yes. It was finally happening.* Digital scans of the contracts would be next, and then everyone would follow his explicit instructions to start destroying the man. Scattering his wealth across the world.

In the meantime, he had new orders for Robert Mercier. It was all prepared, a new email with a new to-do list, and with the click of a button he sent it off.

A new timeline that David had a feeling Mercier would take much more seriously.

Drumming his fingers on the desk he tried to distract himself, avoiding the cameras as much as he could, only glancing at her form once to ensure she'd spit the gag out.

The way she'd screamed...

Groaning low, he grabbed himself through the front of his pants. He wanted to fuck her, to bury himself between her thighs and feel her arch against him the way she'd bowed into the air. But he couldn't, not yet. Switching to the video he'd put together for the first email, he hit play and watched it again. The loft apartment, in black and white, with Lianna curled up on the couch. His eyes devoured the images on the screen, her surprise as he pulled her off the couch. The first reveal of her long legs. He could still remember her pleas, playing in his mind at top volume, and the moment she ran his cock pulsed, so hard it hurt. She had fought, she had been strong — but he was stronger. It had taken so little effort to bend her over the couch, cut her underwear away, and take her.

Unzipping his pants, he shoved his boxers out of the way to grip the steel of his shaft. He could remember the silken wetness of her pussy on his fingertips, remember the way she'd clenched his cock as she'd come, the way she was lying on that mattress now, bound in cuffs and at his mercy. His strokes grew rougher, faster, building as he remembered her soft voice, her muffled sobs behind the gag, the way she'd screamed when the belt snapped against her skin. With a barking shout, he came, ruining his pants, his heart pounding in his chest — but on the screens in front of him was only further torment that the orgasm had barely ebbed.

On one screen she was lying limp over the couch, her hands in cuffs, her legs spread. On the other she was on her back, chained down, crying almost silently. The occasional hitched breath was all that the microphones could pick up. She looked so innocent. So defiled. By him. By all of this shit.

Fuck.

Princess, princess… what am I going to do with you?

Chapter Twelve

LIANNA

Everything was wrong. Everything had gone so terribly wrong. Lying on the mattress with her thighs wide, her body aching from the horrible little metal clips he'd put all over her, she couldn't quite process what had happened. The pain when he'd pulled them off in one swift jerk had felt impossible, both times. And then he'd made her orgasm. Twice.

Lianna bit her lip, not wanting to cry again, but she couldn't stop replaying it. Couldn't deny how wet she'd been after he'd ripped the *zipper* contraption off her. It had hurt, but there had been something else too. A tingling rush, a momentary euphoria that he had taken advantage of as he'd slid his fingers inside her, rubbed her clit, made her fall apart and come harder than she could remember coming in her life.

Cheeks burning, she tried to erase the memory of her moans as the phone had rested on her chest. How would she ever face her father again? After this? Her stomach turned at the idea, and she felt the stupid urge to cry again. Chained down there wasn't much else she *could* do.

The masked son of a bitch had all the power. True to his word, he hadn't let her speak during the last torture session, but it had worked. Her father had signed away whatever companies he'd wanted. *Companies*, more than one. She'd been out of her mind, but she'd still heard that part.

Her father had said he'd signed, but she was still tied down. Still here. Not free.

Which meant he wanted more.

What else could he fucking want?

Lianna groaned, shaking her head from side to side, wishing she could step away from her body. From the constant reminder of the things he'd done to her. Her nipples still ached, cheeks chapped from her tears, but she had finally stopped crying, stopped sniffling, and now there was nothing to do but think.

She knew about the companies they owned. Mostly technology manufacturing operations in countries where labor was cheap, farming their production capabilities out to other companies at a profit. Guilt plucked at her, a twinge that made her stomach twist, but she rejected the idea. This asshole wasn't some humanitarian crusader, demanding higher wages for employees overseas.

No one like that would do something like *this*.

And if that was his concern, he wouldn't have wanted her father to sell the companies anyway. They paid the employees better than the locals ever had, improved the facilities. Yes, it was to increase output, but it was also to protect the workers. Lianna had seen many of them, had seen the improvements firsthand. The grateful employees who were glad to have a job there, glad to work in clean conditions.

Grateful.

That fucking word stuck like a thorn in her mind as thoughts pinged around her exhausted brain, struggling to draw connections between this horror show and the job she'd been doing for years.

Why make him sell the companies?

Why? Why? Why?

Without the corporate connections, it wouldn't be easy to replace the workflow through the facilities. It would take time, effort, and all it did to Mercier Systems was cause a hiccup. Even a handful of companies would only slow the production schedules on a few of their agreements by a month or two, and delays on their own products would just create more demand.

It was all backwards. Confused.

Hours passed as she slipped back and forth in trains of thought without progress, before he finally returned. The man wore his anger like a dark aura, somehow invisible and obvious, but the slamming of the door and the rapid rise and fall of his chest had been more than enough warning.

Her father had missed another deadline.

There was no phone call, no belt, no threats, just him as he stood over her and she bit down on the inside of her cheek.

Eventually, he sat on the mattress beside her just as he had when he'd chained her down, only this time he was completely silent. His eyes moved over her first, then his hand, tracing her skin, leaving shivers in his wake, like a tiger playing with his food.

"*Don't...*" she whispered on a breath as his fingers slid between her thighs, but he didn't even pause. Thick digits slid inside her, and her hips tilted, back arching as she whined.

Still wet enough for him to move back and forth, to summon more liquid heat, to drag it to her clit and grind the bundle of nerves until she was twisting against the chains.

This was slow torture. His silence, the never-ending assault of unwanted pleasure, turning her own body against her until she had to choke off the subtle moans. Pressure was building inside her, tightening, careening her toward another shameful orgasm and those fucking eyes were on her. Watching, waiting for it.

Just as her hips started to lift, as the wet sounds from between her thighs invaded her ears, as the tension in her muscles threatened to snap — he stopped.

Her breathing came hard, nails digging painfully into her palms, and she felt tears prick her eyes as his fingers slid free. Behind the mask he was breathing just as hard, rigid muscles moving over his ribs as they expanded and contracted.

Then he positioned himself between her thighs and urgency took over his movements. Tearing at his zipper, shoving his pants down, he ripped open a condom wrapper. Cock in hand, he slid it on, abandoning the shiny foil wrapper beside them and she looked away.

"Please?" Lianna begged, whimpering, knowing it was useless and trying to prepare as he lined up and thrust deep in one smooth stroke.

For those first movements she craned her head back, staring at her bound wrists, at the wall behind her, refusing to look as he groaned and stretched her. Her body rocked, the chains clattering softly in the silence, and she *felt* how wet she was. It was too easy, every pinning thrust, and as he wrapped his hands around her shoulders and drove in harder she did her best to turn the moan into a cry.

This doesn't feel good.

I don't want this.

His knees moved out, digging into her thighs to stretch her further, ankles straining at the chains, and then he found a new angle. One that stroked his thick cock against a point inside that made her back arch, hips twitching to seek more. She gasped, unable to stop the moan, and found herself looking into his eyes. Face hovering over hers, she stared into the black fabric of the mask, something smooth overlaying a hard shell. Obscuring all his features, all of them except for his eyes, and as he stretched her again she watched his eyelids flutter closed as he groaned low. A hard snap of his hips caught her by surprise and she moaned again, louder, cursing herself as she bit down on her lip, but the damage had been done.

He started to move faster, muscles shifting in his arms and chest and abs as he drove himself deeper inside her. A keening whine escaped between clenched teeth, and she pulled on the cuffs at her wrists, meeting his eyes again to plead. "Don't do this to me. Please."

David

The girl felt like heaven underneath him. Soft skin, smooth curves, and her cunt was so slick, so tight. Even with the condom he was tempted to come already, but he wanted more. More of her cries, her sweet begging as she gripped him and squirmed against the mattress.

Her eyes were so fucking blue, and it made him pause as he thrust deep, feeling the tremors in her thighs, the subtle shift of her hips as she unconsciously sought her orgasm. He hadn't been this close to her, close enough to kiss her reddened lips, to taste her mouth, to see the hints of green in her irises that made it look like staring into the clearest ocean water.

Reaching up he slid his fingers into her hair and snapped her head back, causing her to shut those bottomless eyes and clench his cock inside her. The soft cry of pleasure and pain was one he knew too well, and it made him hungry for more.

Something woke up in the cold, something that wanted to devour the pampered little princess whole, and with all his mental processing power located below his hips he didn't care to fight it. "Take it," he hissed above her as he forced her head back, exposing her throat as he started to fuck her hard.

Everything blurred as she begged, cried out, pleaded with him between moans and whimpers. But all he cared about was the way her limbs contracted, the way her hips lifted, back bowing off the mattress so that her nipples grazed his chest, and the all consuming grip of her cunt around him.

It was torture of the best kind to hold back, to wait, to tease her with the strokes that made her make the sweetest sounds. The little gasps that were pure pleasure.

"*Please…*" she moaned, and he could have sworn she was begging for more as her hips met his with a clap of skin. He wanted to reach down and bend her knees to her chest, but the cuffs were holding her down, keeping her spread.

Next time, he promised himself as he braced the arm gripping her hair and slid his other hand between them. Lifting up just enough to find her clit he worked himself inside her and rubbed. Her blonde brows pulled together, face pinching in a way that almost looked like pain, and then she panted, moaned, hips moving with each swirl of his thumb — and she came.

Hard.

Gripping him in a way that sent a surge of heat down his spine, melting the ice as he braced his other arm beside her and listened to her fall apart.

"No, no, no," she whispered against his ear and he smiled behind the mask, thrusting hard again. Finding that rhythm that had her making sweet, pained sounds once more. She was too perfect. An angel fallen to earth, and he had her chained to the floor, but she felt too fucking good to care about the damnation he'd already assured himself.

Moving inside her was something he wished he could memorize, to feel forever. Like this. Slick, wet, trembling, and softly moaning as he worked them both to the edge this time. The demon inside him was howling, the chains clanking against the brackets in the floor as he fucked her hard enough to shift the mattress, and then he was gone.

Fire stroking down his spine, balls tightening, as he came with a fierce roar.

The world went white for a split second, ears deaf, body crushing her softness as pure ecstasy blasted everything away. She was heaven, nirvana, and Shangri-La all rolled into one.

Perfect, but not innocent.

He could smell her arousal through the mask, hear her panting whimpers as his ears came online, and he wanted her to fall apart again. To come with him inside her.

Growling, he leaned up and grabbed her by the throat, finding her clit again with his other hand. Clear ocean eyes wide, she choked against the constricted airway, but her hips rose, cunt twitching around his slowly softening cock.

Again.

It didn't take long. Stroking just the way her body needed, still sensitive from her previous orgasm, she came in a gorgeous display. Eyes clenched tight, crying out louder than before, lithe body tense and stretched out under him as she gripped him tight until he finally slid free.

Shut out of heaven.

Done with her, but it didn't matter, he'd brought her down to earth anyway. Tears slid over the bridge of her nose as she turned to the side and breathed hard, pants turning into quiet cries as he pushed himself to his knees and pulled the condom free and straightened his clothes.

David licked at his lip as he stood and stared down at her, at the flush in her cheeks, and the shine between her thighs. *All her.* Chained, displaying his marks. It was straight out of a fantasy.

Stumbling backwards when he tried to step, he recognized the post-orgasm weakness in his legs, the daze in his mind, but he couldn't tear his eyes off of her.

Mine. That word, that urge echoed up from the thing inside him, the one surrounded by the slush of melted ice that had kept his mind so clear up until now. Until her.

Lianna Corinne Mercier.

Turning away, he forced himself to pull open the door so he could walk in a daze to his room. David barely managed to toss the condom into the trash before he dropped onto the cot, visions of her flushed skin writhing under him flashing behind his eyes. Breaths stifled, he pulled the mask free and felt the air cool the sweat on his face as he tried to remember what he was supposed to do next.

Something with the girl. The beautiful angel that he'd ripped from her airy world and fucked into a dripping, trembling puddle until she was crying.

Again and again.

Chapter Thirteen

DAVID

A guitar strum jerked him from sleep and he sat up fast, confused and disoriented as he looked around the crowded room that had been his home for months. Another sequence of the guitar strum drew his eyes to the desk where his phone was vibrating against the cheap wood.

"Fuck," David groaned as he hauled himself upright and grabbed the phone. Staring at the screen, he dropped into the desk chair and took a deep, steadying breath before he leaned back to answer. "Yes?"

"David, it's Harry."

"I know," he answered, letting his eyes skirt the monitors that had gone black in sleep mode. Nudging the mouse woke them up, and he focused on the cameras for the cell.

"Look…" The man halted, grumbling for a moment. "Did you— have you done something?"

"I don't know what you mean." Keeping his reply short, he

checked on the girl and could tell she was asleep. Expression soft, eyes closed, breasts rising and falling evenly. If she weren't chained wide with the dark, shiny foil of a condom wrapper beside the mattress she'd almost look peaceful.

"God dammit, you know what I mean. Don't fuck with me." *Nervous*. Harry was nervous, and that was never a good thing after you'd worked with someone.

"Harry, are you alright? I'm honestly not sure what you're talking about."

"Did you take Robert Mercier's fucking *daughter*?" Harry shouted, and then started cursing, but David immediately went still.

"Someone took his daughter?" he asked, keeping his voice neutral as he watched the girl on the screen.

"I swear to God, David, if you took his daughter…" Another round of curses. "He's going to fucking kill you, you know that right?"

Pulling his eyes from the screen, David scrubbed a hand across his face and instantly caught her scent on his fingers. The fact that his cock twitched in his pants was not lost on him, but he didn't have time to think about that. There were only a few reasons Harry would be calling him about this…

Mercier could have reached out to his contacts to look for information. Someone could have reported the girl missing and Harry could have seen it on the news. Or, worst of all, Harry was trying to sell him out to someone who was listening on the line.

His stomach twisted at the last thought, but he remembered one of the last things Harry had said to him. The man owed him no more favors, but he had *also* promised not to name him. Grimacing, David reached for the rum, unscrewed the cap with one hand, and tilted up the bottle.

"Tell me what's going on, Harry."

"Shit…" There was a heavy sigh, and then he heard the flick of a lighter and a deep inhale followed by a cough. "I heard from an old friend that there were questions being asked about Lianna Mercier. He knows I live in the city so he reached out, just to see if I'd heard anything."

"And?" David prompted.

"And I didn't say anything." Another inhale, another exhale broken by coughs. "Of course I didn't fucking say anything, you think I want to paint a target on my back? On my sons' backs? On their families? Jesus Christ, David, I had no idea you—"

"You don't know anything, do you, Harry?" The words came out slowly, but David didn't feel the icy control he'd always had, instead he felt hot inside. All that melted slush boiling until he felt his head pounding from the pressure.

"No. I don't fucking know anything, but do you think Mercier is going to give a shit?" Ragged coughs broke across the line and David tried to get his vision aligned as he pulled his inbox up.

"You're not supposed to be smoking."

"Fuck off."

"I think you should just enjoy your vacation. Weren't you and your boys going to go to Vegas?" David rubbed the bottle of rum against his temple, trying to ease the ache, but the pressure was spreading. Making his ribs feel too tight, his heart beating too fast.

This is too soon. Too fucking soon.

"Yeah, we got here yesterday."

"Sounds like you need to relax, lay off the smokes, and spend time with the family. Go to a strip club or something. You're all away from the wives." He was talking on autopilot, barely paying attention as he scrambled to stop the recording in the room and pull it into the software to trim it down, back to when he'd left her.

"This isn't what your father wanted for you, David." Harry's voice was rough after the coughs, but there were no more prolonged inhales. He'd put out the cigarette, which was good for him, and the family he was lucky enough to have.

"To be frank, Harry, you didn't know my father very well at all." Grimacing, he turned away from the computer and stared at the ceiling.

"I knew him. I knew him for a long time before you even came along, and I knew him after too. You and Miranda were his life, and—"

"I need to go." Cutting him off, David sat up straight, feeling the pressure reach a critical point inside.

"David! You need to fucking listen to me, he wouldn't want this. He tried everything he could to—"

Ending the call, David slammed the phone down on the

desk and picked up the rum, swallowing until the burn in his stomach started to match the one in his veins.

Too hot.

Everything was out of control, off-track, off the plan.

Mercier was reaching out to other people when he should be reaching out to him, when he should be breaking down and doing everything he could to get his daughter back... and the only person who could do that was him.

Just him.

Closing his eyes, David waited for the rum to work its magic, turning the boiling heat inside him into a simmer that thrummed through his veins. When the pressure of his ribs started to fade he turned back to the computer and moved the slider to crop the video until he found the moment he walked out of the room.

Staring at her form against the dull gray of the mattress, and the darker gray of the concrete, he clicked and hit play. The heavy metal of the door shutting echoed over the speakers, and then it happened.

Lianna Mercier started crying, almost too softly for the microphones to pick up, but he heard it. The hitches in her breathing, the quiet whines, the sniffles and the clank of metal chain as she tried to turn and wipe her cheeks on her arms.

The pressure was back, pushing at his skin like something wanting to escape, and he hit the space bar hard enough to make the keyboard jerk on the desk. Her body stilled, the sound gone, but he could still hear her crying as he adjusted the slider to the right point and cut the video off.

He was behind schedule, *way* behind schedule, and Mercier was only making the timeline more important by reaching out for information. Which meant he'd need to make his next deadline that much more explicit in terms of how she would suffer.

Chapter Fourteen

LIANNA

The lock on the door made her exhausted muscles tense, but she knew better than to pull on the cuffs now. Bruised and aching, re-tethered on her stomach during his last visit, her wrists and ankles had to be a multi-colored mess under the leather. "Oh, princess, you lucky girl…"

Lianna didn't speak, didn't react, it only seemed to entertain him when she begged. He ripped her head back by her hair anyway, straining her neck as she tried to brace her elbows against the floor.

"Still in there, princess? Because we're not done yet." A low, dark laugh rumbled behind the mask as he dropped her back to the mattress. She waited for him to hurt her, to bring out some new torment, but instead she felt him working at the cuff on her ankle. "Daddy just sold his controlling shares in Dargen Technologies, and that's one less way for him to launder money."

Recognition bloomed inside her at the name. Dargen was a relatively small company. They made hardware. *What exactly did they make?* She couldn't remember, but money laundering? Somewhere inside the mess her mind had become she tried to connect dots, but then her other leg was uncuffed and he flipped her effortlessly. Intense eyes stared out from the mask, wild in the excitement of his fresh success.

"Tell me, do you think he's finally decided you're important enough to protect?" He brushed her cheek and she turned away from him, refusing to answer as he started to uncuff her hands. Those fingers brushed her arm just below the last cuff. "Or do you think he's enjoying the videos?"

"He's going to find me." The words were rough, her throat too dry, but he'd heard her. A huff of a laugh escaped him, and then she was free from the chains. The man didn't even try to stop her as she rushed to get away from him, scrambling for the wall to curl up against it while her body rang with reminders of pain and the stiffness of being chained down for so long.

Laughing to himself, he gathered the chains slowly, but Lianna had no doubt as his hungry gaze crawled over her bruised skin that he would take great joy in punishing her, taking her again if her father didn't jump through whatever hoops he had concocted next. He paused at the door, holding it open like a taunt. "Just one more question. Don't you think if he could find this place, he would have already come for you?"

She opened her mouth to answer, but he was gone, and she wasn't sure what to say anyway. As soon as the grinding sound of the lock confirmed he wasn't coming back, she dragged the mattress into the corner and curled up where it felt safest.

Still a stupid idea.

She wasn't safe. One thing the man had made *very* clear was that nothing could protect her. Nothing could stop him. If he wanted her chained, he chained her. If he wanted to touch her, he did. If he wanted her to scream, or beg, or cry, or come — she did.

And he proved it again and again as time passed in fits and bursts. Dragging in his absence, with no clock and no change in the strange lighting to signal it… and then there would be another sandwich. A paper plate of lunch meat. A protein bar. Meals that seemed to come at no set interval, but how was she supposed to tell how many hours passed? How long had she even been in this room? How long had it been since he'd come to the apartment, and taken her?

Days? A week?

A hysterical giggle erupted from her lips and she pulled her legs tighter to her chest on the mattress. If only she really were a princess there might be a prince looking for her instead of a father weighing the return on investment to each fucking decision. Because risk analysis and financial reports weren't going to help her escape this prison. ROI wasn't going to do shit for her against a thick, metal door, and there was definitely no negotiating with the villain in this hell.

Her gaze rolled upwards as she wondered if anyone was concerned about her absence, if her friends had even noticed she'd been gone. Maybe if she hadn't just ditched Denise it was possible, but with the way she worked? With the way her father expected her to? It was likely no one even knew.

And the people who *did* know clearly weren't rushing to save her.

It could have been days and days and she wouldn't know. Was there even a point to time anymore with that neutral, half-light coming from the gray ceiling? Neither morning, nor noon, nor night.

It was nothing.

The room was nothing — and she was dissolving inside it.

David

Staring at the screen, he wasn't sure how he felt. Good? Bad? Victorious? Corrupt?

All of the above seemed to fit, and not, at the same time. It was a fucking mess, and one thing he was sure of was that he had no idea how to reconcile it. Harry had called, three times in the last day, and he hadn't answered. At least the man had been smart enough not to leave a voicemail, but the knowledge that Robert Mercier was calling in favors was still eating at him.

Somewhere there was someone who could probably route those videos and emails back to him. It would take time, but would it be enough time to destroy the man before it all came crashing down? *That* was something David couldn't answer.

Thinking over the plan used to be comforting. He would outline every piece of it, down to the last detail, and it had felt solid. Perfect. Unbreakable.

Yet, here he was a full day or more behind schedule because Robert Mercier didn't care enough to save his own fucking daughter.

And you can't stop fucking her.

Kicking the leg of the table, David stood and paced away from the computer.

There was something undeniably satisfying in hurting Lianna Mercier, in hearing her scream and cry out — but there was also no denying the urge he had to hear her come.

Even when he'd uncuffed her ankles to flip her to her stomach, the entire plan had been to take her ass. To make her scream, to make it hurt, and instead he'd just taken her cunt again. Rubbed her clit, made her come before he'd chained her down once more. It was starting to become a problem.

Belting her again had been impulsive. Reactive. He'd been too close, too gentle. *Fuck*, he'd treated her like any other girl he might have taken to bed, and Lianna Mercier was not like any other girl. She was the heir to the devil, the man who had taken everything from him, from his family, and he owed it to them and so many others to get their revenge.

No matter how many graves it took.

But when he thought about Lianna in one of those graves, something reacted in him. Something he couldn't quite describe, but it was twisted up in all of the confusing heat that dealing with the Merciers had caused. But had she been involved? Did she know? There was no more calming ice inside him, no more solid core to lean on, everything was shaky. Everything was melting and breaking down, and that made it hard to think straight.

Picking up the bottle of rum again he was surprised to see it almost half-empty. *Hadn't he just opened it?* Ignoring the magic of disappearing rum, he sat down on the cot and picked up the picture he kept on top of the small fridge.

There were promises he'd made. Promises that meant more than the well-being of one spoiled blonde girl who was the heir to Robert Mercier's corrupt enterprise... right? Staring into the picture he wished he could hear the voices captured there once more, to know for sure if he was correct, or if Harry was the one who was right.

When he leaned back on the wall he could see the monitor with her on it, her pale form huddled in the corner, a shining beacon of pale skin and golden hair.

An angel.

She looked like one, absolutely felt like one, and as he stared at the screen he realized what was really bothering him. The same idea that had come up once before — she had never threatened him. Not with the power of her family, not to kill him, nothing. After everything he'd done to her, after every way he'd hurt her, she had only ever talked about her father finding her.

Saving her. *From him.*

David's stomach roiled, acid etching the back of his throat as he stared at her form on the mattress in the corner. Could she actually be innocent? Could she be good? Could the offspring of the devil still be an angel?

A beep came from the computer and he pushed himself up from the cot, carrying the rum with him as he moved towards it to see what it was. Laughing under his breath he sat down hard in the chair and read through the email again.

"Well, look at that, Dad," he muttered under his breath and tilted the rum up again.

Chapter Fifteen

LIANNA

There were fuzzy things in her brain, as if each thought was covered in dust that blurred the ideas and made it difficult to brush clean. Sound filtered into her head and she realized she was humming again, a half-chewed hangnail hung on one finger that she bit off to keep from tearing it to the quick.

I'm losing my mind... she thought, and the pulse of need between her thighs only confirmed it. He was horrible. A nightmare wrapped in a beautiful package, and some twisted part of her craved him. Some tingling place at the base of her spine woke up when she remembered his hands, the belt, the clips, the way he overpowered her when he came for her. Over and over.

That part of her was evil.

She had to fight it.

Swallowing, Lianna leaned forward and picked up the plastic cup, sipping water carefully before she set it back down. One, two, three, five, eight red lights. Eight cameras.

Eight like the number of legs on a spider, and this was the web. This room a cocoon of silk he'd wrapped her in so he could devour her slowly. Empty her out. Bit by bit. Destroying her at his leisure until she was a simple husk of herself.

And, worse, she was letting him.

"Stop it," she whispered to herself, a harsh hiss. Where was the girl who walked into meetings with her head up? Where was the woman who had presented her Bachelor's thesis to a bunch of smug professors who had doubted her, who had taken one look at her and sneered? The same woman who had then impressed them with her discussion of Titian, and Caravaggio, and Gentileschi? She was still that person.

Even naked and bruised and welted and violated, she was still smart, could still be strong.

The frigid water settled in Lianna's stomach with a shiver that made her sit up, pressing her spine into the concrete wall. A tiny flicker of strength surfaced in the dimness of her thoughts, the color of Titian red. It brushed across the inside of her mind, called her forward to claim her strength. To be brave. To be unbreakable. To seek vengeance.

She would not be a damsel in distress, a princess waiting for a rescue.

Staring at the door, Lianna thought of her captor. The mask, the hard body, the hard— With a shake of her head, she took a deep breath, and drew strength from some unknown well inside her. She had to act or she was going to dissolve in this cocoon.

"Hey!" she shouted, glancing up at one of the cameras.

Why are you summoning the villain back?

"I want to know what you want! What are you doing? Why do you want my father to sell these companies?" As she rattled off questions, emptying her brain of the twisted cloud of thoughts, the camera lights started to tick off one by one. Her muscles tensed, fear zipping up her spine, but the tingle was there too. A warm, buzzing, hungry sensation in her lower belly.

Stop it. You don't want him. You just want answers.

No more red eyes staring down, cameras off, but the lights at least stayed on.

It was only a moment later when the grating sound of the metal lock filled the room, and then he was there. No shirt, no gloves, no pants, no shoes. He was in black boxer briefs, molded to him so closely he may as well have left them behind, and — of course — the damnable mask. Every tanned inch of him was power, and she stared as he leaned his head against the doorframe. "You called, princess?"

"What—" She jerked back because there was a warm, rumbling slur to his voice. "What the fuck? Are you drunk?"

"I'm celebrating." He stepped into the room, a large bottle of some dark liquor in his other hand. The door snapped shut beside him, but he barely twitched.

"Celebrating what?"

"Your father is finally taking me seriously, and I am pruning the tree of his empire branch by branch." Raising one hand, he mimed scissors cutting through the air. "Snip, snip, snip."

"What do you mean?"

The man had let his gaze drift to the side, but he looked back at her when she spoke. "I'm taking everything from your family. Just like I promised."

"Promised who?" she whispered and he walked towards her with slow steps, his bare feet padding across the floor, the muscles in his legs and abs shifting in time with his movements. She fought the urge to run, driving her nails into her palms to stay seated.

No more games.

"You are beautiful." He stopped close to her and set the bottle down on the floor, lowering into a crouch. "Even more so than you are on TV. I think it's the fire inside you. You always look like a lifeless doll on television. But... you're not."

"Not what?" She dodged his hand as he reached out to touch her cheek.

"A lifeless doll," he answered flatly. A low laugh rumbled in his chest as he moved and sat on the other end of the thin mattress. "I thought you would be."

"A doll?"

"Empty. His puppet." His words made her forehead crease, her brows drawing closer together, but her eyes stayed on the bottle.

Keep him talking.

"Why would I be empty? Why would I be a puppet?"

"Because of *him*. I don't know how you exist at all. You *shouldn't* exist. You shouldn't be... *you*." He shook his head slowly and shuffled backwards until his shoulders met the wall.

"I don't understand." Lianna watched as his eyes closed through the holes in the mask, and she carefully inched forward.

"Of course you don't, princess. You're so blind. So innocent." The words were slurring more, and she reached for the bottle just in front of his feet, her hands closing around the neck of it, still warm from his touch.

"Innocent?" she asked softly, trying not to alert him to her movements as she lifted the bottle silently from the floor and moved to her knees.

"Like an angel, like he stole you from heaven. I don't know how you're like this, I never expected you to——" His hand caught her wrist as she swung the bottle hard towards his head, and pain shot up her arm as he twisted his grip sharply. A yelp escaped her as the bottle dropped, undamaged, to the mattress.

Shit.

Tawny brown eyes stared out from the mask, somehow angry even through the watery haze of the alcohol. "Princess," he growled, and she channeled all of her terror and rage, shouting as she reared back and hit his arm hard, breaking his grip on her wrist.

As soon as she was free, she threw herself backwards, almost tripping over her own feet, but she recovered and rushed for the door. Her hand closed around the handle and ripped it open in a single breath. Brighter light, more concrete, but she didn't care. She was out of that damn room, out of the web.

Lianna chose a direction and ran.

The hall ended in metal doors and she was maybe fifteen feet away when a sharp jerk at her hair almost yanked her completely off her feet. Somehow she turned the fall into a simple stumble, smacking into the wall, but he didn't wait as he secured his grip in her hair more fully. "That was *not* smart, princess."

Forcing her to bend forward, he tried to pull her back with him, but she dug her heels into the concrete floor and threw her weight to the side. The ripping sting at her scalp wasn't enough to stop her, and he stumbled with her. His balance imperfect, he wavered on his feet, and they struggled for control. She hit his chest, clawed at his bare hand in her hair, but he was impossibly strong. Eventually he managed to knock her leg out from under her and she landed hard on her knees. With uneven steps, he half-dragged her back towards the room, tears stinging her eyes as the fierce ache ran down her neck, but still she raged. "Let me go. Let me the fuck up! I won't be a fucking pawn for you anymore!"

Collapsing to the floor just before the heavy door to her prison, she forced him to stop short. He turned on her with a guttural, animalistic growl. "Get up."

"No!" she shouted. She wouldn't bow to him anymore, wouldn't be his pawn, his tool. This evil, black masked, bastard. Stubbornly she fixed herself to the floor, her legs out to her side so that if he wanted to move her, he would have to do it bodily. She would *not* walk, or crawl, back into her own prison.

"Do you have any idea what I can do to you?" he threatened, but she laughed bitterly.

"Are you fucking kidding?! I'm covered in bruises from you! Welts! I ALREADY KNOW WHAT YOU DO!" Turning, she tried to kick at his leg, but he barely grunted and she screamed in frustration as she reached back to dig her nails into his bare hands. Air hissed between his teeth as she tore his skin, but it was pure victory when he released her and she scrambled backwards. Breathing heavily, she took in his huge, broad form, knowing that another dash for the doors was useless. "What the fuck do you want from us? Why won't you just tell me?"

"Haven't I made it clear?" He tilted that flat, expressionless mask as he looked down at her. "I want to use you to destroy him."

"I won't let you. I'm done."

"You are so blind, princess."

"Stop calling me that!" The scream was a combination of all of her rage, her shame, her pain, but he used that moment to lunge forward and grab her arm, hauling her forcibly back into the room. Instead of throwing her to the floor, he turned and lifted her, pinning her to the wall, his body flush to hers.

Forcing a knee between her thighs, he spread her as she tried to push his chest back. "What bothers you so much, *princess?* That I call you that, or that Daddy wanted to keep you his little princess forever?"

"Fuck off!"

In an instant he cupped her ass and lifted her from the floor, his hips splitting her legs until she had no choice but to wrap them around his waist. The tingling hum at the base of her spine ushered a surge of shame through her system. She was not enjoying this, didn't want this, she was not—

"Tell me... if I touch you right now, will you be wet?" His voice was a low purr that amplified the sparkling heat inside her and she hated it, hated him, and hated most of all that it was true.

"Let go of me."

"You're wet. I know it. You always are for me." The man leaned forward, brushing the mask across her shoulder as he nuzzled her neck. He took a deep breath against her skin, a groan escaping him as he pressed his hips forward, the growing hardness unmistakable. "You need it as much as I do."

For a moment her hands were still braced against his chest, trying uselessly to push him away, to ignore his words, but then a thought struck like lightning. Before the fear could stop her, she reached up and ripped the mask over his head in a single, fluid motion. Tawny brown eyes immediately went wide beneath sculpted dark brows. He had the features of an angel, too beautiful to be so evil. A seraph with high cheekbones, the beginning shadow of a beard covering his cheeks sloping towards lips parted in shock. The mask hung at her side, gripped white-knuckle tight in shaking fingers, as his handsome face contorted with rage.

He caught her by the throat, slamming her head back against the wall as he snarled. "What the *fuck* have you done?"

"No more hiding," she hissed at him, and his eyes danced over her face.

"That's what you want? You want to see me?" Releasing her throat, he pulled her away from the wall, grabbing her hips, and he almost stumbled as he walked them both towards the mattress. Dropping her onto it, he followed and pushed his way roughly between her thighs, miming a thrust. "You want this?"

"No! I—"

"Are you really going to try and lie to me right now?" His hand slipped between them, and an instant later he swept up her cleft. Soaking wet. Slick with the damning evidence of her twisted urges, and she cursed herself. *Damaged, broken, wired wrong.* Catching her legs, he pushed her knees towards her chest and then spread her wide, sliding down until his shoulders held her open — and then he dragged his tongue through her wetness in a confident swipe.

Oh God.

The pure shock of it made her lift her hips. It had *nothing* to do with the tingling buzz at the base of her spine, or the way his thumbs dug into the tender flesh of her thighs to bare her completely for him.

"Yes…" he groaned against her, the low vibration of his voice making her shiver, but all she could see was the tousle of dark hair atop his head as he started to devour her.

"Please, stop! I don't want this! STOP!" Lianna pleaded in desperation, because no matter what her mind thought, she knew what her body felt. Pleasure stormed through her like an invading army, pushing its way past her borders, starting a war inside that she was ill-equipped to win.

"So. Many. Lies." Each word was punctuated by a deviously long trace of his tongue that ended with a torturous flick over her clit. Just as she opened her mouth to beg for him to stop, he focused in on that bundle of nerves, sending her into gasping moans that cleared the words from her mind.

When she tried to arch her back, to lift her hips against him, he simply pressed her flat with the strength in his arms, pinning her exactly where he wanted her.

Why had she ever thought she could win?

He concentrated all his attentions on her clit until she was a whimpering mess. There was no relief from the constant, vibrant teases that had her on edge in minutes. In one moment he would bring her to the very brink, until she thought there was no way to hold back the pending orgasm… and then he would slow, lapping at her pussy in long strokes of his tongue that eased her racing heart. Then she would inch back, slowly calming until she felt somewhat in control of her body again, but then he would take it back.

It was a twisted game, one that made it clear he could satisfy or ruin her at his leisure. The various bruises across her front and back, around her wrists and ankles, were testament enough. But this? This taunting amusement of bringing her to the cliff, holding her over until her hips were bucking against her will, seeking completion, *this* was pure torture. Pure evil.

Tension coiled inside her, forcing her muscles to a painful tightness, and she couldn't take it.

"I want to come, please!" The plea leapt from her lips before she had even thought it through, and he looked up from between her thighs, his chin wet with her.

"Say it again." Spreading her further, he held her knees painfully apart, straining the muscles as he leaned up. The hard outline of his erection was evident behind his boxers, at the bottom of his carved abs. Forced to look at him, she couldn't make her tongue shape the words. With a low chuckle he moved up her body until he was rubbing himself slowly, deliberately against her. A wicked promise of completion as sparks lit their way up her spine. "Beg me."

"No." Lianna shook her head, whimpering as he started to rock. Teasingly slow, but he never got her close enough that she could push herself over with a shift of her hips, and after a moment she realized she was effectively grinding her clit against the hard ridge of his cock in desperation. "Damn you!"

"I'm already damned, princess. Say it, and I'll give you what you want."

"Oh God... I hate myself," she confessed on a whisper as the arousal turned to fire in her blood, and he laughed, his lips tracing over her collarbone as he slowly rolled his hips above her in a mockery of what she needed.

"Give in. Say it."

She groaned, winding her fingers in her hair to pull at it like she might reactivate the section of her brain that could still function. The part not drowning in this primal need to be overpowered, to be taken by the villain between her thighs.

"If it helps, I kind of hate you too. But a hate fuck will still scratch the itch." He grinned down at her, and the devilish smirk somehow undid her. There was nothing *good* in this situation, nothing redeemable, but somewhere in the chaos, the torture, the nightmare of it all — she'd lost the ability to care.

"I want to come."

"And I want to fuck you," he growled and moved against her.

Clenching her jaw tight, she relaxed her thighs, letting his weight settle over her, and he nuzzled under her chin, his hands sliding up her sides to hold her arms gently above her head.

"I want to hear you say it, princess."

"Say what?" she snapped at him, bucking her hips up towards the hardness between her thighs still infuriatingly encased behind cloth, but he growled down at her. A wordless chastisement.

"Princess…" He nipped at her breast. "Say it or I'll leave you high and dry. Well, high and very, *very* wet anyway."

"I can't." The words were a whine, and he laughed softly as his tongue traced her skin, his hips starting to pick up a rhythm that was more torment than pleasure.

"Do you want me to fuck you? Do you want me to make you come, princess? Just nod for me."

It was exactly what she could have never said aloud and even though she cursed herself, hated her weakness — she nodded. A satisfied groan escaped his lips as he propped himself on an elbow to shove his boxers out of the way. She caught one glimpse of his hard shaft before she forced her eyes back towards the ceiling, not even fighting as he lined up and thrust hard.

Instantly, achingly full.

The gasp was half shame and half satisfaction, but he wasn't waiting for a second invitation. He swung his hips back and slammed into her again, and again, and her hips met him every time. Low grunts of effort left his parted lips, but he nuzzled against her neck like a lover. His mouth tracing firebrands of nipping kisses over her skin, damning her with each thrilling pulse of pleasure from between her thighs.

"Why?" she whispered, biting back the moans as he groaned above her.

"Just accept it, accept that this is what you wanted. This is what you've always needed."

The painful truth of it silenced her, and those visions of strength, of being unbreakable, were shaken to their core. Something about him seemed to burrow under all her defenses, all her well-formed logic, all her intellect and day-to-day strength, and it left her bare and raw.

Each thrust stoked the growing fire inside her, the one that had her spreading her legs wider, that kept her from struggling when he forced one knee to her chest to send the next thrust even deeper, making her ache. Making her want him to do it again, because with the pain came some kind of absolution for the pleasure she was taking. If it hurt, it cancelled out the sparkling heat that wound its way up her spine, blurring the thoughts in her brain until all that mattered was that he would keep going. Keep pushing her towards that intolerable horizon she knew was waiting.

And it was close. Too close.

"Please," she begged on a hoarse whisper.

Give me more. Give me enough to end this. Give me oblivion.

His fist found its way into her hair, winding until his grip forced her head back, baring her neck to him like some sacrificial lamb. He nipped at her like he might tear her throat out, but his teeth pressed into the place where her shoulder began instead, and as the sharp shock of pain crashed into the swell of pleasure — she came.

It was lightning and thunder in the same breath, the world shaking under her and inside her all at once. She cried out something senseless, digging her nails into his back to leave deep furrows in their wake, and then he growled low against her skin and joined her. His cock kicked deep, and she barely flinched when she felt the warm rush of seed filling her, pulse after pulse.

Damned.

Their breaths were a cacophony, his teeth lifting from her skin to leave the soreness behind, but even that quickly faded into the myriad of bruises and welts that covered her. A map of their interactions painted across her skin in reds and deep purples, blues, and fading sickly greens. Her body was a book she couldn't bring herself to read, to even acknowledge.

Traitor.

"Fuck…" he hissed as his cock slid from her, but he stayed poised above her, tawny brown eyes finding hers in the aftershock of what she'd done. "You are so beau—"

"No, no, no…" Tears threatened to choke her as he froze, and she swallowed them down, breaking the stare to turn away from him.

"What is it, princess?" There was a hint of humor in the

languid tone of his voice, the sated beast had returned. Luxuriating in her pain, in her shame.

"I can't believe I—" The words wouldn't come and she groaned and covered her face with her hands. "I hate this, I hate *you*. I hate myself," she whispered.

He laughed quietly as he pushed himself off her, and then she felt him settle on the mattress near her legs. "Take this, it helps."

Peeking between her hands, she saw the offered liquor bottle and rallied herself into a sitting position, feeling the wetness between her thighs like a needling reminder of her weakness. Grabbing the bottle without another word, she unscrewed the top and poured a hearty amount into her mouth. The burn almost made her choke, but she swallowed hard and then coughed, her eyes watering as the fiery, sweet rum hit her stomach like a bomb going off. Remnants of the explosion immediately crashed into her bloodstream, her body taking it in as if it had been waiting for it, and before she'd opened her eyes again she felt the first rush. "You're right," she rasped, and took another hard drink, feeding the fire. "This is what I needed."

"Okay, share." He took the bottle back and tilted it up, swallowing with no visible reaction to the burn.

"I want more."

"Of me?" His lips formed a lopsided, cocky smile, and she rolled her eyes and turned away from his angelic face. There was a throbbing pulse between her thighs, the lingering sparks of her orgasm refusing to be ignored as her nervous system tried to wind down.

Too much adrenaline. Too much pleasure. Too much fear. Too much futile rage.

"Will you just tell me why you're doing this?" There wasn't even desperation in her voice anymore, she felt hollowed out by all the torment, the mind-games, the violence. When he offered her the liquor again, moving the bottle into her line of sight, she took it gladly.

"You know why. It's all to destroy your father, and — I might add — it's working."

"But why him? Why us? My father has never done anything to deserve—"

The man scoffed hard, a scowl passing over his lips as he looked away from her, snatching the bottle back. "Don't be naïve, *princess*, we both know he's not as perfect as he pretends to be."

"He has *never* hurt me." The accusation from before popped up in her mind, and she denied it again. He had always been a good father, sometimes absent, sometimes distant, but always *good*.

Except he let you suffer here, lectured you about selling companies while this beautiful villain hurt you over and over again. Didn't that count as hurting?

"Then I guess you really do live a charmed life." Just as the masked villain went to take a drink, she took the bottle from his hand and drank instead.

"He's a good man," she insisted, but she wasn't sure whom she was really trying to convince. Him, or herself.

Selling a company takes time, Lianna.

"Do you really believe that?" There was open disgust in his

voice, and she looked over at him, finally able to study his features. His dark brows were pulled together, his lips parted as soft breaths moved in and out. Too gorgeous to be so evil, so full of hate.

"Yes. I do," she answered, though it felt like a lie.

He huffed out a bitter laugh and stood, popping his boxers back into place, then he held out his hand for the bottle, mute and sullen. When she didn't offer it, he growled and turned on his heel, moving to the door in furious silence. The lock grinding into place removed any hope that he'd forget in his distracted state, but she still had the liquor — and that was better than anything else he'd given her. Even better than the lights, or the toiletries. She could still feel her pulse between her thighs, her clit pounding out the rhythm of her heartbeat, and what small, sane piece of her could still feel guilt was wracked by it.

Fortunately, there were still several inches of rum in the bottle.

A few minutes later, when the lock on the door shifted again, there was one less inch in the bottle and she was rapidly heading towards drunk. The man hadn't bothered to gather the mask, but he did drop a stack of photos onto the floor. They scattered, some flipping over and sliding across the concrete. "Why don't you look at these and tell me what you think of daddy dearest, princess."

She didn't even open her mouth to speak, cradling the bottle against her bare chest as she stared numbly at him. He waited, as if she were supposed to have some line in this little play they were acting out, but then he shook his head and left.

The door shut, locked again, and she looked at the

scattered pictures for a few minutes before she slowly moved towards them, gathered them, and then found her way back to the mattress. With another drink, ignoring the wetness lingering between her thighs, she flipped the first one until it was upright.

Chapter Sixteen

LIANNA

The photos were a strange mix of old and new. Different sizes, some in color, some in black and white, and one smaller picture had a faded orange hint to it that reminded her of those taken in the seventies.

Lianna sat at the edge of the mattress, crossing her legs to create a nest for the bottle of rum, laying the photos out in front of her. Eleven in total.

And her father was in several of them.

Picking up one she studied the man her father was shaking hands with. Both of them were smiling like someone had told a great joke, both wearing fine suits, standing in front of a restaurant. Nothing about the other man sparked a memory no matter how long she stared at his face, so she gave up and picked up another.

The next picture was large, taken through the window of a house like some kind of creepy stalker photo, and all it showed was her father sitting at a table with two other men. He was in profile, but she knew it was him. The dark haired man facing the window was someone else she didn't know, and the last man was turned away. Flipping the photo over she saw three names: *Alain F. Marc F. Denis G.*

What the hell?

She turned the picture back over and stared at the shape of her father's face, the light catching his blond hair, and she was sure it was him, but his name wasn't on the back.

Huffing, Lianna took another drink and grabbed the next photo in line. This one was at night, a gritty black and white picture showing men in dark coats standing around big boxes. One was open and a man was lifting out a gun, a big one that was probably some kind of rifle. On the back it simply read: *Faure November 2011.*

The photo beside that one showed a group of thin women in short dresses huddled together beside an SUV. There were three men in the picture, two beside the women and one leaning on the car, and she didn't know any of them. They were all dressed in warm looking clothes, and when Lianna leaned closer she could see shadows of bruises on the women's lean wrists as they wrapped their arms around themselves. Rage plucked at her from beneath the growing haze of the rum, because her wrists looked even worse. Dark purples and blues like thick, uneven bracelets.

She wanted to rip the photo to shreds, but instead she tossed it away from her and let it slide across the concrete. What the fuck was she supposed to learn from these photos? They made no sense, and she felt crazy for even looking at them. After everything he'd done to her, why was she even entertaining him?

Lianna leaned back, swallowing the sweet taste of the rum

that didn't seem to burn anymore. Her eyes skirted the remaining photos and she nudged one with her foot.

That's him.

The next two pictures were taken at the same place, one showing her father hugging another man she didn't know at some outdoor party, and the next was him from the back with Uncle Mike standing beside him. They both looked younger and when she turned it over she saw why: *Faure-Molet wedding, June 1997.* Twenty-years ago. She would have been six.

Dropping them she pulled another towards her and skimmed it. Another grainy black and white, but this one showed men climbing out of cars. Turning it over she was surprised to see *January, 1983* written below a list of names: *Jean, Marc, Alain, Jean-Luc, Joseph Blanc, Roland Boyer.* Staring at the front again she tried to make out the faces, and then she saw the two young men with light hair. Both looked stoic, but the one on the right looked almost like...

The click of the television coming on made her jump, and then rapid Spanish came over the speakers. *What the fuck?* Standing up, she stepped over the photos, taking the rum with her to watch the screen. A male reporter stood outside the gates to a large house where police were walking back and forth. Subtitles rushed across the bottom of the screen and she tried to keep up, but only caught bits and pieces of the story. *Family murdered in their house. Two guards also dead. Seven people total. No suspects.*

As the man continued speaking a gurney rolled behind him, and the shape of a child's arm and small hand peeked out from under a sheet. Lianna's stomach turned, and she was about to ask out loud why he was making her watch this when she saw the caption on the screen. *The Jacinto Manufacturing facility will continue operations.*

"Jacinto Manufacturing?" she muttered the name under her breath. Something about it felt familiar, but she couldn't place it before the clip stopped and another started. It was another news report, and she shook her head, speaking to the ceiling because she knew he could hear her. "I'm not watching any more of this shit."

To make her point she moved back to the mattress and sat down on it, back to the wall with the television on it. The sound continued for a minute, the light playing across the smooth concrete, and then it stopped completely and turned off.

That's right, asshole. No more games.

Glaring at the photos in front of her she didn't understand what she was supposed to make of them. It was like he'd given her a handful of puzzle pieces, refused to show her the box they came in, and expected her to divine the meaning of it from the universe.

Laying down on her side, Lianna propped her elbow up so she could still drink the rum. The photos taunted her, scattered around the edge of the mattress, and she snagged the small one with that orange seventies feel. It was a family photo, three boys standing in front of a father and mother, everyone smiling in their Sunday best. They looked like a nice family, a happy one. The faded writing on the back of it made her forehead crease, it was from 1974, but they were the same names.

Lianna sat up to scramble for the photo of everyone getting out of the car. Placing the two side by side she matched the names on the back. *Jean, Marc, Jean-Luc, and Alain.*

Those names were in both photos, just nine years apart. The mother, *Liliane*, wasn't in the car photo, but the father, the boys... As she flipped to look at the pictures again a chill inched down her spine, raising the hairs on the back of her neck. Faces changed, from childhood to adulthood, but there were always some of the same features. A nose, a smile, ears... or a set of dimples.

Grasping for photos she set them side-by-side, staring at an impossible answer that still didn't answer anything. Didn't explain anything. Didn't mean *anything* — and it couldn't be true anyway.

None of it.

Raising her eyes to the cameras, Lianna contemplated speaking but she was enjoying the silence. Nothing but the strange hum of air that felt like a texture against her skin. Out of habit, she reached for the rum and tilted it up, a few sweet drops touching her tongue before she sighed and pushed the empty bottle away. It rolled across the photos scattered in front of the thin mattress, and then onto the concrete. With a soft *clink*, it stopped against one of the rings embedded in the floor.

The same one he'd chained her wrists to the day he'd given her the mattress.

Rubbing her face, she groaned and tried to chew on her thumbnail only to find it bitten down all the way. "Fuck this," she whispered to the room, to *him* if he was listening.

There was an ocean of confusion around her that she didn't have the energy to tackle while drunk, so she turned away. Turned away from all of it to face the wall, resting her cheek against her arm. Her bloodstream was alight with the fire of the alcohol, brimming with the buzzing after-effects of adrenaline, and a portion of her was wondering if the man would return if she called. If he was listening, standing just outside the door, waiting to see what she made of his strange offering.

But that was too much to think about, and she had no interest in another confrontation. No interest in fighting him or arguing with him. So she closed her eyes tight against the dim light, and pleaded with her mind to let go of the things she'd read and seen.

To stop trying to draw connections from names scribbled by a psychopath.

She was either going to throw up or sleep off the rum soon — and she was very much hoping it was the second.

David

Watching Lianna curl up on the mattress, all of the evidence at her back, David felt his fist tighten around the bottle of vodka.

The girl was smarter than this. Smart enough to look at the photos and figure out who her father really was — but instead she was going to sleep. He toyed with the edge of the folder on his desk, plucking at it with his thumb, tempted to go rip the door open and toss it in with her.

No. That's too far.

He almost laughed as the idea surfaced in him. After

everything he'd done to her, every fucked up thing in his attempt to break her, to ruin her father, to punish her for things he now believed she had no idea about... *this* was too far?

Apparently, yes.

He pushed his hands into his hair and even with all the alcohol he could still smell her, still taste her, still see her body arching above him as he'd delved his tongue inside her. It was messing with his head.

Grabbing the vodka he stumbled to the doorway and barely caught himself against the frame before he hit the floor. The hallway was tilting and that meant there was either a severe foundation shift he wasn't aware of, or he was shitfaced. When he took a step forward and had to catch his balance he knew which one it was, he just couldn't bring himself to care.

The plan was progressing, and soon Mercier's corrupt corporate empire would be dust, and the family would be hobbled. It wouldn't matter that the girl had seen his face, none of it would matter because it would be done. It would finally be over.

Brushing his hand across the door to her cell, he kept walking, one hand on the wall to steady him, until he found the bathroom. With the water warming up for a shower, he leaned against the wall and swallowed another mouthful of vodka. He just stared when he caught sight of himself in the mirror.

He looked like hell.

He needed a shave, and a haircut, and to not look like a drunk.

None of those things were happening tonight though. The best he could do was a hot shower, brushing his teeth, and going to sleep. In the morning there would be one less puppet company for Mercier to use, one more family avenged.

And Lianna Mercier? The ruined princess, the fallen angel, the damned daughter of the son of a bitch that had inspired all of this?

Well, she'd still be there. After all, Harry had done a hell of a job with the door.

Chapter Seventeen

LIANNA

There was someone crying. A heart wrenching sound, deep and full of despair. The tile was cold under her feet as she walked towards the door, nervous energy tickling its way up her spine.

She wasn't supposed to be here. She was supposed to be sleeping.

The doorknob was practically eye-level, and she wrapped her hand around it to twist, but it barely budged. From the other side of the wood the crying stuttered and slowed.

"Lianna?" It was a woman's voice, still on the verge of tears. But she couldn't speak, couldn't respond. Thin, pale fingers reached under the door, stretching until they brushed against her small toes. "Lianna." The voice came again, another sob, but she stepped back. Scared.

This was bad. She was going to get in trouble.

The fingers disappeared and a soft tap on the door was almost completely muffled by the sniffled sigh inside the room. "You have to go back, darling. Go to bed."

"I can't open the door," she whispered.

"It's okay. You need to sleep. I'll be quiet, I promise. Go back to bed. Hurry. Run." There was a pause where Lianna was frozen to the spot, trying her hardest to think of how to make the knob turn. *"Go! Now!"* The urgent whisper felt like a push, and she obeyed. She turned, ran back towards her room — and woke up.

Lianna flinched, rolling to her back as a latent nausea quickly reminded her of all the stupid choices she'd made.

"You're awake," the man's low voice made her lift her head, and she groaned and fell back against the mattress.

Ah, yes, there was one of her stupid choices in the flesh.

"I brought you water. Toast. Something for the headache."

Turning to the side, she saw that he had, in fact, filled her water cup and provided toast and two pills on a paper plate. A bitter laugh slipped past her lips. "You think I need pain relievers *now*?"

Muttering, he pushed a hand through his dark hair and clenched his fist at the root. He was half-dressed again. Dark colored jeans, but no shirt, no shoes — and he'd left the mask off. A quick glance at the ceiling told her the cameras were off. It was just the two of them. "I brought them for the hangover. I'm sure you have one."

"So, these pills are *not* supposed to help the bruises or the other marks? Just the headache?" She sat up, and realized her temples *were* pounding, but the broken skin and splotchy bruises around her wrists were impossible to ignore.

"If you don't want them, don't take them."

"I'll take the whole bottle if you're offering." The dark

comment seemed to come from nowhere, but it made his eyes snap up to hers.

"You don't mean that."

She shrugged. "I might. Are you going to kill me now?"

"No," he growled under his breath, cradling his head with his hands like *he* was the one with the vicious headache.

"Then what are you going to do with me? I've seen your face."

"Did you look at the photos?"

"You didn't answer my question."

"Answer mine first." Leaning back against the wall near the door, he stared across the room at her, knees bent so he could rest his arms on them as they let the silence stretch between them. Such a reliable negotiation tactic.

Her eyes went to the scattered photos, and the names wormed their way back up from memory. Strange and concerning connections forming now that she wasn't drunk — and as much as she didn't want to give in, she *did* have questions. "Yes, I looked at them."

"And?"

"And I don't understand."

"What part?" He seemed to relax slightly, the tension in his shoulders dropping.

"Any of it. I agree that this is my father in some of the photos, but the older ones?" She shook her head, rubbing her fingers against one throbbing eye. "It may look like him, but it can't be. My dad was an only child, his parents died a long time ago. I think you're confused."

"I'm not confused." An edge of threat was back in his tone, that anger resurfacing, but she was too tired and too hungover to entertain it.

"Apparently you are, because his name isn't on the back of any of these."

"His real name is."

"Bullshit."

"I'm not lying to you." Shaking his head, he blew out a slow breath. "Come on, Lianna. You're smarter than this."

"I *am* smart, it's why I refuse to just believe a bunch of random photos that you've scribbled on!" She leaned forward and ripped a handful of photos from the floor. "You think a bunch of grainy photos are going to turn me against him? To convince me my father is some monster?"

"I think the truth will."

"The truth." She laughed, tossing the pictures into the air in front of her so they fluttered down across the others. "You don't get to pretend to be all noble now. You, of all people, don't have a fucking leg to stand on when it comes to this. *You* are a monster."

He turned away from her and despite her pounding headache, and the sour taste on her tongue, she pushed herself off the mattress and strode to the photo she'd avoided, snatching it off the floor.

"Look at this." Turning, she threw it towards him. "You want to talk about the truth? Look at those girls, look at their wrists, and then look at mine. Look at all of the things *you* have done to me!" She laughed, her sanity frayed at the edges. "And you want to sit there and say *you* can tell me the truth? As if *you* aren't exactly like the assholes who did this to them?"

The man picked up the photo that had landed beside him, and there was a flicker of a flinch. The barest reaction to the image before he was stone faced again.

"Talk to me! How is that any different than what you've done to me?"

His voice was almost too low to hear when he finally spoke, "You don't know what happened to them."

"I'm not an idiot, I have a pretty good idea." There was heat in her voice, her rage finally finding an outlet that seemed to work. His shoulders hunched forward, and his head dropped into his hands as he took a slow breath. When he didn't speak, she threw her hands up with a huff and turned away from him.

Bastard. Spineless, insane –

"I wanted to destroy you." The sudden, harsh words stopped her in place, but he continued in a growling tone. "I wanted to *decimate* you. Tear you down off your privileged, golden pedestal and break you down until you were nothing. I didn't just want to hurt you, I wanted to ruin you forever so that even when he got you back, you would never be the same. So, *he* would never be the same."

Lianna turned around slowly, watching as his eyes traced the photo in his hands before he let it drop to the floor, shrugging like nothing he said bothered him.

"I admit that, I admit all of it. I even admit that I've enjoyed it. I love the way you scream, the way your body tenses and arches when I hurt you. I love the way you fight, the way you refuse to break no matter how hard I push you. I am *addicted* to the way you respond to me." Tawny brown eyes lifted to hers, that powerful gaze catching her off guard. "But I have *never* lied to you, princess. I told you right away what I was going to do to you, before I even took you out of his fucking apartment."

"And?"

"And what?" His expression was blank, unfettered by guilt as he stared up at her.

"And have you destroyed me? Have you decimated me like you wanted to?"

"Not yet." His eyes stayed on hers, and she felt a tremor rush through her muscles. A quiet reminder in the back of her mind that he was *allowing* her to speak to him this way, that at any moment he could stop her if he chose. "But here's the difference, princess, I don't pretend to be a good man. I know that I'm damned. I *know* I'm a monster, a demon, a nightmare. Even right now I want to pin you to the floor, I want to feel you fight as I take you, and then I want to feel you come under me. I want to make you scream, I want to light up your skin with my belt again, I want to do so many obscene things to your body, but... right now there's something more important."

The pulse of need between her thighs brought on by his words made a blush burn its way up her chest and into her cheeks. There was definitely something wrong with her. With both of them. None of that should have excited her. "You're sick."

And so am I.

"I won't argue that. I won't argue any of it." With a shrug, he gestured towards the photos scattered across the floor. "But all of that is real, and I didn't write on the backs of them."

"I don't believe you." Her hands formed tight fists at her sides, ragged nails biting into the skin as she tried to stay calm, her rational mind fighting its way forward. "This is just a skewed sampling of data, put together in an attempt to prove some ridiculous hypothesis that my father was—"

"Tell me your last memory of your mother."

Lianna rolled her eyes and turned away from him, walking back over the pictures to drop onto the mattress. She was done with this insanity. Done with this damn conversation, done with trying to reason with a villain, and done with the throbbing ache behind her eyes and the hum between her thighs. With a growl, she swallowed the two pills with a sip of the water.

"You're going to want to eat the toast if you took the medicine."

"Since when do you give a shit how I feel?" she snarled at him, but ripped a bite of the toast off anyway and devoured it. Picking at the crisp edges as she glared down at the pictures.

He sighed. "Tell me your last memory of your mother."

"She died when I was little. I don't have any memories of her."

"Try harder, princess. What's your last memory of her?" He was so calm, so monotone, while she was a ball of tangled thoughts and rage. As the fire in her belly grew, she was about to scream at him, but then there was a flash. *A woman with blonde hair smiling at her, laughing.* It disappeared as quickly as it came, taking with it the vicious words she'd planned to shout. "Are you remembering?" he asked.

Lianna shook her head, the mental cloud of the hangover was making it hard to think clearly. Making her imagine things. "There's nothing to remember. She died in a car wreck when I was three."

"Did she?"

"Yes." Lianna nodded, swallowing the suddenly too dry bread. She chased it with more water. It was the hangover, it was messing with her head. *He* was messing with her head. This whole fucked up situation was doing nothing but mess with her, and he'd already admitted that was exactly what he'd wanted all along. She was just playing into his game now.

"Are you sure?" he asked, and she let out a scream of frustration.

"What the fuck do you want me to know? Why won't you just spit it out?" Leaning forward she shoved her hand through the photos, spreading them out further. "This shit isn't helpful! It doesn't explain anything! Not why you're doing this, not why you hate my father, not why you want to hurt me, none of it, so go fuck yourself!"

"Did you find your father in each of the photos?"

"He's not in all of the photos," she hissed before she popped another bite of toast in her mouth, her stomach rumbling with the need for food.

"Yes, he is. Want me to point him out?" The asshole

started to get up and she raised a hand, wanting him far away from her and the thrumming sensation between her thighs that reminded her of the explicit feeling of his mouth.

"Stay over there."

"Alright," he conceded, sitting back down. "Your choice, do you want to know or not?"

Grumbling she crawled forward to grab the photos together, flipping through the ones where she recognized him. Lifting the one of the family getting out of the car, she turned it toward him. "This one?"

"He's the shortest one. The blond teenager near the rear door. His brother Marc is next to him."

Lianna watched him as he spoke, and there wasn't a twitch in his face. His eyes were steady. No hint of a lie, but she slammed the photo down and grabbed for the one she hadn't looked at closely the night before. It was a group of unsmiling men sitting around tables, many with their heads down, and she raised it so he could see.

"On the left side, second table back. I believe he's almost looking at the camera in that one." A smirk threatened to tilt his lips up. "You should have caught that one."

"Fuck off," she spat, turning the photo around to play the most screwed up version of *Where's Waldo* she'd ever attempted — but there he was. Younger, yes, but still him. Glancing at the date on the back she saw *Feb. 2002*. That photo joined the pile of failures and she lifted the one of the men around the guns, almost smiling as she held it out.

He nodded slowly, closing his eyes for a second as his head

dropped back to the wall. "I think he's the third or fourth guy back on the right. Behind the open crate."

No. Pulling it close to her face, she studied the grainy faces, some obscured by the lapels of their coats, but then she saw him. His nose, his face, him. Her ears buzzed, lungs tightening, and she wanted to scream, but there could be explanations. It could make sense... somehow. Tossing the rest of the photos to the side she pointed at the one beside the asshole who had joyfully admitted to wanting to destroy her. "And that one? The one of the abused girls?"

"You mean the sex slaves? The girls your family bought and used and sold?" He lifted the picture towards her and tapped his finger against the SUV. "Your father is the driver."

Everything shifted and she shook her head, trying to push the idea away, but the son of a bitch kept talking.

"This was taken in 1984, the year he moved to the US. The year before he changed his name."

"You're a fucking liar!" she shouted, but she was shaking. Hands trembling, breaths too shallow, and she couldn't get enough air.

"You don't recognize a single one of your uncles, do you." It wasn't a question. He knew without her even answering. "Never met your grandfather? The grandmother whose name yours is so very close to? Liliane Faure... Lianna Mercier... they're similar, aren't they?"

"He was an only child. His parents are dead." *Right?*

"They're dead now, but you can see him shaking Jean-Luc's hand in 2015, so I can assure he does *not* think he's an only child. He just lied to you, princess. He's been lying to you your entire—"

"Shut up!" she screamed, fighting the urge to look at the photo on the mattress, but her eyes shifted to it anyway. The other man had lighter hair too, did they share features? Did they look like siblings?

"Okay, enough about the Faure family. Let's get back to my question then, what's your last memory of your mother?" For some insane reason *he* was the calm one. Sitting against the wall like he could do it forever, while she felt like the ground was breaking apart beneath her.

"She died! That's my last memory of her. Me asking about my mom and wondering where the hell she was. My father loved her so much he hasn't been with anyone since. He just opened a women's shelter in her name for fuck's sake!" Kicking out in frustration, she sent several photos spinning away, mixing all of the horrible pictures together. "You don't know anything! Not about me, not about my father, not—"

"I know why your mother died."

The words rocked her, a dizzying heat flushing up her chest that left her speechless. When her lips finally parted to speak, nothing came.

"I know *how* your mother really died."

"No, you don't know anything. You're a liar." She shook her head as she tried to block him out.

"I've never lied to you, princess. She tried to leave with you. To take you away from your father, away from that family, to free the both of you — but he caught her." His voice was too soft, and in her head she saw the doorknob from her dream. Heard the soft cries beyond it.

I can't open the door.

Were those dreams, or memories? How many times had she dreamed those things and brushed them off? She rubbed her eyes and finished the water in the cup. "You're wrong. He didn't, he wouldn't—"

"Do you really think he would have let anyone take his heir away from him? You're all he has here. The only one groomed to take over when he's gone. You've got the MBA, the experience, and I'm sure he would have told you about your uncles, about what you were *really* inheriting... eventually."

"Stop." Her chest was tight, her head pounding, and there was something just out of sight, like a word on the tip of her tongue, something pushing at her mind, wanting to be seen.

"Your father's real name is Alain Faure, youngest son of the Faure crime family. Your uncles are Marc Faure and Jean-Luc Faure, who is the current head of the family."

"You couldn't possibly know all of this."

"But I do," he spoke softly as he stood up, but her head was spinning in circles. Too far gone to feel the fear at his presence.

"This can't be real."

"But it is, and I can tell you all of it. Every secret he's kept, including the real way your mother died."

She raised her eyes to his, realizing he was now so close he was towering over her. Carved marble perfection, angelic features, offering a devil's deal.

"If you want to know the truth, princess, now's the time."

"What are you going to do to me?" she whispered.

"If you'll let me, I'm about to ruin your life."

Chapter Eighteen

LIANNA

He was offering to ruin her life as he held out his hand, and for some insane reason, as her eyes flicked over the photos, filled with faces she didn't recognize and names she didn't know — she took it.

More gently than she thought him capable, he pulled her to her feet and led the way out into the hall, releasing her as he headed in the opposite direction she'd fled the day before. He stopped at an open door, waiting patiently for her to follow.

No threats, no aggressive movements.

Nothing.

As she slowly moved towards him, he tilted his head at the interior. "Come on."

It felt like a dream as she approached. Part of her was screaming at her to run, to flee out the doors, but when he flipped on a buzzing fluorescent light revealing an overcrowded room, she knew she wasn't going anywhere. A small cot was pushed against one wall, there was a desk covered in computer parts and a table that seemed to be a makeshift kitchen against another — but the rest of the room was lined with tall, black filing cabinets. "What is all this?"

"Your father's sins." He turned away from her to open a drawer, digging through the files.

Leaning against one of the cabinets, she counted them in her head — three, five, seven. Seven filing cabinets? Seriously? "*All* of these files are about my father?"

"There are a lot of sins to cover." Dropping a thick folder onto the little table that filled the only space left in the room, he reached back into the cabinet and removed another, setting it next to it. "You want the truth? Go ahead and look, princess. Alain Yves Faure woke up one day and decided he wanted to make something of himself. Do something more for the family than just be a lackey to his eldest brother."

"What the fuck are you talking about?" She crossed her arms at the doorway, and he pointed at the folders.

"*Look.*"

Pulling over a stiff, metal chair, Lianna sat down with a huff and flipped open the folder in front of her. There were papers confirming Alain Faure's immigration to the United States. An official looking photograph of a much younger version of her father, still a lanky, tall teen. Twenty at the latest. Underneath were details about where he lived, notes confirming where he worked.

"That first folder is still from when he was being legitimate, the next one shows the sudden name change. New identity."

Opening the file, she saw a slightly more filled out face, a man that looked closer to the father she knew, but still in his youth. *Robert Edward Mercier.* There was a set of signatures on the forms, and she knew her father's handwriting. Knew the way he looped his lower-case e's, the way he dropped below the line with the first letter of each name. She swallowed hard as the man kept talking.

"Then he started his company, with a hefty influx of startup capital from the family of course, and Mercier Technology came to be." He moved to another cabinet and pulled open the second drawer down, bringing out another dense packet. "But then he wanted to grow. After all, in 1985 the options weren't as diverse as they were now. Your father still had an eye for business opportunities though."

He held out the next folder to her and she took it, flipping it open to find printouts of obituaries, articles, and lists of companies that her father had apparently acquired. Next to each was one of two words, *legitimate* or *corrupt*. "Wait, so you're basing all of this on a name change and the fact that he bought companies? Lots of businesses expand by acquiring existing companies."

"Keep listening, then tell me what you think, princess."

"Asshole," she muttered under her breath and he glanced at her as he slammed a file drawer shut again.

"Your father is smart. While I hate the bastard, I can admit that, and I know you agree with me." Another cabinet. Another folder. "So, he knew exactly which companies would make a difference. The ones who had the right production capabilities in the right markets, but lacked the connections that he was building rapidly with the backing of his family."

"None of this is a crime." Shutting the folders in front of her, she looked up at him, sensing the seething rage under his skin as he started to pull out narrower folders from a variety of drawers.

"You're right, it wouldn't have been a crime. Except your father didn't take no for an answer. If someone didn't want to sell to him, wanted to keep their company in *their* family instead of his — shit happened." He dropped a tall stack of folders onto the end of the table. "I won't burden you with the fucked up details of the various ways your father had people killed, entire families, children, it's all in the cabinets if you want to read it. But he did it all so he could launder more and more money for the Faure family, so he could be important here in the states, and important to *them*."

"That's not possible," she whispered as she opened folder after folder. Each one started with an outline of a business and information on the family that owned it, then details of their deaths, some of them gruesome, and then came the date that Mercier Technology, or Mercier Systems, acquired the business. Looking around the room at the cabinets, Lianna's skin went cold. "There's no way this could have happened, with this kind of repetition, and no one noticed."

"Oh, someone noticed." He dropped another folder in front of her. "INTERPOL knows about the Faure family. Fuck, they even know that Alain Faure is Robert *fucking* Mercier — but do you think they've done a damn thing about it? Do you think they've moved a single fucking inch in his direction while he's collected millions of dollars soaked in the blood of families he's destroyed? While he's cleaned millions more in dirty money that your fucking family sends?"

Swallowing, she opened the folder and saw exactly what he described in INTERPOL reports that seemed to be official. How he'd obtained them she couldn't even guess, but the names she recognized. Jean Faure, Marc Faure, Jean-Luc Faure, Joseph Blanc… her hands trembled for a moment, because next to that name in parentheses was *Michael Turner*. Her father's head of security, the man she called Uncle Mike, but apparently that wasn't even his real name. He was someone else as well. *Joseph Blanc.* Some kind of captain to this family of criminals she'd never known? Shutting the folder and moving it away, she looked at him. "If they know this, if they have all of this, they would stop it. The government wouldn't just let this happen. There's just no way."

"Of course there is, princess. Your family is connected. They have friends in high and low places, and no one in the US is going to give a fuck about a small business disappearing to make way for the latest and greatest. Especially if it happens overseas."

Lianna flipped through another folder that detailed a factory they still owned, one based in Mexico, and she flinched as she looked back at the family picture that had been used in a newspaper discussing their death. Her Spanish wasn't great, but everyone knew *muerto* when they saw it. Dead. All of them. And eight months later Mercier Systems bought it.

How was this possible? Could he have really done this?

"He was never legitimate. He bought companies to spread his wealth, he diversified, he left behind the drugs and the guns... but he never lost his taste for blood. He went on for years, killing his opposition, expanding, building a name for himself, an empire here in the states. Mercier Systems was already earning a powerful reputation, and then your father met Vanessa Scott." The name stopped her heart cold, and she found her eyes glued to the drawer his hand rested against. "I guess you're not completely blind, are you, princess? You may not remember your mother, but you know her maiden name."

"Let me see." Pushing back from the chair, ignoring her nakedness, she moved to the filing cabinet, and he stepped away, giving her room as she ripped the top drawer open and took out a file at random. There were typed pages of interviews with people who had known her mother. Talking about her father wooing her with elaborate dates, trips, their marriage, and then how she disappeared from everyone. Wouldn't return calls, wouldn't answer them. When she couldn't take anymore, she slammed the folder down on top of the cabinet and faced him. "I'm not reading through all of this. What happened?"

"Are you sure you want to know? This is the kind of thing—"

"That will ruin my life. I heard you. Don't try and pretend you care, just say it."

A muscle in his jaw twitched as he stared down at her. "She got pregnant with you, and your father married her." He tapped the third drawer down with his foot. "There was one hell of a pre-nup, by the way."

"And then?"

He shook his head, a wry smile lifting one side of his mouth. "And then he had everything he wanted. His empire, power, and an heir. *You*."

"You're speculating," she grumbled, slamming the drawer back into the cabinet before resting her head against it. There was a pounding behind her eyes that was only getting worse the more he talked.

"Well, *princess*, do you want to know how your mother really died?"

Turning to look at him, she braced herself for whatever horror he'd share next, but he just raised an eyebrow. Exasperated, she snapped, "I'm waiting."

"I'm waiting for you to ask me."

"You're such an asshole!"

Reaching forward, he grabbed her by the hair, flipping her around to slam her back against the next set of cabinets, his body crushing her against it. The handles dug into her ribs, air hissing between her teeth as the sting raced across her scalp. "It is taking every ounce of my self-control not to fuck you over the end of this table right now, and if you want to continue being a disrespectful little brat I can treat you like one. So, do you want to hear the rest of Mommy and Daddy's story, or do you want me to chain you up again?"

"I want to know the rest."

"Then ask me nicely."

"How did she die?" Lianna forced the words out as he brushed her hip, and she tried not to think about him bending her over the table, ignoring the pulse of need between her thighs.

"Say please," he purred, angling her head back until she had to meet his eyes.

"*Please.*" The word came out between her teeth, but he smiled and released her, moving back to one of the filing cabinets.

"That wasn't so hard, was it?" Running his hand over the front of the place she'd found the first file about her mother, he shrugged. "Your mom didn't know about your father's family. Didn't know any of it, but she was with him for several years. Heard him on the phone, heard him meeting with people. He even took her on a few trips... and apparently *she* was clever enough to put two and two together, to figure out what he *really* did. But she was still stupid enough to think she could run."

Her skin was on fire with the aftershock of his touch, her mind twisting in knots as she tried to find a hole in the story he painted, in the information he'd provided. But the photos seemed to be real. Those horrible obituaries seemed to be real. The fucking INTERPOL file seemed to be real. The companies listed in the files were definitely real because she recognized at least one of them.

And Vanessa Scott was absolutely my mother.

Lianna swallowed, her eyes tracing the drawers of her mother's cabinet, full of a history she wasn't sure she wanted to know — but there was one thing she couldn't ignore. "You said you knew about her death."

A low laugh rumbled out of him as he paced across the other wall, in front of the filing cabinets full of a bloody and evil history. "Yes, princess…" He crossed his arms over his broad, firm chest and leveled his gaze at her. "Do you finally believe me?"

"I don't know what to believe."

"Can you tell me your last memory of her yet?"

"No."

"Try," he urged, his voice taking on a strange quality like he was waiting for something.

"I don't remember her!" she shouted, dropping heavily into the chair before she cradled her head in her hands.

So many twisted flashes, broken images.

Real or not real?

"What do you remember then?"

A frustrated scream escaped her chest. "You want to know what I remember? I remember a woman crying behind a door that I couldn't open. I remember my father reading me stories while a woman shouted and begged in the apartment. I get quick flashes of things that I can't *really* remember. I thought they were just nightmares, but I don't actually remember anything, and I don't remember *her*. She died in a fucking car crash when I was three, so NO! I DON'T REMEMBER HER!"

"Fine." In a few steps he walked to the desk and ripped a folder off of it, slamming it onto the table and opening it with a flick of his hand. "What about now?"

Lianna's eyes went wide as she took in the pictures.

Oh God.

Morgue photos. It was her mother. The woman whose photo was tucked in a drawer in her bedroom. The woman that sometimes appeared in dreams, smiling and laughing, but there was no more laughter now. She was dead, and the bullet hole just right of center on her forehead was definitely not from a car accident. As Lianna stared at the face, it was as if the world shuddered around her. A rush of images appeared and disappeared in her mind, and the harder she tried to hold onto them, the faster they faded. Like capturing water in a sieve.

No, no, no... it can't be.

"Daddy dearest doesn't take betrayal lightly, as you can see."

"He did this?" she whispered.

"What?" He was digging in another filing cabinet now, but he stopped to look back at her.

"How could you possibly know he killed her? How?"

"Who else would have killed her for trying to leave with you?" A sharp slam of the latest drawer made her jump, a chill settling on her bare skin. "When your mother tried to leave he killed her so he could keep you. His perfect little princess, perched on a throne of corpses, and he kept you blind so you could pretend it was gold."

"How do you know this, how do you know *any* of this?" she shouted at him, the threat of tears in her voice as she stared at the last images of her mother until something started to tear inside her and she slammed the folder shut.

When she raised her eyes to him, she saw the deathgrip he had on the handle, his knuckles white, and the aura of rage bloomed around him again like some dark halo. "I know all of this shit because *my* fool of a father tried to help her escape. With you."

Her already unstable world completely flipped, body rocking back in the chair like she'd taken a blow to the chest. "*What?*"

"My father tried to help your mother, and when daddy dearest found out he killed her, and then spent a year ruining our lives after he failed to kill us all." The man growled and dropped the folders in his hands to the floor, going for another cabinet.

"I don't understand," she breathed, suddenly lightheaded.

"*You* don't understand? I don't fucking understand it. Why he ever thought it was a good idea to get between one of the Faure family and his fucking child..." He cursed under his breath. "*That*, that insane choice, I will never understand."

"Wait, how did he even know him? Who the fuck are you?" Lianna stared at him, twisting in the chair to watch him as he dug through another cabinet.

"My father used to help out on odd jobs, things people needed done." The man shrugged a shoulder. "Officially, he was involved in construction, but the list of things he used to do was long. From what he told me, your father wanted him to make some updates on his buildings in the city, including his apartment. Somewhere in that time he met your mother, and somehow she managed to tell my father she needed help, and like the fucking fool that he was, he agreed."

"What happened?" Lianna asked, rubbing at her sternum as she stared down at her mother's death folder. The longer she looked, the more uncomfortable she felt, remembering her father's agitation every time she'd asked about the accident. Asked him to talk about her mom. Asked to see her pictures. Asked, and asked, until she'd stopped. She'd just stopped asking about the woman who had tried to save her.

He's right, you've been so blind for so long. So willingly stupid.

"I don't know everything. I know that he built a way out, used *his* connections to find you both a place to go, with people who weren't friends to the Faure family. She was going to trade information about them for safety."

"And?" she prodded. Her chest hurt, and she couldn't tell if it was the hangover causing the nausea or the new knowledge that was settling like an acidic weight inside her.

"And you know the end of this story, princess. I didn't lie to you. My father gave her a way to get past all of the tricky little passcodes that locked the doors, picked a day and everything, and then just before it was all supposed to happen — *poof*. She disappeared."

Brushing at the tears on her cheeks, she looked up at him. "What about me? What happened to me?"

"You were three. You stayed with him."

"Goddammit!" She shoved the folders in front of her off the table, standing up fast enough to knock the chair over. Papers fluttered out, but she didn't care as she willed herself to summon one real memory of the woman who had cared for her enough to die trying to save them. "Why don't I remember her? I had over three fucking years with her!" A sob broke past her lips. It felt like her chest was caving in, the pain of a loss she didn't even have words for, didn't even have memories for — just an emptiness, an absence. Something she had never mourned, because she'd never known just how much she'd lost.

"You were a kid, Lianna." His voice was quiet, and when she looked up at him to find his brows pulled together in some version of concern, she flinched and tore her eyes away. "I've been hoping you could tell me the one thing my father never understood. How Mercier figured out what was happening, and how he found out my father was the one helping her."

"Why does that matter? She's dead."

"It matters because your fucking father killed my mother too, and then spent a year destroying my father! *My* family!" Ripping a thick folder from one of the cabinets, he stormed around to the other side of the table and dropped it, flipping it open to point at an obituary. "This was my mother, Elizabeth Gethen. *She* actually died in a fucking car crash. Brakes stopped working. Coincidence right?" He growled. "Do you think that's why he told you your mom died in a wreck? Because he tried to kill us at the same time? Well, it didn't work. She was alone in the car when it slammed into the barricade, and when he found out we were still alive he blacklisted my father's name to everyone. There wasn't a job anywhere that he could get. The other families, all of his connections, none of them would hire him to drill a fucking hole because it would mean making an enemy of Alain *fucking* Faure."

Alain Faure.

His real name, which meant nothing in her life was ever real.

"Do you want me to say I'm sorry?" Lianna picked up her chair so she could collapse into it, chewing at the shredded edge of her thumbnail. She felt a twist of guilt that had both nothing, and everything, to do with her. It was all her father, it had always been her father, but his blood ran in her veins. Faure blood ran in her veins. "I'm sorry, okay? He's a bastard, is that what you want me to say? Just tell me what you want."

"Do you believe he's a monster now?"

She avoided his gaze, but she nodded. It was a painful admission to connect the man who had seemed to love her, the man she had good memories of — with this monster who the files described.

"That's what I wanted, princess."

David

He moved away from her, and he could feel her eyes on the tense muscles in his back as he tried to let the rage go, tried to forget the memory of his mother's death, the never-ending pain his father had been in before his heart had finally given out. Digging through his duffel bag he nudged the gun aside to pull out a clean shirt, and then grabbed the vodka from the little fridge with two cups.

Setting it all on the table he held out the shirt towards her, trying to keep his eyes off her breasts, the rosy nipples, the sweet curve of her waist. *Stop.* "We're going to drink now, and you're going to put on this shirt because otherwise I'm going to fuck you — and trust me, as wet as I make you, now is not the time."

He shook the shirt at her and she took it, glaring at him as she pulled it on. It only took a second, pulling her hair through the neck, but then she was covered and he could think a little clearer.

"What do you say?" he prompted.

"Thanks," she whispered, and he made a noise of acknowledgement as he poured a few inches of vodka in each cup.

Lifting his, he waited. After a long moment, she sighed, lifted hers, and then they both drank. It was cheap, nowhere near as good as the rum, but she'd finished that off solo. And now he'd told her all of it. Lianna Mercier knew the truth about her father, and his company was hemorrhaging. The plan was finished. He breathed out as he stared at the pages scattered all around them, and wondered why he'd ever thought this would make it all better.

"You know, after my mother died, it was all my father could think about, all he could ever talk about. Destroying *him*." David swallowed the rest of the vodka and reached to refill, doing the same for her when she nudged her cup forward. "That's how this whole thing started. Figuring out how to destroy him. We watched you both for years, went everywhere trying to dig up proof, to gather enough evidence."

"Seems like you succeeded," she mumbled, gesturing towards the cabinets.

"When my father died, I couldn't just let it go unfinished. This plan was my whole life. I wanted to tear down his empire, I wanted to destroy him... but I really wanted to destroy you too. I'd hated you both for so long. Making millions, a silver spoon in your mouth from birth bought with dirty money, all while we were barely able to get by." That bitter rage filled his mouth again, but she didn't even react with fear. Lianna only sighed, pretty blue eyes lifting to his.

"You've made your point, I get it."

"Then tell me, did I destroy you, princess?"

She rolled her eyes and finished her vodka, reaching to refill. The question hung between them, and eventually she just shrugged. "Honestly, I don't know."

"Well, you're still the golden heir to Mercier Systems. What's left of it anyway." He almost laughed into his drink at the absurdity of it, of leaving her the rotting shell of her father's corrupt company when all of this was done.

Even with Mercier Systems destroyed, nothing was truly fixed. His parents were still dead, all of those families the Faures had killed were still dead. The Faure family would eventually find new avenues to protect their money and themselves — but looking across the table at Lianna Mercier, his corrupted angel that he'd pulled down to earth and ruined with his bare hands, with his words, with the truth... he felt something else in him. Something that plucked at a long dead humanity, something almost like guilt for the damage he'd done.

If only he could actually regret taking her, fucking her, then there might be some hope of salvaging himself in all of this.

But he didn't regret any of it.

"You know... you weren't a part of my father's plan, but I had watched. I knew what would make Alain Faure do what I wanted. I knew if I could get you, I could get him to destroy his own company piece by piece. It took him a while to start responding, but he did it... because you're his. His blood. His name. His only legacy."

"No." Lianna flinched. "I'm not his. Not anymore. Not after... this."

"Well then, that deserves a toast." Adding more vodka to their cups, he lifted his from the table. "To not being his."

She didn't repeat it, but she nodded and swallowed enough vodka to make her choke and squeeze her eyes shut. The back of her hand pressed to her pink lips as she cleared her throat. "So, what are you going to do with me now? You still haven't really answered that question."

"I'm going to let you go, like I always planned to."

Lianna looked surprised, and he sighed and stood up, wandering back to his bag to dig out what he needed. Disbelief peppered her voice as she spoke, "You're just going to let me go. Even though I've seen your face."

With a smile tugging at his mouth, he approached her again and shrugged. "That was always the plan, although I never expected you to have the balls to go for my mask. That was pretty fucking stupid, because I *could* kill you." *Which would be smarter than this.*

"I know." She swallowed hard, and his cock twitched in his pants at the clear fear. It confirmed for him just how fucking far from human he was, and it was exactly why she needed to go.

"I'm not going to kill you, Lianna. This was supposed to end differently, but I honestly don't care anymore what happens to me." He closed in on her personal space, watching her arm twitch as he laid the item down on the table in front of her, but he kept it covered by his hand so she would look at him again. "This will help when you go to the police."

"What is going to help——" The kiss silenced her instantly, and he tried to memorize how soft her lips felt against his, how warm, and he couldn't resist slipping his hand into her hair to gently hold her still. His tongue danced out to open her mouth, sweeping in to taste the lingering vodka, but when she let out a quiet, feminine moan he pulled back.

It's over. You have to let her go.

Chapter Nineteen

LIANNA

The kiss was like nothing she'd ever experienced. Simultaneously a cool rain after a forest fire, and somehow like adding fresh kindling to it at the same time. She felt soothed and burned in the same breath. But then he pulled away, ending it as quickly as it began, leaving her heart stumbling over itself. And as if she weren't stunned enough, on the table in front of her was a driver's license.

His driver's license. Terrible photo and all.

David Gethen.

His name was printed in perfectly standard ink on the little plastic card and she could barely believe it. David Gethen had taken her, hurt her, tortured her, shattered her entire life by telling her the truth, and now he was giving her his name, his information, and letting her go?

"David?" she breathed his name in disbelief.

"Yes?"

"You kissed me."

"Yes."

"Why?"

He shrugged. "I just wanted to know what it felt like to kiss a princess. "

"For the last time, I am *not* a princess." She touched her lips as he settled into the chair across from her, his ribs expanding and settling back in a deep breath.

"You're the modern equivalent, whether you want to admit it or not. Mercier is the king of his little kingdom, and you are his heir." He took a drink, and smiled. "Although, I guess if the empire does fall, you'll be a pauper like the rest of us. Like your mother was."

"My mother..." She flinched, her mind still full of gaps and holes. His knowledge about her life, her unknown family, was overwhelming, and as she looked around at the filing cabinets, aware of the millions of pages that were lurking inside them — all she had were questions. "What else do you know? Have you really read everything in here?"

"You can ask me anything, I don't care anymore." His lips twitched. "I did tell you I'd ruin your life, didn't I?"

Lianna sighed, looking for answers in the vodka. "How can you ruin something that wasn't real?"

"I guess that's true. Go on, ask away. I promise I'll tell you anything I know."

"I don't even know where to start." She reached for one of the papers on the table, but didn't bother trying to read it. "How many family members do I have?"

"A lot. Your uncles had kids too, some of them have kids now. Most of them live in England, France, some in the rest of Europe, but from what I know they're all familiar with the family business."

Remembering the faces in the photos, the men standing around the guns, standing beside those women, she wasn't sure she ever wanted to know them. Ignorance really was bliss, but she didn't have that luxury anymore. "Are you going to kill my father?"

"I think I've done worse than kill him, don't you?"

"How?" She caught his eyes as he glanced up at her.

"I've taken you from him, haven't I?" David gave that strange, lopsided smile, and then it disappeared as a long beep emanated from his computer. Jumping out of his seat he rushed over to the desk, shaking the mouse as he pulled out the office chair. His screens came to life and he cursed under his breath.

"What is it?"

"I made a mistake somewhere. *Fuck*, what did I do?" His hands flew over the keyboard, and she watched as windows opened and closed on the screen. For a few minutes he muttered under his breath, the clatter of the keys the only noise besides the hum of the computer. "DAMMIT!"

The shout made her jump, and then he started to laugh quietly. A quality of madness to it that made her nervous. "What happened?"

"*You*. You happened. I let you distract me, I let you inside my head, and I sent the last email to your father unencrypted." He grabbed one of the monitors and turned it so she could see the framework of surveillance cameras, and in the bottom left square were two figures. "And now he's here."

Part of her was relieved. Rescue, escape, freedom. No more locked room, no more violence, but a smaller part, the part that hummed at the base of her spine when she thought of his hands on her, felt regret. A twisted sense of losing something. "Where are they?"

"At the double doors — which are locked by the way." David sighed and turned around in the chair, rubbing his face before he pushed his hands into his dark hair. He was so beautiful, so damaged, so corrupted by everything her father had done. He had let it destroy him, had let it eat him alive until he was barely human anymore, and she couldn't suppress the pity as he raised those tawny brown eyes to her. "I feel like I should apologize, but I told you I wouldn't lie to you."

She ignored his comment, a sense of urgency rising in her. "I have more questions."

"You better ask them fast, or you're going to need to make an appointment at the penitentiary." He was too calm now, too accepting, and it made her angry.

"But I don't even know what to ask, I don't even know what pieces are missing!" The metallic bang of a door swinging into the concrete wall made her turn towards the doorway, panic rising inside her. David stood and moved to lean against the filing cabinets on the back wall. His chest bare, all that carved muscle on display as he crossed his arms and waited. Like a defiant criminal waiting for the hangman.

"Just don't let him lie to you again, Lianna. Don't let him

empty you out and turn you into the little doll he wants. You deserve the truth, don't let him strip it away." She turned to meet his eyes, his blank, solemn expression, and then she heard a familiar voice.

"LIANNA!" It was a shout of relief from the man she'd called Uncle Mike, and he had a gun in his hands as he stopped just inside the doorway. "We're here, we've got you. Over here, quick, come to me."

Her father appeared next to him, slightly wide-eyed, but relief passed over his face as soon as he saw her. "You're okay. You're alive," his voice was warm and soft, the confident tones of a CEO reassuring reporters, but when he took a step towards her, she pulled back in her seat.

"Lianna, come on, sweetheart. We'll handle this, and you don't want to be here for it." Mike nodded at her, his eyes intensely focused on David, but when she saw him adjusting his grip on the gun she shook her head.

"Go ahead, Lianna." David took a step forward, and she closed her eyes tight as he spoke. "Time for you to go home."

"No, I'm not leaving yet." She stared at Michael, ignoring David's words. "You can't kill him, I still have questions."

"This is ridiculous," her father muttered. Lianna had been avoiding his gaze, unable to face him, but he suddenly grabbed Mike's gun, immediately re-aiming it at David, and before she could think about it she'd jumped to her feet to stand between them. Stumbling back several steps, her arms wide as she tried her best to block his chest.

"DON'T! You can't do this, he needs to be alive. I have—"

"You are clearly upset, Lianna, but I will fix this, and then everything can get back to normal. Now, come over here." Her father was speaking to her like she was still a child, but he wasn't lowering the gun and that meant she couldn't risk moving.

He wants to erase this like it never happened.

Just like he erased my mother, and David's, and all of the people who had owned those companies.

The papers under her feet caught her eye, and she found herself shaking her head. "Normal? You want things to be *normal?*" A bitter laugh passed her lips. "No. There is no normal anymore. Do you know what this room is? What's in all of these filing cabinets?"

"It doesn't matter." Her father sighed. "You're safe now. Michael and I have found you, and we can put this behind us."

"Are you insane? I can't put this behind me! There's no *normal* after reading that!" She kicked some of the papers towards him, and he lowered the gun to lean down and scoop them up. After a moment his jaw went tight, and his eyes flicked to the stacks of folders and papers across the table.

"What is this?"

"This? This is your family. *My* family. This is what you apparently did to all those other families just to get their fucking companies! Tell me, tell me if you really did this. Tell me if you're really Alain Faure! Tell me the truth!" There were tears in her eyes, her voice breaking as she tried to hold onto her composure, to bring back the anger so she wouldn't break down.

Robert Mercier wadded up the papers in his hand and tossed them onto the table. "You're upset, but while I'm not sure what he's told you, I can assure you it is all easily explained. I can help you understand, but now it is time to move so Michael and I can finish cleaning up the mess you've made."

"Me?" Another laugh burst from her lips, her eyes flipping to Michael, who avoided her gaze so she had to look back at her father. Baby blue eyes, pale blonde hair, immaculately put together — *a monster*. "You're calling this *my* mess? I was taken because of you! So, what about the mess YOU created, Dad? What about all of this shit you've done, I mean, who the fuck are you? What did you do to these people? To my MOTHER?" Her voice rose until she was screaming, but the only reaction she got was an exasperated sigh.

"I am done coddling you, Lianna. You're old enough to understand the requirements of building a business. Success is never handed to you, you have to reach out and take it, and sometimes that requires sacrifices. Now, if you're done with your temper tantrum, it is time to go."

"And what happened to my mother? Was she just another sacrifice?"

"That woman is not your concern, Lianna. You should be grateful for everything I've done for you, every advantage I've provided you." He gestured at her, his voice growing colder. "I gave you the best tutors, put you through the best colleges, I have given you *every* opportunity. You are poised to inherit Mercier Systems, to be someone worth so much more than she would have made you, and for *that* you should be incredibly grateful."

"Grateful?" She scoffed, anger surging inside her, and she saw the flicker of rage on her father's face underneath the perfectly composed shell. "I should be *grateful* that I've benefited from every terrible thing you've done? Grateful that you destroyed others to turn me into some kind of puppet to carry your name forward? Well... guess what, *Dad,* I don't want to be your fucking heir!"

This was her father. The monster, the real villain. The same one who had tucked her in at night and read her stories with happy endings, all while he killed innocent people — such a load of bullshit. Her entire life was bullshit. A lie.

Lianna laughed. "In fact, I'm going to tell everyone what you've done. I'm going to be on every news station, in prime time, telling all your dirty secrets. Telling all of them about *you*, about the fucking Faure family!" She was seething with righteous anger, burning brightly, when she felt David's fingers slowly wrap around her arm.

"Lianna, stop." His whisper came from close behind, a touch of warning in his voice, but she shook him off.

"I'm going to destroy your fucking legacy. Whatever piece of Mercier Systems is still standing, I'll personally make sure it gets burned to the ground. For Vanessa, for Elizabeth, for *everyone* you tore apart."

"All right, Lianna." Her father nodded. "If that's how you feel, if you don't want my legacy, then you won't have it." He lifted the gun, and for the first time she truly saw the emptiness in his eyes. The soulless darkness underneath the charming façade — and then the world spun. The gunshot rang out too loud in the small room, someone shouted, and she found herself crushed against a warm chest, muscular arms tight around her.

Looking up, she realized she was staring into David's tawny brown eyes, too wide for a moment, and then he wavered on his feet, pain twisting his features as he released her. She let out a scream and tried to catch him as he collapsed to the floor, but he was too heavy, and she ended up on the floor with him. "Oh no. No, no, no, what the fuck did you do?"

Her head spun. He'd protected her, taken the bullet her father had meant for her. In a panic, she reached over his broad shoulders to search for the wound, and when her fingers found it he hissed air through his teeth.

"Why did you do that? WHY?"

A rough laugh slipped from him as he turned his neck to look up at her. "I have no idea. Being a fucking fool must run in the family."

His words made her chest ache and she looked back at her father. "You were going to kill me?" Everything in her world shuddered, the last shreds of hope crumbling as she saw no hint of remorse in the man who had been *Dad* until a few minutes before, and then she turned her gaze to Michael. "You have to get help, you have to—"

"Oh, no, we don't *have* to do anything, Lianna, and we will definitely not be bringing any police into this." Lifting the gun to point it at her again, her father shrugged. "It's such a pity to lose you, you were coming along so well, and you did look so nice during the photo ops."

She flinched, and just as she prepared for the gun to fire

again, Michael touched her father's arm. "Sir, I can handle this. There's no need for you to be the one."

Robert Mercier was gone, but Alain Faure sighed, his tone frigid when he spoke. "Well, you took care of the mother, might as well handle this as well."

The words stole the last of the air from her lungs on a sob, and she looked up at Michael to see if he would argue it, to see if it was a lie — but she could tell it wasn't. He wouldn't even meet her eyes.

Monsters. She'd been surrounded by killers and lies her entire life.

Tears streaked her cheeks, and she felt David squeeze her arm as she looked down at him. His voice was weak, but she could still hear him. "I should have left you with the lie. I never—" A fit of coughs cut him off, blurs of red on his lips when he stopped.

She shook her head. "Uncle Mike, please, you can't do this."

"Handle it, Michael. I'll be in the hall." Her father passed the gun off like a dirty object, and turned to leave as she stared after him in disbelief.

"Close your eyes, Lianna," Michael commanded, but he wasn't looking at her. He moved the gun into his other hand, raised it to her father's head — and fired.

The spray of blood and other matter made her scream. It was unreal, a nightmare. She covered her eyes as the dull sound of her father's body collapsing to the floor filled her ears, and then there was a strange, buzzing silence.

"Lianna, sweetheart, are you all right? I—" Mike's voice was like a knife twisting between her ribs.

"Don't." With a steadying breath, she looked at the man she had viewed as family her whole life, and felt a wave of disgust. "You killed my mother?"

"I've always regretted—"

"You've worked for the Faure family all this time. You knew about them, about everything he did, all the people he killed."

"It was my job, Lianna. I've just done my job for your father, but you… I couldn't let him hurt you. He didn't even want to respond to the videos. He said he wasn't going to negotiate, I had to *beg* him to help you, and — *shit*, I'm sorry. I'm so sorry."

"You think sorry is enough for this? For everything you've done?"

"No." Michael looked down, wiping the gun off on his shirt before he placed it back into her father's hand, wrapping his hand around it a few times. He stayed in a crouch beside the shape that had been her father. The monster. The man who had wanted to keep her like an empty doll, to have her carry on his bloody legacy. Michael sighed and stood. "What can I do?"

"Save him." She looked down at David who opened his eyes to look at her, his brows pulled together in pain.

Mike scoffed. "Absolutely not, he—"

"I said to save him. He's the only bastard in this room who hasn't lied to me. He's the only one who will tell me the truth. I don't care what else happens, but he lives. Understand?"

Michael paused for a moment longer than she wanted, but

eventually he nodded and dragged over the cot, lifting David face down onto it with her help. Snagging a towel and the bottle of vodka, he poured the alcohol over his back, which made David jerk and groan, and then he splashed some on the towel before pushing it into her hand. "If you want him to live, apply pressure, push as hard as you can. I have some calls to make."

Moving to her knees beside the cot, she overlapped her hands and pressed. A deep groan escaped him, and she could hear Michael in the hallway on the phone, but her mind was still a chaotic blur. "Listen to me, *David*. You don't get to die. You're not getting off that easily. You promised you'd answer any of my questions, and you don't break promises, remember? You don't lie. You don't fucking lie, and so you can't die now."

"Now, you're really starting to sound like a bossy princess." His voice slurred, and then he coughed again.

She rolled her eyes. "Shut up and focus on not fucking bleeding to death."

"You should be nicer, I saved your life. I—" David's voice trailed off and she leaned forward to see his eyes closed. A rush of panic surged inside her.

"Uncle Mike! Tell them to hurry, he's not conscious anymore!"

"Apply pressure!" he yelled back into the room and she did, putting as much of her weight as she could onto the spot. Shaking her head, she stared at his profile. Those angelic features combining with the memory of every twisted thing he'd done, and she hated him for putting her in this situation. The place where she had to admit he had saved her life in more ways than one. Saved her from a bullet, from her father's lies, from a life of forced ignorance. Nothing in her life had been real.

Except this.

He'd been her villain, and her savior — and she had no idea which version of him was stronger, all she knew was that she needed him to live.

Chapter Twenty

LIANNA

Two Weeks Later

Lianna double-checked the room number as she turned down the hall, and paused outside when she heard voices. The chiding tone of a doctor, followed by a gruff acknowledgment.

"You'll need help for the next few weeks, and I have to encourage you not to lift anything heavy or exert yourself. You still have a lot of healing to do."

"How will you be getting home?"

"Taxi."

"Of course, I'll call you—"

"That won't be necessary." Lianna walked into the room, and all three faces turned in surprise. "I'm here to take him home."

"Oh, well, that's wonderful." The nurse smiled at her, and

then moved to slip past her. "Let me just get the final paperwork."

"Think you can keep him from doing anything strenuous for the next few weeks?" The doctor looked at her, a joking tone in his voice, and she turned on the smile she'd practiced over years and years.

"I'll do my best."

"All right, well, you have the post-op instructions in your folder. I'll go talk with Sandy and get you discharged. Hope you're feeling better soon, Mr. Gethen." The doctor shook his hand and then nodded at her as he left the room.

David was almost too still on the edge of the bed, his gaze floating somewhere in the middle distance between them.

"Are you going to say anything?"

He shook his head slowly, staring down at the floor as he gripped the edge of the hospital bed.

"All right, maybe start with, 'Thank you for saving my life, Lianna'. Go on." She smirked when he looked up at her, those dark brows lifting just a fraction.

"I believe I saved *your* life."

"But I kept the pressure on you until Michael's medic friends arrived." Tugging her purse higher on her shoulder, she leaned against the wall and spoke a little softer. "And you did kidnap me, and… did a lot of terrible things to me."

"So, we're even?" His lopsided smile reappeared, but she just rolled her eyes.

"You owe me a lot of answers."

David nodded and tried to stretch, but flinched and stopped short, groaning. "I believe you may have mentioned that when I was dying."

"And you stayed alive like I asked. I appreciate that."

His expression darkened and he looked away from her again. "Why didn't you tell the police about it, about what I did?"

It wasn't just that Michael's cleaning crew had erased the hard-drives on David's computers, torn down the cameras, and obliterated any trace of her being there. It also wasn't the strange confusion she'd felt in the last weeks when the memory of his touch would appear like a phantom on her skin, and she would react with a surge of heat, not fear. The way his voice would buzz in her mind as she touched herself, remembering his strength, his hard body pressed against her. No, it had been something more inexplicable. Something darker, something no one but the two of them could possibly understand. Lianna swallowed, and told the truth. "I didn't tell them about it, about any of it, because I wanted you back."

His eyes snapped up to hers with such a look of shock that he almost looked angry. "You *what?*"

"I want you. *You.* The person you finally let me see, the one under the mask. The real you. The one who referred to hating me in the past tense, the one—"

"Stop."

"You saved me, you took a *bullet* for me."

"Yes, I did, and I've spent two weeks in a hospital because I was that foolish." His words froze her tongue in her mouth, making her flinch as he turned away from her again. "It's time for you to go."

"No, *listen*. David, I—"

"Get out!" He shouted at her and she took a step backwards, shocked by the sudden outburst of rage. This was *not* how she'd imagined this going in her head.

Turning, she shoved the door to the room closed and then rounded on him. "No! I'm not going anywhere. You promised me answers."

"Fine. Ask away, princess," he growled, his knuckles growing white as he clenched the bedding in his fists.

"Do you still hate me? Do you still want to destroy me?"

"Oh, there are a *lot* of things I want to do to you right now for being this fucking stupid."

"Answer the question! Do you still hate me?"

"No." The word came out through gritted teeth, and she could see the dangerous man underneath the beautiful exterior, the flash of darkness, but she was hopelessly drawn to it.

"Do you still want to destroy me?" Her voice wavered as those tawny brown eyes met hers with a fierce glare.

"Right now I want to get a belt, bend you over the end of this bed, and whip you until you're sane again." David shook his head and looked away from her. "But no, I do not want to destroy you. That would be such a waste."

"I know you're trying to scare me, but it's not going to work."

He surged forward off the bed, stopping just in front of

her as she rocked back on her heels, but she held her ground as he stared down at her. "You *should* be afraid of me, princess. I'm still a demon. I'm just a demon with a bullet wound right now."

"A bullet you took to protect me, and I don't care. You just got caught up in the same shit that I did, only you've known about it. It's been inside you, twisting you, shaping you. Making you this person."

"And you were blind to all of it. So innocent and wide-eyed." He stroked her cheek, and then shoved his hand into her hair, painfully ripping her head back. "Tell me you're not scared."

"I'm not scared of you. I'm grateful. You showed me the darkness that had always been there, you took away the lies."

His other hand caught her hip and he shoved her back against the wall, his body crowded close, the fist in her hair keeping her face angled toward his. That tingling hum at the base of her spine returned with a flush of heat. "I almost got you killed using you like a pawn. I took out my rage on you instead of your father. I tore out all of your innocence, and I forced in all of my darkness. You can't forgive that."

"I wasn't innocent, David."

"You were whole, and beautiful, and pristine, and I tried my best to destroy it." His grip in her hair tightened, the sting sending lightning down her spine. "I *liked* trying to destroy you."

"But you failed."

"I know." He leaned in close, breathing in at her neck, his

lips brushing her skin in the lightest of touches that made her silently plead for more. "But I can see the darkness in you now, princess, and I did that. I put it there."

"Yes, you did." She gasped as his body leaned into hers, pressing her against the wall, his hand inching up to her waist to squeeze.

"You would have been happier if I'd left you with him, you know that, right?" Even his voice was a growl, a texture against her skin that had heat stirring between her thighs.

"It would have been a lie."

"You'd lived the lie long enough, you could have lived it forever. Been the good little heir, followed in Daddy's footsteps." With a nudge, his knee was between her thighs, his thigh rubbing against her, and she chewed on her bottom lip as he traced his mouth over her collarbone.

"I want real. I want honest." She hissed when his teeth nipped at the side of her throat, but it turned into a moan as his next movement delivered a delirious friction between her legs. "I want you," she breathed, and he laughed low.

"You don't know what you want, princess."

"Yes, I do." She nodded against the grip in her hair, trying to keep her thoughts straight as her body turned into a bed of coals that he stoked at his leisure. "I want someone who understands the darkness in my history, the shit they're talking about on every news station. I want someone who knows the truth, who can see me for who I am. Someone other than a lifeless doll, a hapless victim of circumstance."

"Lianna…" A low groan left him as she used his own words against him, his hips rocking against her. "No. I won't. I've already ruined your life, I won't be responsible for filling you with more darkness."

He released her and pulled away, leaving her heart racing, her skin hot, but she caught his arm and pulled him back. "That's *my* choice, not yours."

Leaning up on her tiptoes, she wrapped her arms behind his neck to bring his lips to hers, and she poured everything she had into the kiss. Desperate to get through to him, to not lose this connection, no matter how terrifying and unpredictable it was.

David was stiff for a moment, and then the hum of a growl buzzed against her mouth and he had her pressed to the wall. He nipped at her lip, and when she took in a breath he deepened the kiss. Their tongues clashed, warring for a moment, and her skin was alight with energy. It was like all the color in the room was amplified whenever he touched her, like the world was half-asleep until his touch woke it up.

"Dammit, princess," he broke the kiss, pressing his forehead to hers. "I'm not a good man."

"You're not good? My father is responsible for so much horror that there's a court case being put together about it." She twisted her hands in his shirt and pulled him harder against her. "I've got plenty of darkness to share."

"None of that was your fault. I was being an asshole." His hands squeezed in at her waist, and she lifted up to press another kiss to his lips.

"What happened to your mother and father wasn't your fault either, and you got your revenge. Everyone knows the truth now. The world is digging through those files. You finished his plan."

"I'm still not a good man." He rubbed himself against her, the erection straining the front of his pants, his hands roaming up to brush her breasts through her top, and then his lips were on her neck. "Even right now I want to hear you scream again."

"That's fine, I've been fantasizing about it anyway." A smile spread across her lips as he leaned back to look at her in surprise.

"Have you?" he asked, a low rumble in his chest.

"Yes." It was the truth. He was at the center of the storm with her even though his name wasn't in the media. They were two halves of the same fucked up coin, except she'd only ever seen the light, and he'd only had the dark. It was time for them to share. He deserved some light, and she'd realized she craved the dark. *His* dark. Lowering her voice, she traced the hard ridge of his cock through his pants. "When we get back to my apartment, I'll scream for you, I'll cry for you, I'll beg you to fuck me. I want you, David, and I'm not confused about who you are."

"If I touch you right now, will you be wet, princess?" That wicked grin spread across his perfect lips, and she shifted her feet a little farther apart in invitation. One fist caught her by the hair, holding her back against the wall, and the other slid down her side until he could gather her skirt up and push her panties aside. The first brush of his fingers between her lips made her hips buck forward, and he teased her clit for a moment, too light, his eyes tracing her face as she bit down on her bottom lip to stay quiet. Then he thrust two fingers deep, and she couldn't hold back the gasp as heat blossomed and rushed through her veins.

"David," she whimpered, and he captured her lips again as he teased and tormented her, winding her up until she was slick and grinding against his hand.

He stopped as suddenly as he'd started. Lifting his fingers to his lips, he drew them in and groaned as he tasted her. "You still taste like heaven."

"Does this mean you'll come with me?" Lianna asked, breathless.

"I'm going to ruin you."

"You've already ruined me, I'm just asking you to fulfill your promise." She rolled her hips against him and he growled and pinned her back against the wall.

"What do you want from me? It's yours."

"I want to know all of it."

"All right," he nodded, his hips rubbing against her in a method that was almost too distracting.

"I want you to always be honest with me."

"If we don't leave soon, I'm going to fuck you on the floor until you're in need of medical attention." He bit down on her shoulder, and she felt a growl in her own chest as she squirmed against him. "How's that for honesty?"

"Perfect." She had to stifle a moan, focusing. "And I want a promise."

"Anything."

"Don't call me princess again." A moan slipped from her

lips as he rocked between her thighs. They were making out like teenagers and she could barely think straight.

"Okay, I'll go with angel. My fallen angel. Now choose where I'm fucking you, because it's either here with Nurse Sandy as an audience or somewhere else."

"My apartment."

"How far?"

"Ten minutes."

He pulled her away from the wall and with great effort pried himself back. His eyes were wild with energy, his beautiful face flushed, his hair a mess from her hands in it. "Lead the way."

"You're not going to walk with me?" She smiled when he growled.

"I'm going to follow you, and then in the car I'm going to describe in detail what I will do once I have you naked behind a locked door."

"Do I get a hint?"

"It's going to make you scream." Heat hit her cheeks and she had to swallow as a dizzying wave of arousal almost made her knees buckle. "You should start moving now, angel. I've spent enough years waiting to have you."

Lianna ripped the door open and started back down the hall, but she could feel him behind her, like a stalking animal, and it had slick heat pooling between her thighs. As she paused by the nurse's station for him to gather his papers, she saw yet another news broadcast about the dissolution of Mercier Systems, a flash of the building on the screen that had been her home for her entire life.

But not anymore.

No more ignorance, no more naïveté, no more lies.

She was going to be someone new. Someone stronger. Someone that didn't flinch back and hide from the darkness. Now, she was going to make the darkness hers.

Chapter Twenty-One

DAVID

It was only the fact that his hands were clenched around discharge papers and a sack of meds that kept him from grabbing her as they walked away from the elevator. The building was nice, still very expensive based on the security at the door and the spacious lobby, but nowhere near what he knew she could afford. Still, she was Lianna Mercier, only daughter of Alain Faure, and she'd brought him home.

Oh, the irony.

He smiled as she fumbled with the key, her hands trembling, and he leaned close to whisper in her ear. "Thinking about what I told you in the car?"

Lianna dropped the keys, cursing, and he chuckled.

"You sure you want this, angel?"

The look she gave him was full of fire, and the heat in her cheeks matched it well, making her blue eyes shine.

Opening the door, she held it wide and tilted her head inside.

He shook his head as he walked in, because while she seemed sure about this insanity, he definitely wasn't. Yes, he wanted her. She was all he'd thought about since he'd been conscious.

Was she okay? Had the Faure family come for her? Would the world make the same assumptions he had about Lianna Mercier and condemn her right alongside her father?

Sitting in that damn hospital bed, he'd wanted to protect her from all of it. To keep her safe from the destruction he'd wrought on Mercier Systems and that fucking bastard who had tried to shoot his own daughter.

But then clarity would return and he'd realize the only question he had any right to ask was *when would the police show up to handcuff him to his bed and read off the list of crimes he'd committed against her?*

Fuck.

"So," she spoke from behind him and he turned to find her in the shadows near the front door. The skirt and top were subdued, barely hinting at the curves underneath them. Probably work clothes.

He wanted to rip them off her, and bend her over the elegant gray patterned chair at the edge of her living room, but the stinging tug of sutures in his back as he rolled his shoulder reminded him that he wasn't capable of that. *Yet.*

"So…?" He smiled, watching as her weight shifted between her heels.

As nervous as a rabbit ready to run.

"Would you, um... how about I make us a drink? Rum?" Lianna smiled at him and walked into the open kitchen, flipping on a light before she pulled a cabinet open.

"Sure." David moved to the bar that served as the separation, ignoring the chairs she had neatly tucked underneath as he set his things on the top. "Do you have the same bottle we drank?"

Her body stilled, a distinctly different bottle clutched in her delicate fingers as she lowered it. "No, I don't. Do you not drink—"

"Whatever you have is fine."

The tension in her eased a little, shoulders relaxing, movements not quite so sharp, as she gathered glasses and dropped ice cubes into them, but the moment she turned to face him again she stiffened slightly. Her throat worked, eyes dancing across her almost empty countertops, and then she set the glasses and the bottle of Kraken rum onto the bar. "I don't even remember the brand you had in..."

"Your cell?" he finished, tilting his head to watch as the flush returned to her cheeks and a nervous smile spread over her lips.

"Right."

"Let's sit down." Snagging the bottle, he left her to get the glasses as he moved toward her living room. Floor to ceiling windows let the late afternoon sun stream in, and he took the gray chair, which forced her to choose between the couch and the matching chair on the far side of her coffee table.

She chose the couch, in the seat closest to him, and arranged two coasters with the precision of a hostess.

Before she had the chance, he shifted forward and poured the rum as silence settled over them. Reality had a funny way of showing up when he least appreciated it, and as David stared at her on the couch — he could hear it knocking. Picking up his glass he took a long drink, savoring the spice on his palate before swallowing. "We don't have to do this, Lianna. I can walk out right now."

"No." Shaking her head, all that golden blonde hair tumbling over her shoulders, she sat back on the couch with a heavy sigh and drank. Brows pulled together, she had her thumbnail between her teeth a moment later.

"It was Sailor Jerry."

"What?" Her eyes lifted to him, a little too wide.

"The rum," he answered.

"Ah, yeah, there was a girl on the bottle."

He nodded, looking around her apartment. No photos, no knick-knacks, nothing that made it *hers*. It looked like it could have fallen out of some trendy upscale magazine. All clean lines, inoffensive colors, except for the artwork. A huge painting hung where most people would have had a television, and there were two others on the other wall. None of the three seemed to match, and his eyes were drawn to the one in the middle, a splash of different paints across the canvas that seemed to be more an accident than anything he would call *art*, but he wasn't the one with a degree in the subject. Still, it was like she didn't live here at all. Anyone could have walked in and made it their home. "Who painted that?" he asked, pointing at the messy one.

"Pollock."

"Jackson Pollock?" he asked, turning to look at it again.

"Yeah." She shifted on the couch, her knees pressed together as she leaned forward. "You know his work?"

"Not really, I just recognize the name. Must have cost a lot, right?"

Lianna shrugged and sat back again. "I'm not sure, *he* bought it for me."

"Your father."

Nodding, she took another drink before sitting up straight and tucking a strand of hair behind her ear. "I don't want to talk about him, okay?"

"You just want me to shut up and fuck you?" He grinned when her mouth dropped open for a split second before she struggled to compose herself. "If that's what this is, just tell me. I'm not going to argue."

"That's not what I said." The blush was back in her cheeks, her legs squeezing together, and he would have bet money she was wet.

"Then what is this?" he asked.

She finished her drink and reached forward to pour another, so he followed suit. Upending his and offering it for a refill. "You promised me answers."

"We can talk and drink all night. I'll tell you whatever you want, we don't have to fuck." It felt good to say it aloud, to confirm it for himself and her.

"That's not what I meant," she groaned, and he laughed a

little, leaning back in the chair to stare at her high ceilings, painted with the orange of the evening sun.

"Then what *do* you mean, angel? Because I already described everything I want to do to you. I want to make you scream for me again, I want to make you come again, and then I want to wake you up and do it all over again. You told me not to lie, and I'm not going to, but I have no fucking idea why I'm here right now unless you're planning to kill me for the evil shit I did."

With the sun behind her hair she was glowing like an actual angel, the golden light turning her hair into a halo, the pale blouse shining. If wings had sprouted from her back, he wouldn't have been surprised.

She sighed softly, tilting her glass back and forth. "I don't want to kill you. I mean, I thought about it. In the— in the *cell* I thought about it a lot. I'll admit that, but all I've thought about since they got you into the hospital was how much I wanted you back."

What the fuck? *Those* words surprised him more than spontaneous wings ever would have.

"But *why?*" he asked.

She made a frustrated sound, kicking her heels off onto the carpet before pressing her bare toes into the weave. "Why are you making this so complicated?" she snapped.

"Why the fuck are you bringing the man who kidnapped and hurt you into your fucking house?" The question made him clench his fist, and once he'd asked it he felt the same protective urges he'd felt in the hospital. Only now he wanted to protect her from himself, because he was the danger. *Talk about complicated.* "You should have called the damn police, Lianna. I deserve it."

"I want you here."

"That's not an answer." He leaned forward, wincing when he pulled the healing muscles in his back. Another swallow of rum was the only medicine he needed right now, the pain meds would put him on his ass. "I hurt you. Badly. I did things that... You shouldn't let a man like me within a hundred feet of you."

"I don't care," she muttered into her glass as she drank again.

"You don't *care?* What the fuck, Lianna? You deserve better than that! Better than me!"

"I don't WANT anyone but you!"

He may have raised his voice, but she *yelled*, anger flashing in her eyes and he leaned back on the couch, as his mouth hung open. Useless, and stunned.

"Fuck!" she shouted again, standing up and taking her glass with her as she walked away from him. "I thought you understood this. I thought you got it, but I guess I was wrong. Shit, maybe I am crazy."

"Got what? What am I supposed to understand?" he asked, feeling more confused than he'd ever felt in his life.

"THIS!" Gesturing between the two of them, she let out a short scream and then thrust her hand into her hair, pouring the rum down her throat as she swallowed twice, three times. "Oh my God, I've lost my mind. I've really lost my mind."

"Would you just explain whatever is going on in your head

so I don't have to play this guessing game? I promise you I'm terrible at it." He waited until she faced him again and then he tilted his head toward the couch. "Come on, sit down and talk to me, angel. I like the way you look with the light behind you."

For a moment she only stared, beautiful concern passing over her face, before finally returning to her seat. David shifted in the chair, trying to hide the way his cock hardened as the light slid across her thighs. He could taste her on his tongue again, from the hospital, from the cell — and all of it felt wrong. Being *here* felt wrong. She should hate him. Hate would be so much easier to handle than whatever this was.

Fuck. This was not what he was good at.

"Talk," he commanded, and her body tensed.

"I don't know what to say," she whispered, nursing the last of her drink.

He shrugged the shoulder that didn't cause his back to twinge. "Why do you want me here?"

"Because you know everything and you won't lie to me about it." Lianna stared down at the glass in her lap, letting the shadows grow across her apartment floor as he waited to see if she'd say anything else.

"I won't promise I know absolutely everything, but I know a lot."

"You know more than I do."

"You don't know much, pr— angel." Clearing his throat, he took another sip and sat up straighter, hoping she hadn't caught the slip but the look in her eyes said she had.

"Why are you calling me angel?"

He chuckled. "You're avoiding talking to me about what you think *this* is." Gesturing between the two of them he set his glass on the coaster to refill it, and did the same for her, well aware they'd be drunk in no time if they kept this up — which may not be the worst end to the night.

"You first," she taunted, lifting her chin as she started drinking again. The girl wanted to get drunk, but he couldn't exactly blame her. She'd brought a nightmare home for a nightcap. Getting drunk was pretty much her only sane decision of the day.

"Alright, fine." David took a breath and tried to think of how to phrase it without sounding like a psychopath. "I knew your father called you princess, so that's what I called you. I did it on purpose to mock you, and because at first I saw you that way. You were the heir to his company, and you were wealthy, privileged."

"Right." She gestured around the room like it explained everything.

"I thought you *knew*. About what he was doing, about the Faure family, all of it. I thought you were in on it, his pretty little clone. Getting ready to fill his shoes." David shook his head, remembering how the realization had slowly crept up on him that she had no idea why she was suffering, no idea of the terrible things her father had done. "When I finally figured out how innocent you were, I'd already done— *shit*."

He drank more, deciding he agreed with her unspoken decision to just get trashed. It would be easier that way to make it through whatever the fuck this was.

Forcing a breath he said the words out loud, "I'd already taken you, fucked you, hurt you, done so many fucked up things to you and *enjoyed* them… I couldn't believe — didn't *want* to believe you'd been innocent in all of it. It made me the bad guy, ruined my whole revenge plan, tainted it. And then I couldn't believe someone like you could belong to him."

"I don't belong to him," she whispered, and he could hear the rage in her voice. Towards her father, not him, which was satisfying and somehow troubling at the same time.

"I know. I really don't know why he kept it all from you. I don't know why he hid it from—"

"Michael said it was because he wanted me focused on the company. Apparently my father thought if I knew about the family my goals would change, and he wanted me to learn the company first. Before he, you know, told me how he did it." Her voice trailed off, eyes dropping to the sleek wood and glass table.

"Ah." He paused, not sure what to say as he ran his fingers across the condensation, tracing patterns in the tiny water droplets. "Well, once I knew you were innocent I couldn't shake it. Couldn't stop thinking about it, about everything I'd done to you, everything I still wanted to do… and the image of a fallen angel just fit in my head. You had been so pure and so good, and I had pulled you down and defiled you. Ruined you, and then I went ahead and took away everything else because I'm a bastard." David swallowed, and then eased the lump in his throat with more rum. "So, when you told me to stop calling you princess, I was fine with it. I'd been calling you *angel* in my head for a while."

She was smiling when he looked at her again, the sun

lower in the sky, painting the room in that red-orange haze that turned her hair to golden fire. "It's weird, but I thought you looked angelic when I pulled off your mask. I'd been expecting something monstrous, but you reminded me of baroque paintings of—" Lianna stopped and rolled her eyes. "Don't look at me like that."

"Like what?"

"Like you're surprised to find out you're attractive."

"Tell me more." He grinned and she huffed, but she still laughed a little as she relaxed back against the cushions.

"*Anyway*, I thought the same thing. That after all the evil you'd done, you still looked angelic."

"Even Lucifer was a fallen angel," David replied.

"And we all know looks can be deceiving." Lifting a shoulder she toyed with her glass, moving it between her fingers as it rested on one of her thighs. "But I know why you did everything you did, and I get it."

He lifted an eyebrow, to the best of his ability, and stared at her for a second. "You get it?"

"Yeah."

"You *get* why I fucking assaulted you? There's no excuse for—"

"Would you stop trying to play the fucking martyr here? Christ!" Lianna groaned, and he growled under his breath. "Yes, I do understand why you did what you did. Was it fucked up? Yes. Was it wrong? Yeah, it was fucking wrong, but like you said you thought I was in on it all. You wanted to make me suffer, and you did."

"This is exactly why you should just tell the cops everything. Shit, it's why every day I expected them to show up! It's why I gave you my fucking information!"

"But you stopped, David."

"I stopped after I'd wrecked you, and even then I just got drunk and fucked you again. I could have let you leave that night, I could have opened the fucking doors, and instead I chased you down and dragged you back, and fucked you again." He groaned, putting the glass down so he could rub his face with both hands. The conversation wasn't helping at all, it was making it worse. Making him remember everything he'd done to her, and *fuck* if it wasn't making him hard as a rock.

"This isn't going to work." He pushed himself out of the chair and took a few steps backwards towards the door. "Look, I appreciate you not going to the cops, prison would be terrible, but this is wrong. I don't deserve your fucking forgiveness, I deserve for you to—"

"All I had my entire life were lies." Lianna cut him off, standing up with the glass at her side. "They were pretty lies, *beautiful* lies, that gave me a beautiful life. I had money, privilege, and anything and everything I wanted. It was everything good, everything wonderful, and my father hid every shred of darkness from me. I didn't know about his family, I didn't know about what *really* built his company… I didn't even know how my mother actually died."

David flinched, remembering his own mother. "I know."

"And you?" She took a step toward him, and then another. "You're only four years older than me, so… what? You were *seven* when my father killed your mother? When my father alienated yours from the world and shut you both out?"

He felt his jaw clench tight, memories clashing inside him as he tried to stick to his new plan. The plan to get the fuck out of Lianna's life and leave her in peace.

"And for all those years all you knew was your father's pain, caused by one man. And you learned all of his secrets, every dark and fucked up thing. You *grew up* knowing every shred of evil he'd ever committed, and knowing that all of it had led to your mother's death. That *I* had led to your mother's death." Lianna stepped closer to him, and he had the strongest urge to run from her as she moved nearer. "All you ever had was darkness, David, and all I ever had was light. Two sides of the same coin, and when you took me, when you did everything you did, you saw my light, and I saw your dark. *That* is what I meant. That's what we have."

Her fingers wrapped around his hand, and he didn't pull away, which felt like a damnation all on its own, but when she stepped in and moved to her toes to kiss him and he leaned into it — that was when he resigned himself to whatever hell the universe decided to send him to after this life.

This was worth it, *she* was worth it.

Chapter Twenty-Two

LIANNA

Kissing David shouldn't have felt this good, on some level she knew that, but as his hands moved to cradle her face, as he bent to make it easier on her and their tongues clashed — she didn't give a fuck. Everything felt right when one of his arms shifted down to caress the small of her back, pulling her against him, and she wished she'd set the damn glass down so she could return the gesture but with her one free hand wound in the fabric of his shirt it was still good.

So good.

Her pulse picked up, the heat reigniting at her core as he nipped her lip and changed the angle of the kiss, licking his way between her lips again until she was moaning against him. Hungry for the intensity of him, the fire that made him so dangerous, so unpredictable. He pulled her tighter against him and then stumbled.

"Fuck!" Pulling air between his teeth, he hissed and stood upright, pain etched across his face.

"Sit on the couch," she commanded him, even going so far as to pull him towards it by a belt loop, and he chuckled as he followed.

"I had no idea you were so bossy."

"Drop your pants," she clarified, with more than a touch of sarcasm, ripping his belt open so fast the metal fixtures jingled. Then she pulled the button free, and dragged his zipper down. "Come on."

He walked the rest of the way without an argument, let his pants drop to the floor, and sat down, letting her abandon her glass on the coaster so she could inch her skirt up and straddle him. The moment her knees landed on either side of him, he went wide-eyed. Hands in the air above her legs. Trying to be the fucking good guy. But she didn't need a hero anymore, and she didn't want the villain, she wanted the man. David Gethen. *Him.*

"Kiss me?" Inching forward, she put her hands over his and brought them down to her hips, staring down at his tawny brown eyes. When she leaned closer he met her halfway, capturing her mouth and tightening his fingers around her hips, thumbs digging in at her waist as he pulled her closer. Their groans echoed each other as his erection rubbed against her, and a moment later they were grinding, making out like teenagers again.

"Fuck, angel..." He licked and nipped his way down her neck, tugging at her top until he cursed under his breath. "Take this off."

"Take your boxers off." Standing, she smiled at him as she tugged her shirt over her head, and he quickly leaned forward to nudge his boxers to his thighs. Reaching forward she pulled them down his legs, and he toed his shoes off so she could toss it all aside.

"Skirt?" he prompted, and she smiled as she unzipped the side to let it fall. "Panties too, angel."

"And your shirt?" she asked as she slid them down her legs.

"Afraid you'll have to help me a little with that." He grinned as she climbed onto his lap again, wrapping her fingers around the fabric she slid it up his hard abs, letting her fingers graze his skin until he pulled one arm through and winced as she helped him maneuver the other side free to rip it over his head. "Almost perfect," he whispered, sliding his hand behind her back to unhook her bra with a single flick.

"How much have you practiced that?" She dropped the bra to the side and shifted forward on his lap as he ran his hands up her sides to cup her breasts.

"A gentleman never tells." Leaning down he took one nipple between his lips and sucked, nipping the flesh until she whined, tingles rushing over her skin.

"Since when are you a gentleman?" she asked, breathless, and he chuckled as he gave the same treatment to the other breast, before pulling her forward until his cock brushed against her and she shifted her hips.

"It's something new that I'm trying for a girl I'm interested in."

"Well don't try too hard." She smiled down at him and he laughed low, moving his hands to her thighs, and then higher, and higher.

"Oh, I doubt I'll be very successful." He leaned closer, whispering against her cheek. "Are you wet for me?"

The words made her shudder, a warm tingle rushing over her skin as one hand dipped between them to stroke up her cleft and gather the wetness they both knew was there. He started to roll his thumb over her clit and she gasped, the noise dissolving into a moan as she leaned back to give him more access. "Fuck," she hissed, appreciating the groan as he slid his hand lower and pressed two fingers deep.

"You are so perfect."

Perfect. If it weren't for the buzz of pleasure between her thighs, she might have laughed. She had never felt so far from perfect in her life. Everything was upside down. Everything was wrong. Even *this* was so fucked up it should have felt wrong... but it didn't. For some reason David Gethen was the only thing that made sense. The only part of her universe that seemed solid and real, and his body was out of this world.

So much hard muscle.

His bicep bulged as he worked his fingers inside her, and she grabbed onto his shoulders, pushing him back into the couch so he wouldn't strain the stitches. From the bullet wound he'd taken for her. *Fuck.* Just remembering that moment had her rocking her hips against his hand. His strong arms around her, body shielding hers — he was good. Down deep, *very* deep, he was a good man. The kind of man who fulfilled his father's plan, avenged his mother, protected a girl too spoiled and stupid to realize her father was a soulless killer.

"I want you," she whispered, moaning as he stroked her g-spot.

"You do?" Sliding his fingers free he lifted them to her lips, and she opened her mouth without a request, nodding as she sucked them in. Tasting herself for no other reason than he'd wanted it. "Fuck, angel, that's hot."

Teasing one finger with the tip of her tongue she leaned back and smiled. "Well?"

"Ride me," he commanded, large hands palming her hips as he lifted her slightly until she was poised over his cock — but he didn't pull her down. Instead, his fingers dug in to her flesh, gripping and massaging, and she was the one who reached between them and slid him inside as she slowly eased down.

"*Fuck.*"

"Yesss," he hissed, head angling back on the couch as his hips twitched.

This was what she'd wanted, as fucked up as it was. Him inside her again, and it was somehow better with her in control for the moment. Lifting and dropping, before grinding her clit against him. All her pleasure, while he made desperate sounds and lifted off the couch to plunge deeper. Her nails dug into his shoulders, back arching as she sought her own orgasm regardless of his, and with the hum of alcohol in her veins she didn't see the point in second-guessing her instincts.

Logic was bullshit anyway.

Reason and 'thinking things through' would have led her to an existence of abstinence, when all she'd really craved was *this*. Him. Hard body, hard cock stretching her core, making her ache when she spread her legs further and let him drive in deep. She wasn't perfect, but *this* was.

"That's right, ride me," he purred, a low rumble in his chest as he slid one hand between them and started to stroke her clit with his thumb. She was soaked, the wet sounds of their bodies colliding only pushing her further towards oblivion.

When she opened her eyes he was outlined in dim gold, and it was criminal how gorgeous he was. He had taken her, hurt her, shattered everything she'd known… but now he was all she wanted.

No more empty wealth, no more shallow friendships, no more workaholic tendencies — Lianna had decided to live in the physical. In the real. In this. This place where she didn't have to think, she only had to feel.

Static skirted over her nerve endings, lighting the ends like the popping of firecrackers, and she dug her fingernails into his skin as she arched her back to grind herself down. Reaching, surging forward for that impossible bliss that she knew waited just beyond the tension, the crippling pleasure that thundered through her muscles and made her shake. David picked up the pace, pulling her closer, soft feminine curves pressed against hard muscle.

Then it all exploded into glimmering fragments, leaving her breathless as the orgasm took her, and he continued to pull her against him, which only stretched out the horizon on her ecstasy until it seemed endless. Lost in a haze of alcohol and sex, draped over his hot, firm chest, Lianna rested her cheek against his shoulder as she felt him come, tightening around him on reflex. His groan brushed over her neck, and then he pressed a kiss to her skin as they were both caught up in the bliss filled silence.

What could they have been if they had met under different circumstances? Could it have always been like this?

Could it be like this forever?

Past and future taunted her as she struggled to stay in the present. To ignore their history, and the looming uncertain future. Tonight was not for thinking, too much of that had been done already. Too many confessions, too many discussions about her, the *cell*, their corrupted pasts. If she let herself, she'd taint this bliss — and that would bring back the reality of everything else.

"Come to bed with me," she mumbled against his skin, nudging her hips forward so he shifted inside her.

"You want me to stay?" he asked, and his voice was almost too soft to hear over her own breaths.

"Yes."

"Are you sure?"

"Shut up." Lifting her head she kissed him, and he wrapped his arms around her back, squeezing her close. It might have been insanity, or just the dangers of the world he'd opened her eyes to, but the only person she felt safe around was him. She wanted his arms around her, wanted him at her back, and if he slept in her bed she might finally sleep an entire night.

"You know what happens when you get mouthy with me?" he asked, leaning back enough to look in her eyes.

"I'm not afraid of you anymore."

"I can tell." Brushing his thumb across her cheek, he cupped the side of her face. "Why are you forgiving me?"

"I never said I'd forgiven you, did I?" With that, she turned out of his hand and climbed off his lap, feeling him slip from her, but she still held out her hand for his. She wanted him in bed, wanted him in *her* bed. Real and here.

"Guess not," he answered, grabbing the rum as he let her lead him down the hallway toward her bedroom. It was much darker, but it wasn't difficult to find the bed and pull the sheets back.

Climbing in, she scooted over to make room for him, and they both settled back against the pillows, staring at the dull gray ceiling. He offered the rum, and she sat up just enough to drink from it. "I don't want to talk anymore."

"Alright." Without another word, he took the rum back and swallowed a mouthful. They continued that way for a while. Cooling down in silence under the crisp sheets as the alcohol suffused their limbs and left them still in post-orgasmic bliss.

Lianna woke up for a moment as he tucked her against him, skin to skin beneath the covers, but her alarm didn't last. Even through the drunken haze and exhaustion she remembered wanting him in her bed, wanting him against her like this, and everything felt right for the first time in a long while.

Maybe ever.

Chapter Twenty-Three

DAVID

He'd barely slept, and his dreams had been abrupt and violent — more nightmares than anything else — but Lianna was in his arms. His angel. She was curled into a ball, his arm around her ribs. Too thin. She'd lost weight in the weeks since everything had exploded, and he was forcing himself not to breathe too deeply out of fear of waking her. For once, he just wanted to watch her at sleep, her features serene, her body molded to his.

Peaceful.

It was troublesome to realize that he'd never seen her like this before. She had always been awake and terrified. Angry, or cold, or in pain. Guilt pulled at him again and he gently drew some of her hair off her face. There were parts of him that still craved her pain, her screams, and another completely oppositional piece that only wanted her happy, pleasured, and moaning.

Maybe this was why he'd never attempted relationships.

Well, this and the whole obsessive plan and stalking he'd

been doing since he had been old enough to help his father. *Fuck.* Both of their lives were a wreck, and she was right. He'd been aware of it for years, had lost whatever childhood he may have had to the pursuit of Alain Faure, and Lianna's childhood was a farce. It had probably been filled with extravagant gifts and trips and toys that other children only dreamed of — but it had been with Robert Mercier. The man who had killed her mother, and kept her blind to the evils surrounding her, leaving her open for him to take her.

Lianna groaned in her sleep, and David realized he'd tightened his arm as he'd been thinking about everything. About her, about their pasts, and what he'd done to her... it made him want to pull his touch from her completely, just as much as he wanted to pull her closer and bury his face against her neck to breathe the sweet scent of her skin.

One thing was clear, he didn't deserve her. Never had.

Not out of vengeance. Not out of hate.

Not at all.

But he still wanted her.

It made the heat of her skin feel like a brand against his, yet he was happy to burn as he kept them close together. With one elbow propping his head up, he was able to study the gentle rise and fall of her chest, the soft pinch of her features as something happened behind her closed eyelids. Golden hair in a tangled cloud around her head, she looked exactly like the tainted angel he'd told her she was. And if he burned in hell for what he'd done, for enjoying this moment with her, he'd accept it. He'd walk into the flames with his head held high.

He just hoped that the devil would wait to collect his dues.

"Hmm?" A soft murmur escaped her, and then she yawned, jaw stretching so wide he thought it might crack, and then he found himself yawning as well. She twisted, curling into his chest, and mumbled sleepily, "Morning."

"Morning, angel." Brushing her cheekbone with his thumb he leaned down to kiss her softly, and she smiled against his lips.

"You stayed."

"Did you think I was going to leave?"

"I thought you'd run as soon as you could."

"Not a chance, beautiful." Pulling his fingers to the tip of her chin, he pinched lightly to lift her eyes to his. "Do you still want me here?"

"Don't start that." Lianna groaned and pulled her face from his fingers to turn and bury it back in the pillow, her ass pressing against his hips as she burrowed into the covers.

"Start what?" he teased, gliding his touch down to her waist so he could grind his growing cock into the tender flesh of her backside.

"The martyr shit."

"Who's being a martyr?"

"You," she clipped, snagging his hand as he moved to slip it between her legs. Lianna rolled enough to meet his eyes again. "I know this is crazy, so I don't need you pointing it out too, alright?"

"I didn't say anything about crazy." *Even though this is.*

"Right." She tossed the covers aside and sat up, moving to the edge of the bed in a quick swing of her legs, but before she could stand he grabbed her arm and pulled her back. Ignoring the argument from his back, he pressed a hand to her sternum, teasing the base of her throat with his fingertips.

"Listen to me, Lianna. I didn't lie when I said I wasn't a good man. I'm not, and I'm definitely not going to let you get away with acting like a brat just because I feel guilty."

Wide, blue eyes stared up at him for a second before they narrowed. "I thought you didn't regret what you did to me."

"Different things," he answered, tracing the hollow of her throat with one finger. "I can feel guilty for assuming you were aware of all of it, for hurting you *because* of that, but that doesn't mean I regret taking you, or telling you the truth."

"Semantics."

"Yes." His eyes roamed down her body, cock twitching with the urge to be inside her again. "But words matter, sometimes they're all you have."

"And your words are that you feel guilty for what you did to me, but you'd do it again?"

"Absolutely."

Lianna drew her bottom lip between her teeth, nibbling it as her eyebrows pulled together, and he had the strongest urge to pluck it free and bite it himself. Take her mouth, slide between her thighs and claim what was *his*. She reached up and pushed his hand away, sitting up on the bed so that all he saw was her back in the dim light of early dawn. "You'd do all of it again?" she asked, facing the thin curtains over the window.

"I told you I wouldn't lie to you."

"*Fuck*," she cursed softly, pushing a hand through her tangled hair. "I'm going to take a shower."

"What do you want me to do?" he asked as Lianna stood, the soft angles of her body in shadow.

"You don't need to do anything. I'm not telling you to leave, I just—" Turning to face him she sighed, that look of concentration still etched into her brow. "I just need to think for a minute. Alone. Okay?"

"Okay." David nodded, and she walked around the end of the bed towards the door on his side. "Mind if I make a phone call?"

"Go ahead."

"I need your phone, mine wasn't in my stuff."

"Shit, that's right. Uncle Mi— Michael, *shit*, Joseph, or whatever his name really is, destroyed it with the rest of the stuff you had down there. Said you might have had recordings of the calls on it." She pointed to the door. "My phone is in my purse, passcode is four seven twenty-two."

"Four-seven-two-two, got it. Thanks."

Lianna stepped inside the bathroom and then paused and glanced at him. "Just don't do anything fucked up with it, okay?"

"Sure."

The sound of her cursing under her breath as she shut the bathroom door almost made him smile, he could feel his lips tugging upwards, but he eased himself out of bed before he could give in. Standing beside it, toes digging into the carpet, he finally noticed the room. Lianna had taken every scrap of his attention since she'd woken up, and before that the room had been too dark to notice all of the colors.

But there were so many.

Her bedroom was cobalt blue, vibrant, with framed prints of paintings covering the walls. Their colors popped in the early light — oranges and reds and purples. One was a still life of flowers and fruit, a ripe pomegranate split open on its side. Another was a whimsical splash of paints, possibly a print of another Pollock. There were portraits and landscapes and a large tribal looking mask hanging beside her bed, above the stained glass style lamp on her bedside table. The bedding was a pattern of mint-toned leaves over a tan background. None of it seemed to match at all, and he liked it.

Liked it a hell of a lot more than the sterile, bland look of the rest of her spacious apartment.

Shaking his head, he wandered out into the living room to collect his boxer-briefs from the floor so he could tug them on. As he stared down at the pale couch memories threatened to overwhelm him. Memories of her kissing him, of her climbing on top of him because *she* wanted it, the feel of her skin against his... none of it felt real. It shouldn't have been real.

"And yet it is," he muttered under his breath as he turned away. "Who's the crazy one now?" David rolled his eyes as he looked for her purse. It was still on the edge of the counter where she'd abandoned it, and he nudged it open so he could dig out her phone. Tapping in the code he tried to avoid looking at her apps, or any notifications she might have, and pulled up the phone screen to dial the number.

It rolled to voicemail and he hung up and dialed again. "Come on, old man, I'm sure you've been losing your shit. Answer the damn phone."

"Hello?" The gruff voice was wary, but David still felt the tension ease a little inside his chest as he heard it.

"Hey Harry."

"*David?* Is that you? What blocked number are you calling from? Where the fuck are you? What the fuck happened?" Harry's voice gradually grew more irritated with each question, and it made him smile as he started to poke through Lianna's cabinets.

"Yes, it's me, and I don't think you'd believe me even if I told you where I was."

"Are you okay? Are you somewhere safe?" Concern warred with the irritation in his tone, reminding him of his own father. Bittersweet.

"I'm fine, healing up, and I'd say I'm about as safe as I deserve to be." The only threat in the apartment was Lianna, and if she decided to kill him he still hadn't decided if he'd try to stop her or not.

As he opened another cabinet filled with nothing but dishes and glassware, he knew his brain was leaning towards letting her do whatever she wanted.

Guilt was annoying as fuck.

"Healing? What do you mean? What happened?"

Cursing, David shut the cabinet door a little harder than necessary and opened the next to find her liquor stash. "I took a bullet, but I'm fine."

"You got shot?" It was Harry's turn to curse on the other end of the line, while David gave up hope for food in the cabinets and opened the narrow pantry door. The shelves were mostly empty. A can of coffee, a few spices, an opened box of microwave popcorn, a package of cocktail napkins, and a stack of hand towels.

Where the hell is her food?

"It's not a big deal, Harry. I'm fine."

"Not a big deal? I swear, if this has to do with you-know-who you've painted a damn target on your back. If you killed him... dammit, David, this is *not* what your father would have wanted!"

"It wasn't me, Harry." He sighed as he opened the fridge and leaned down to stare at more empty shelves. A handful of salad dressings, a few take out containers, and a carton of half-and-half.

"Swear to it. Swear on your mother's grave that you had nothing to do with this shit."

David cringed and shut the fridge to lean back against it. The mention of his mother was still like a knife twisting deep, even though the bastard who'd ordered it was dead. "I swear I didn't kill him. On my mother's grave, I swear. All right?"

Harry let out a long breath. "Okay. That's good, that's very good. But it doesn't explain how you got shot."

"I was protecting someone," he answered, and saying it

aloud felt… nice. Despite all the bullshit between them, he still cared what Harry thought of him.

"What? Who were you protecting?"

Grinning, he cracked the knuckles on his hand as he debated whether or not to tell him, but her name found its way to his lips anyway. "Lianna Mercier."

"WHAT? I thought you, *fuck*, David, I would have sworn you'd been the one to take her. I'm so relieved to know that it was—"

"I'm not saying you were wrong, old man, I'm just saying that in the end I took a bullet for her."

"Jesus Christ." There were a few more muttered curses he couldn't make out, but eventually Harry groaned. "I don't want to know what you did, but she's his only daughter. You've got to know she's connected, that she can come after you too."

"Well, that wouldn't be hard considering I'm at her apartment right now." He chuckled as his eyes landed on the coffee maker and he decided that putting coffee in their stomachs was better than nothing.

"Listen to me. You need to leave. It's over, you've done more than enough for your parents and that girl doesn't deserve—"

"Calm down. She invited me here."

Harry was silent for a moment as he set up the coffee to brew. Finally, the man spoke again, "Why would she do that?"

"I *did* save her life."

"Who tried to kill her?" Harry's voice was hushed, low.

"Who do you think?" he asked, and the curse that answered him was surprising.

"Mercier was going to do a murder-suicide with his own daughter? That… that's fucked up."

David didn't bother to correct his assumption. "I think she's safe for now."

"For now?" Harry muttered again. "How much does she know? Enough to cause trouble?"

"She knows enough to understand why things happened the way they did."

"Look, I'm sure you've been watching the news, but she's at the center of this. Being anywhere near her is putting yourself at risk. You need to walk away."

David opened his mouth to answer, but movement caught his eye and he watched Lianna walk around the corner from the hall, her gaze finding his over the bar. "I don't think I can."

"You need to, that family is powerful. If she had anything to do with her father… she's a walking target. Just let it go, let *her* go, and leave."

Lianna braced her arms on the bar, hair still damp, wearing a simple navy top that scooped low enough to tease at the swell of her breasts. *Beautiful.* The crease between her eyebrows only made him want to smooth it away. "I know, but that's exactly why I can't."

"David—"

"I have to go. I'll call you when I get a new phone."

"Please, listen to me. You don't want to get involved in this shit!" Harry sounded desperate, but there was no helping him now. It had been instinctive to protect her, even after everything he'd done, it was like his mind had decided for him when he'd put himself in the path of the bullet, and it felt the same way now. He had to stay, had to make sure she was safe. She was still too blind, too naïve to handle what was coming, and like she'd said the night before... he knew all of the darkness. He'd always known, and she was so damn innocent.

"Bye, Harry." Pulling the phone from his ear, he hung up and deleted the number from her call log. The coffee maker beeped and he smiled at her. "I made coffee. I was going to make breakfast, but you don't have any food in your apartment."

"Who was that?"

"An old friend. I figured he had been worried about me, and I was right." Moving to the cabinet that held her coffee cups, he pulled down two identical white ones. "Want a cup of coffee?"

"What were you two talking about?" Lianna was focused on him, and he felt that strange protective urge again.

"Nothing important. I'm guessing just half-and-half in your coffee? I didn't find any sugar."

"You went through my kitchen?" she asked, accusation in her tone, but he just chuckled as he poured.

"I don't know about you, but I'm hungry."

"If you'll give me my phone back I can order us some breakfast." Lianna held out her hand, sighing. "And yeah, half-and-half is fine."

David placed the phone on her open palm before he swung by the fridge to grab the cream, adding generous amounts to both cups. "So, you're just going to order us breakfast?" he asked, setting her coffee in front of her.

"You may have noticed, but I don't really cook."

"I did." He couldn't help but smile into the cup as he took a sip, the heat of it sinking into his hands and warming him from the inside out.

"Don't smile at me like that. I'm guessing you're some secret chef, and those sandwiches you gave me were just part of your torture plan?"

The laugh escaped him before he could stop it, and then he laughed harder when she glared at him before staring down at her phone. "No, angel, I'm not a chef, but I get by. I didn't exactly grow up with the money to just order in for every meal."

Lianna swallowed and shrugged a shoulder. "Well, it's not like I had anyone to teach me."

"I'm not judging you, angel. It makes sense." Bracing himself against the counter he watched as she scrolled through something on the little screen. "So, what's on the menu?"

"What do you want to eat?"

"Honestly, I'd like to take you back to bed, spread you out, and lick you until you're screaming my name…" He grinned as a blush turned her cheeks a deep pink. "But, since I think you're talking about eating breakfast, I'm starving. Eggs, bacon, pancakes? The whole nine-yards."

"Um, okay. Just, here, take the phone and choose what you

want." She held it out, and he took it from her shaking hand.

"If you're worried I'm going to force you into bed, I'm not." He stared down at the phone so he didn't have to look at her, guilt stabbing at his ribs, making his lungs feel tight. "I won't do that." *Again.*

He left the last word unspoken as he scrolled through the menu of some local restaurant, adding one of the breakfast plates that appealed to him, along with a side of hashbrowns. When he tapped the cart he saw his order, and a single order of egg whites with fruit.

"Is this seriously all you plan on eating?"

"I'm not hungry."

"Bullshit, you look like you haven't eaten well in weeks. Too thin." Saying it aloud made him remember the way her hipbones had been a little too sharp, the skin over her ribs missing that feminine layer that left them smooth. Gave him something to squeeze, to hold onto.

"There's been a lot going on."

The snark in her tone made him chuckle, and his hands tingled with the urge to grab her. One fist in her hair so he could bend her over the side of the chair he'd sat in, and then he'd spank her bare ass until she struggled. Until she screamed, and cried, and fought him — and then he'd fuck her.

No.

"I've seen the news, and I'm ordering you real food anyway. Then you're going to eat every bite."

"You can't just—"

"I can." Deleting her order, he moved back to the menu and ordered her an omelet with meat and veggies, a whole-wheat English muffin, and a side of fruit. Nothing ridiculous, but enough real calories and protein to help her fill back out. Confirming the order, he handed her the phone. "And I just did."

"God, you're an asshole."

David smiled into his coffee, watching her stare at the order.

"I can't eat all of that."

"Most of that is for me, but you will eat what I ordered for you." Pointing at her cup, he tilted his head towards it. "And you need to finish your coffee."

"You need to stop telling me what to do. I'm not your prisoner anymore," she hissed.

"I know." The words sobered him, but he wasn't backing down on the food. "You're still going to eat while I'm here, but… you can always just tell me to leave."

"And you will?"

"Absolutely," he answered, even though his stomach tightened at the idea. *Shit.* He really didn't want to leave, and after the call with Harry he'd been reminded of exactly why she shouldn't be left alone.

"Tell me what you were talking about on the phone."

"No."

Chapter Twenty-Four

LIANNA

Glaring at David standing in her kitchen in only his fucking boxer-briefs like some kind of Greek god of domesticity, Lianna felt the strongest urge to scream.

She'd lingered in the heat of the shower, taken her time drying off, dragged her feet putting on clothes, all because she hadn't been sure what she wanted now that he was here. In the two weeks since her father's death, since her whole world exploded, he had been the focus of most of her thoughts. Getting him back in her life. Getting him *here* so she could ask him questions, and so she could touch him again and feel *something* — but now that he was here she had no idea what to do.

Then she'd caught the end of his conversation.

She knows enough to understand why things happened the way they did.

David Gethen had all of the answers, she was sure of it. He knew more about her life, her *real* life, than she did —

and now he was playing games? Keeping things from her? Ordering food for her?

"Fuck you," she growled, grabbing her phone to stomp towards the living room. This time, she dropped into the chair he'd taken the night before. *Her* chair, her favorite spot when she sat out here.

He followed her, the soft pad of bare feet on the tile getting closer until he passed in front of her to take the spot she'd had on the couch the night before — well, the spot she'd had until she'd put him in that spot and fucked him. *Dammit.* Everything was out of control.

The dull *clink* of her coffee cup settling on a coaster made her look at him. "I'm not drinking that just because you told me to."

"Would you rather have water? Alcohol? Because those are the only other options you have here." He settled back into the couch cushions, sipping his coffee as if he didn't have a care in the world.

It was annoying.

"I want to know what you were talking about on the phone."

"I was just reassuring my friend that I was okay." David took another sip before resting the cup on his toned thigh. Every inch of him was as perfect as she remembered. Muscular, tanned, with dark hair and tawny brown eyes that she'd memorized while he'd tormented her. Tortured her. Hurt her over and over.

I'm completely insane for bringing him here, but I'm going to get my fucking answers.

"What did you mean when you told him I knew enough to understand why everything happened?"

He stiffened and she felt a sense of victory, but his expression quickly locked down. "You know about your father, about his family. That's all I meant."

"What don't I know?" she asked, and he cursed and lifted his coffee again. "Just fucking tell me. You promised you would answer my questions!"

"Have *you* been watching the news, angel?"

Grumbling, she reached for her coffee. "Of course I've been watching the fucking news. I've also been reading the articles online. Everyone knows what a bastard my father was. Hell, I'm sure I'll have to testify in court about it along with the entire board from Mercier Systems."

"Have you noticed what they *haven't* mentioned?"

Oh, that. "They don't know about the Faure family, *my* family."

"I thought you turned everything over."

Lianna laughed, a bitter burn rising in her throat. "Yeah, I wanted to. I wanted to burn them all down, but Michael, or whoever he really is, wouldn't let me."

"What?" David leaned forward a bit, bracing his arms on his knees.

"When the medics were working on you in the cell, Michael started cleaning up. Asking me about the pages you'd pulled out of the filing cabinets, grilling me about what I knew, what *you* knew." She shrugged. "I told him everything I knew, and he made more phone calls. A bunch of men showed up, men I still don't know the names of so don't ask…"

"And?" he prompted, and she sagged in the chair. Feeling the same weight of despair she'd felt in that concrete room.

"They dug through them. Removed every reference to the Faure family, removed every piece of evidence that I'd been there, but they left my father where he was." Swallowing down the lump in her throat, she tried to bury her own guilt. "Michael told me how dangerous it would be to implicate the Faures, he kept me there for hours as they went through everything. There were bags of papers they pulled from the cabinets, and he kept going over and over the story."

"What story?" he asked, and she looked at him, confused to see what looked like honest interest on his face.

"*The* story. The one to explain all of it. The files, my father's apparent suicide. All of it."

"I don't know what you're talking about."

Lianna had her thumb nail between her teeth before she could even catch herself, chewing at the shredded edge that hadn't had a break in the two weeks he'd been healing in the hospital. "I thought Michael spoke to you."

"No one came to see me, Lianna. Tell me what he did."

Wrapping both hands around the lukewarm coffee cup, she chewed at her lip instead for a moment. "Michael called the police. I mean, he *had* to. My father couldn't disappear without a lot of questions, and that meant we had to have a reason for all of it that didn't involve—"

"A story that didn't involve you, or what I did to you," he finished.

"Right." She nodded. "Michael wanted to protect me. He didn't want me involved at all, and so he said he was going to take the fall for gathering the information on my father. He promised that the police would know I had no idea about what he'd done, and he'd tell them that the idea of being exposed to me, to the public, was what drove my father to kill himself."

"But those files, my father wrote a lot of them himself. He—"

"I know. Michael knew who you were, or at least he figured it out after he saw your driver's license and your mother's obituary." She felt sick, staring down into her lap as she said the next words. "He remembered the order to kill your family, he... he helped set it up."

"He killed my mother?" David's voice was too steady, too cold, and she sensed the threat in him when she raised her eyes.

"I don't know who did it, but my father ordered it, and Michael most likely made sure it happened." She raised her hand when he started to speak, too tired to try and argue the corrupt and evil history of the men who had raised her. "He came up with the story to resolve it all. Said that he'd confess, tell the police *he* was the one who helped your father research everything, that he wanted to bring my father down. To make him stop it all."

"*Why?*" David's voice was hollow, empty, and she felt the same.

"He kept asking me what he could do to make it up to me,

to make me forgive him. I told him that if you died, if he took the one person who had been honest with me away — that I'd never forgive him." Her voice cracked, but she forced out the next words quietly. "I told him he may as well be dead alongside my father, because I'd never forgive him."

"You shouldn't have tried to protect me like that."

"Well, I did. And it all worked anyway. The building was in your father's name, and from what I know the files they kept were his." She shrugged. "I'm not sure though, Michael sent me home. *Here*. While they finished cleaning up, tearing out your cameras, destroying your computers and stuff, so they could call the cops and turn it all over. It was like I was never there, like *you* were never there."

David was too quiet, staring at the floor, his ribs expanding and contracting steadily and she wished she knew what he was thinking. Bringing all of this up, every fucked up piece of their shared history, it felt like an impossible chasm between them. Too much to step over, too much to forget. Whatever solace he'd brought her the night before had probably been a one-time thing, driven by lust, by this fucked up attraction — but at least he was free. Michael had made sure of that, as fucked up as *that* was as well.

"The building was in my father's name? Not mine?"

Nodding, she watched him closely. "Yeah."

He laughed, a bitter sound that had no real humor in it. "Fucking Harry… I should have known."

"Harry?"

"So that's why the cops never showed up at the hospital? You never named me, Michael covered it up, and the investigators are sifting through thousands of documents on all the shit your father pulled, but they have no idea it was the Faure family that really led to all the killings." He finished his coffee and set the cup down on a new coaster, lifting the glass from the night before. "I think we need something stronger than coffee for this."

"David…"

"What?" he snapped, and he finally met her eyes again, but she couldn't decide how she felt.

Did she feel guilty for every crime her family had committed? For all of the suffering Michael and her father had put him through? Or was she angry with him for everything *he* had done to her? For every secret he was still keeping from her?

"A drink sounds like a good idea." Setting down her own coffee and picking up her glass, she offered it and he snagged it from her hand as he walked into the kitchen. The sounds of cabinets opening and closing, and of ice clattering in the freezer, meant she'd have a drink in her hand soon. Before nine in the morning, but it still felt appropriate considering the discussion.

Why hadn't Michael gone to see him? What if he had told a different version of the story?

As David returned with a bottle of bourbon under one arm, and two full glasses in his hands, she took hers. Setting the bottle down, he dropped onto the couch in silence. Eyes glued to the coffee table.

They both drank, and she cringed as the burn tingled in her nose, making her eyes water. Still, it was good bourbon. Blanton's, one of her favorites. Something her father had enjoyed regularly. "David, just tell me what you know."

"I don't even know where to start, angel." The anger had left him, buried under another swallow of bourbon, and she felt helpless. More helpless than she'd felt trapped in his fucking cell.

"You're the only person who can help me make sense of all this," she whispered.

"I know." Another drink. "And I'm not going anywhere unless you tell me to leave."

"I don't want you to leave."

"Good." He lifted the glass, and she watched the amber liquid shine as it slid toward his lips.

Fuck the fact that morning light was pouring in through the floor to ceiling windows, they existed outside of time for now — and she was fine with drinking. It was the only thing that seemed to make these discussions easier.

"I'm glad you listened to Michael."

His words surprised her, and she wet her lips before she spoke. "About the story?"

"About keeping the Faure family out of it."

"Are they really that dangerous?" she asked, and he gave a low, humorless laugh once more.

"You have no idea, angel."

"That's the fucking point! I want to know! I'm sick of being in the dark about all of this, I'm sick of being sheltered." She finished her bourbon in two burning swallows, and hissed through her teeth as she slammed it onto the coaster, making the ice clatter. "You *promised* me the truth. The whole fucking truth, and it's time you paid up."

"Okay." David finished his bourbon, leaning forward to pull the cork free on the bottle and pour more into both of their glasses. "You're right, I made promises. I promised to tell you anything you wanted to know."

"So, tell me."

"The Faure family is all over Europe, in all the major countries. They have connections that cross the ocean, that cross borders, span fucking continents, and your father used that to build Mercier Systems."

"I know that already," she grumbled, snagging her drink back.

"You're not really listening to me. They have *real* connections. If Michael hadn't killed your father, he could have made all of this disappear. You, me, the files, that basement — all of it. It would have taken a phone call, and it would have been like it never happened. Well, except for the companies he couldn't get back." A smile tugged at the edge of his mouth as he shook his head. "Michael killing your father, agreeing to take the fall for this, it allowed all of it to come to light. It put the target on him. Took it off of you."

"And you," she added.

"Because you asked him to, but either way he's betrayed the family. Exposed Robert Mercier's crimes, and it was those crimes that let them launder so much money through his company. Even if the authorities don't make the connections, after this… he won't live long, angel. You get that, right?"

He said it all with such a steady tone, such confidence, but she hadn't really thought it through. She had imagined Michael cutting a deal with the authorities and going into witness protection, or at worst serving a few years in prison… but being killed over it? The thought had honestly not crossed her mind, and despite his betrayals, his lies, and the fact that he'd killed her mother with his own hand — she still felt nauseous at the idea that he'd die over it.

"You had to know what he was doing," David added.

"I didn't think about that. There's been so much happening. The board has been calling me constantly about the accusations, about the unapproved sales of the international facilities, and the police have come by a few times. I've been distracted, and I just stuck to the story." Swallowing more of the bourbon, she stared at the replica of Édouard Manet's *A Bar at the Folies-Bergère*. It wasn't an original, that painting hung in the Courtauld Gallery in London, but the version in her apartment was close. The woman's eyes had haunted her from the first time she'd seen a print of it, and she'd been ecstatic when she had seen it in person. Finding a hand-painted replica had taken time, but she had, and now she found herself drawn once again into the woman's expression.

Trapped in her role. Stuck in place for eternity with the stroke of a paintbrush.

She wasn't free. Hadn't escaped her past or stepped away from her father's tainted company. She was still there, stuck behind the barrier of everything her unknown past was.

And all of it blocked her in, painted her as who she really was...

Lianna Faure.

Mother murdered. Father dead. And the man who had been like an uncle to her had offered himself up like a sacrifice to the family she'd never known.

"You really think they'll kill him?" she asked.

"Do you really think they'll let him live with all he knows? With the fact that he's outed so much to the authorities already?"

They fell silent again, and she pulled her eyes from the painting. Maybe she had subconsciously loved Manet's painting because it was how she felt. Trapped in a role she didn't want to be in, forced to be the perfect face of Mercier Systems since she was too young to argue. Staring into the bourbon, she took a steadying breath. "I just want it all to be over."

"Michael Turner has done what he could to protect you, and the Faure family will take care of everything else. *That* I'm sure of, and..." David cursed softly, bringing the glass to his lips again as he kept his eyes away from her. "I just want to make sure you stay safe."

"Do you think they would come after me? Just because I'm his daughter?" The question made her voice wobble, because somehow in their discussion the Faure family had once again become the bogeyman. A nameless, faceless shadow organization that could pull strings and have her dead if they wanted.

"I don't know," David answered, and then her doorbell chimed and she jumped.

"That's breakfast." Moving to set her glass down, she saw him standing in her peripheral vision and she gestured for him to sit as she stood. "You are *not* answering my door while practically naked. Sit."

"You need to stop telling me what to do, angel."

"Then put some fucking clothes on," she snapped as she walked towards the door.

"At least check the damn peephole before you open the door."

Lianna rolled her eyes as she approached it, but glanced through to make sure it was one of the building security people who carried deliveries to the apartments. Opening the door, she propped it against one foot to sign, taking the bag in one hand. "Make sure you add something for yourself to my fees, okay?"

"Yes, ma'am." The security guard nodded and she smiled as she shut the door.

"Food is here if you still have an appet—" She dropped the bag on the counter, for there, standing in all his sculpted, bared glory, was David.

Clutching a knife.

Chapter Twenty-Five

DAVID

The hilt of the kitchen knife felt slippery in his palm. *Sweating.* A hint of a tremor as he adjusted the hold, because just the idea of someone on the other side of that fucking door hurting her had made his heart race.

"I'm sorry," he said, placing the knife onto the coffee table before he lifted his hands into the air. The door was locked, she was safe, but she still looked afraid. *Of him.* "I only had it because—"

"You thought someone would come here to hurt me?"

"I just want you safe."

"Jesus…" she muttered, before she turned away and started rifling through the large plastic bag. "Would you come get your monstrous breakfast?"

"Sure." Leaving the knife, he walked over and helped her sort through the containers. "I don't see a dining table. Where do you want to sit?"

"Normally I eat at the bar, but I can turn on the TV if you want."

"You have a TV? Where?" Leaning back to look at the walls, he was confused until she laughed softly.

"It's hidden." Lianna was smiling to herself as she gathered the silverware, snagging some paper towels from a roll on the countertop. A few trips back and forth from the kitchen, and they were finally both settled on the couch, the array of food laid out in front of them. She'd collected a set of remotes, and one of them made the section of wall between the two paintings drop away, drawing down blackout blinds over the windows behind them.

"That's fancy," he commented, smiling over at her as she rolled her eyes.

"Yeah, yeah." The television clicked on, and sound came from all around them, a commercial about a sale at some store. "Just please tell me most of this food is yours."

"I got you an omelet." Nudging the container towards her, he plucked the English muffin from another and set it beside the omelet. "And a whole wheat muffin."

"I can't eat all of this," she whined, and he grinned as he passed over the little plastic bowl of fruit.

"Hush, angel. You've got fruit too."

"What the fuck? No one eats this much before noon." Lianna stared at the little omelet and sides like it was a feast, and he grumbled as he pulled the rest of the containers towards his side of the table.

"People don't usually drink bourbon before noon either.

Just eat or I'll have to make you eat." Snagging his fork and knife, he started in on the eggs first before they could cool.

"I thought you weren't going to force me."

David swallowed the mouthful of eggs, reaching for the bourbon to wash it down before he answered as steadily as he could. "I said I wouldn't force you into bed with me, I never said I wouldn't force you to take care of yourself. Now eat before we have to find out what else I can force down your throat."

Her jaw clenched, and the twinge of guilt he felt should have made him apologize, but he didn't take it back, didn't even move until she dug her fork into the omelet and pushed a bite between her lips. "Happy?" she asked as soon as she swallowed.

"I'll be happy when you finish your breakfast, angel."

"*Asshole,*" she muttered, but he just shrugged and continued eating. Watching the commercials until the news came on. First up was a report on some bullshit in Washington, D.C., which was a whole other clusterfuck he didn't want to think about. They had too much drama in their own lives to worry about the country.

Then it changed stories, and the words *Mercier Systems* floated over the surround sound and they both froze. A picture of her father appeared on the screen, and both of their hands went for the remote on the table. He let her take it, and she switched the channel.

"Movie?"

"Sure," he answered, and a moment later she was scrolling through another screen before he recognized several that he'd enjoyed. When she chose *John Wick*, he felt the grin in his cheeks. "You like this one?"

"I watch it a lot." Lianna popped another bite of omelet into her mouth before she looked at him and swallowed. "I can pick another one if—"

"Are you kidding? I love this movie." He gestured towards her food. "Keep eating."

"Stop bossing me around," she muttered, but picked up one of the buttered pieces of English muffin.

They ate in silence for a while, but just as John Wick started slaughtering people in his house she sat back against the couch with her glass of bourbon, half of her food left untouched in the containers. "You're not done."

"I am. You keep eating."

That urge to grab her resurfaced, and his grip on the fork tightened. "Take a break then, but I expect you to finish eating. You're not wasting away."

She huffed under her breath, taking a sip. "It's more than you fed me," she muttered.

His fork clattered against the coffee table as he let go of it, and his fist was in her hair before he'd thought about it, leaning over her on the couch with his other hand lightly circling her throat. Those crystal blue eyes were wide, but there was still so much ferocity in them, so much strength. It made him smile like a monster baring teeth as he stroked the column of her neck with his thumb, the dull twinge of pain in his back somewhere in the background. "Do you want me to admit that I mistreated you, angel?"

"*Yes*," she hissed.

"Okay, I was cruel. I was an asshole. I hurt you. I kept you like a prisoner, because that's what I wanted you to be." His fingers tightened around her throat, and the flash of panic in her face made blood surge to his cock. "But I *did* feed you. You weren't this thin the day I planned to let you go. *You* did this to yourself, and as long as you have me here, as long as you want me around, you need to know I'm not going to put up with you starving yourself. Understand?"

"Fine." The word came out strained, higher-pitch, and he leaned down and took her mouth because he could, because in that moment she was his. Her hands were in her lap, fingers clenched around her glass to keep it steady, and she hadn't even tried to push him away. She tasted like bourbon and butter and warmth, and with a groan he tightened his fist in her hair to angle her back further.

It was the moment that she nipped his lip and moaned into the kiss that he knew he was done. Lost. Completely caught by the woman under his hands. She could destroy him if she wanted to, and now he was sure he would let her. No matter the consequences.

Shifting his hand to her jaw, he held her head in place until he could feel her body shifting, her soft sounds echoing back his own need as the kiss turned into a war of nipping teeth, greedy tongues, and swollen lips.

Not now. She needs food.

With more effort than he wanted to admit, he pulled himself back, keeping his hand in her hair to hold her still. Lianna whined, her hips lifting, the glass of bourbon dangerously tilted at her side and threatening to ruin her couch. The erection tenting his boxers didn't give a fuck about her couch, and neither did he really, but he did want her to eat. Needed her healthy. Whole. "Eat your fucking breakfast."

"Fuck me," she demanded in return and he chuckled.

"Not unless you eat, angel."

With that, he released her, leaving her panting as he tried to gain enough motor control to pick up his fork and pretend to be interested in eating. The first bite he put in his mouth might as well have been cardboard, because he couldn't taste it no matter how long he chewed. Still, he kept his eyes glued to the screen. Watching the movie like it was the most interesting thing in the world, even though all he wanted was to push Lianna to the couch and tear those fucking jeans off her legs and— and *nothing*.

If she didn't eat, didn't take care of herself, none of it would matter.

"You're a tease." The grumble as she stabbed at her omelet again made him laugh, glancing sideways at her to see if she was serious, and the lack of a smile on her lips had him grinning.

"Why don't you finish your breakfast so you have the strength for me to fuck you like I want to?" He winked when she turned her head towards him.

"You were easier to deal with when I was in the cell."

"So were you," he answered, but this time he kept his eyes on the screen, and smiled to himself when he heard her digging into more of the food.

Chapter Twenty-Six

LIANNA

One Month Later

The sound of the front door unlocking made her tense, but a second later she saw David's broad shoulders, his biceps bulging as he carried a bunch of plastic grocery bags. She plugged one ear to block out the racket as he walked into the kitchen, trying to listen to the lawyer. "What did you say?"

"It's a complicated matter, Lianna."

"I really wish you'd stop using that word." *Too close to her father's excuses while she'd been tortured.*

"Fine. The things your father has been accused of are extensive. Honestly, if Michael Turner hadn't turned himself in and pled guilty to his knowledge of it all, worked out the deal to testify, the focus of this investigation could have been on you. You were Robert's only child, you worked at the company." Maria sighed. "If you had worked in *any* other department except for acquisitions it wouldn't have looked so bad, but that's where you've been for over two years."

"Do you think they're going to charge me?" she asked, feeling her stomach clenching again. Movement caught her eye and she raised her eyes to David, concern darkening his beautiful features as he crossed his arms.

"I can't say. We've built our case around Mr. Turner, and he's been very vocal that the reason your father killed himself was because he couldn't face *you* knowing about it. Truly, it was the kindest thing he could have done for you, because it's a convincing argument." The lawyer let out a slight groan. "That was insensitive. I'm still very sorry for your loss, he clearly loved you very much. I'm just saying he helped you a lot with that terrible act."

"Thank you." She forced the right words out, even though she wanted to tell Maria Espinoza that she didn't give a fuck that the bastard was dead. Not really. Even if she felt like an orphan, and occasionally reached for the phone to call him on instinct before she remembered *he* was the reason for all of this shit. "So, what's the latest update on the company?"

"That's being handled by another team at the firm. Paul Mahaffey is the lead on it. From our last meeting I can tell you that the dissolution is continuing, despite the attempt to block from a couple of people on the board. Assets are being liquidated, but…"

"But?

"You know your father violated the bylaws that *he* set forth with the board in selling those companies without calling a meeting and seeking approval. Technically, he was the owner and retained the right to do it, but they're contesting the sales. I'm not sure how much Paul has told you, but they can't even find the company he supposedly sold to. Operations at the facilities have already been shut down, and in two of the cases the properties have already been resold."

Maria was flipping through papers on the other end of the line, but all Lianna could think about was his voice lecturing her about the complications of selling them while she begged and screamed. When David walked towards her, she held her hand out and paced further into the living room.

"It all looks extremely questionable, and although his suicide has helped our case in supporting your innocence in all of this, it doesn't speak well to his state of mind in the erratic business decisions he made leading up to his death." She sighed. "Really, you need to talk to Paul about it. I can ask him to call you."

"I'd appreciate that, thank you." Lianna rubbed her eyes, wondering if the blinding pain behind them was an aneurism waiting to take her out and end this shit show in a truly spectacular fashion. "So, when will we know what they decide about me?"

"Maybe a few more weeks. But, really, they could press charges even after they say they won't. The investigators have only had the files for six weeks, and if they found evidence—"

"There isn't any evidence, Maria. I didn't know anything."

"I believe you, Lianna. I do, but that doesn't mean other people will." A phone ringing in the background had Maria sighing again. "Listen, I know this sucks, but you're going to have to stay put for a while. You can't leave the country, and I wouldn't recommend it anyway. Until the financial stuff is sorted out with Mercier Systems, you want to save your money. We don't know how that's going to turn out. All right?"

"I understand."

"Good. I've sent Paul a message asking him to reach out and update you, but I have to go. I know it feels impossible, but try not to obsess over this. We're all working hard for you and Michael, and you're doing everything you can."

"Thank you, Maria. I really appreciate it."

"Have a good day, Lianna." The call ended and she let the phone hang at her side, staring out the windows at the soggy skyline, blurred by the rain. Normally, this would be her favorite kind of day. The sky heavy with gray clouds, the patter of rain against the windows, the peaceful haze of the city cloaked in stormlight.

But there was no peace for her. Robert Mercier, Alain Faure, had ensured that.

The sound of plastic bags rustling in the kitchen pulled her back to reality. Walking over to the bar, she leaned her arms on it, watching his back flexing through his soaked shirt. "You're being domestic again."

"I'm better at it than you are, angel." He winked before pulling the fridge open to deposit more food inside it.

"I know," she mumbled, and he turned to face her as he let the door fall shut.

"Lianna…" Walking around the end of the bar he stopped a couple of feet from her, one arm reaching for her before he stopped himself. "Can I?" he asked, and she scrunched up her nose.

"You're soaked."

"So?" That lopsided grin transformed his face with warmth and she rolled her eyes and stepped into his chest so his arms could come around her, squeezing her against the cool, wet cloth.

"Did you just stand in the rain?" she asked, unable to hide her smile as she breathed deep. Warm male skin, a hint of his cologne, and that unique smell of rain hitting hot concrete.

"I had to unload the bags from the trunk of the car." David rested his cheek against the top of her head. "Are you going to stop complaining?"

"The doorman would have helped you."

"I don't need servants to help me carry groceries."

His tone made her eyes roll again, but she wrapped her arms around his waist anyway. "For the last time, they are not servants."

"Mmhmm." The noncommittal sound made his chest rumble against her cheek. "So, are you going to tell me what the lawyer said?"

"Nothing really. Everything is still fucked up, I can't go anywhere... and she suggested I be careful with the money I have."

David leaned back and tilted her face up by her chin, his smile still in place. "You've got millions in your account, angel, I think you'll be fine."

"Stalker. It's annoying that you know that."

He chuckled and leaned down to kiss her, warm lips melting against hers, sending a rush of heat over her skin that pooled between her thighs. "I told you I know everything about you," he whispered against her mouth.

"Still annoying," she whispered back, and he spanked her ass hard, jolting her into his chest with a yelp.

"Get your ass in the kitchen and help me with the groceries." David nudged her forward and she plucked at her shirt, unsticking it from her skin.

"I'm soaked now, and you're an asshole."

"Keep smarting off and I'll be fucking your tight little asshole in a minute." The low growl in his voice had her clenching between her thighs, with far more arousal than fear. In fact, there was almost no fear now, just a craving for his darkness, for the hungry, possessive look in his eyes.

She reached into a bag and grabbed a container of mixed greens, just as his hands braced on the counter on either side of her. Caging her in with his hard body, grinding his stiff cock into her ass.

Lips brushing her ear, he spoke low, "You liked that, didn't you, angel."

It wasn't just her shirt that was soaked. Warm, liquid heat was spreading between her legs, and she found herself panting, unable to respond as one of his hands stroked up her stomach. That large hand cupped one breast, kneading it before he plucked at her nipple through the thin bra. Pinching until the zing of pain made her nerves hum and her ears buzz. She licked her lips, gasping as he finally released the bud and wrapped his hand around her throat.

"Say it." Nipping her ear with his teeth, he breathed out a warm laugh, and she shivered.

Her hands were planted on the counter, fingers splayed as he bent her forward just enough to make her back arch, held by her throat against his chest. Her brain was overloading, heart pounding against the inside of her ribs as she squirmed. "I like it," she said, a hint of a moan making the words breathy, desperate.

"I want to hurt you," he growled, fingers tightening around her throat, and her knees almost gave out as arousal burned through any attempt at complex thought.

"Please."

"*Fuck.*" He turned her around with a sharp jerk and kissed her hard, taking her mouth violently. Biting her lip, nipping her tongue, that low moan meeting hers as his hand held the back of her neck in place. Shifting his hands to her ass, he lifted and then he was walking, her legs wrapped around his hips as his teeth traced her neck, clamping down at the beginning of her shoulder.

She groaned, watching the ceiling, the door frame to the bedroom passing overhead, and then he dropped her onto the bed, immediately flipping her to her stomach with a hard grip on her thigh.

"I'm going to make you scream," he hissed, fingers sliding into the waistband of her yoga pants, yanking them down with her underwear. "I'm going to make you beg."

The metallic sound of his belt buckle coming loose had her fisting the rumpled sheets, whimpering in anticipation as her pants tangled around her ankles.

Then he ripped her head back by her hair, making her pull

air between her teeth as the sting spread. "And then I'm going to fuck you. Hard."

Words were impossible now, mouth dry from the rapid breathing, but she managed to nod against the powerful grip in her hair as she licked her lips.

He dropped her head back to the bed, and then she heard the belt, the silken sound of leather sliding over skin, coupled with the tinkling metal of the fixtures. Every nerve ending hummed, taut in anticipation, and then the first line of fire landed across her ass and she gasped, barely able to draw air back in as another and another struck.

Vicious spikes of pain, and she yelled, started to push herself up on the bed, but his hand landed in the small of her back and slammed her back down. "Don't fucking move."

"Please!"

"That's right, beg." He stepped back and then rained down the belt across her ass and thighs, over and over. Line after line of brutal fire, leaving a deep ache behind that she could barely process as the sharp pain doubled, multiplied.

A scream ripped out of her as a lash landed at the delicate place where her ass met her thighs, and then she was crying. Hiccupping as she kicked her legs, tried to push herself up, to shift away, but every time she moved he was there. Holding her down, making the next strike of the belt that much harder. Twisting the sheets in her fists, she whimpered, screaming again as the pain blurred into one high note, held too long, making her skin buzz and her ears ring. "Stop, stop! Please!"

The belt snapped across her thighs again, and she sagged

against the bed, feeling it dip as his knee landed beside her, and then his fingers were in her hair, craning it back. "I'm not done."

His eyes were almost black, pupils dilated so fully, that hungry look in his face that had her whimpering and desperate at the same time. Arousal, edged with a taste of fear, clit pulsing in response. She hated it. She loved it. She needed it.

"Put your fucking face in the bed so no one calls the cops, angel." Pushing her head down, he moved off the bed and she bit down on the sheets just in time to take the next strike. Muffling the scream against the mattress, she felt the bedding grow damp against her cheeks, drool soaking in, as the pain returned full force. Brilliant lines of fire, the heat spreading, tightening every muscle in her body and then she felt it cresting — agony awash in blinding light.

There was no thought, just a desperate surge of fight or flight, and she pushed off the floor, halfway across the bed when his fingers caught her ankle and yanked her back. She turned, feeling her bruised ass burn against the smooth sheet as she tried to kick her foot free, but he was faster. Stronger.

"Did I say I was done?" The belt was out of his hands as he pushed her down on the bed, forcing her onto her stomach as he climbed up, moving behind her. Hand wrapped around her throat, he squeezed hard enough to choke and ripped her upright onto her knees. "Did I?"

Back pressed to his front, she whimpered, coughed, nails digging in at his wrist as she shook her head hard. His low laugh rumbled against her ear, tongue tracing the hollow just behind it before nipping her neck. He released her to rip her shirt over her head, leaving her gasping in air to ease the buzzing in her ears.

"That's right. I'm not done yet, angel." Leaning them both forward for a moment he grabbed pillows and piled two in front of her and then bent her over them. Ass lifted just enough for him to grind the bulge of his erection directly against her core, likely soaking the fabric, and she trembled as every movement teased her and made the welts ache and sting.

He spread her legs wide, digging his knees in, and then she heard his zipper and the arousal took over everything. The pain, the burn in her skin, the lingering hints of fear, it all melted into pure need. At the first stroke of his cock at her entrance, she tried to lean up on her elbows to push her hips back, but he landed a hand between her shoulders, pinning her down.

It was animalistic, raw, powerful as he thrust into her slick heat, the weight of his body pressing her into the bed. He growled, pushing in deeper, making her body adjust and accept him, primal sounds escaping her as he drew back and slammed in again. "Mine," he snarled.

Yes.

Words were impossible now, but she spread her thighs further for him, met each drive of his cock with her hips, reveling in the feel of his hard body against hers. Hot skin, carved muscles straining as he fucked her with every ounce of strength. Bottoming out, making her ache, making her moan and whine.

It hurt. It felt so good. It was perfect.

Capturing her wrists he pinned them to the bed on either

side of her, using them as leverage to take her the way he wanted. Completely in his control, at his mercy, and she lost herself. Pleasure building in growing waves, higher and higher, echoed and lifted by the tingling bursts of pain. It was light and darkness, swirling into a tidal wave that stole her breath, sent her mind spinning, and then he bit down on her shoulder and the wave crashed, drowning her in bliss as she came hard. Body contracting under him, around him, clenching tight as she cried out against the sheet.

Ecstasy washed the world away and left her floating in warmth.

Under him, safe, in the perfect gray between light and dark.

"That's right," he purred, slowing his strokes until he was teasing the flickering edges of her orgasm with each sinful pulse of his hips. His tongue traced the bite in her shoulder, but she could barely feel the ache of it as he settled over her, moving deep. "I know what you need."

Lianna nodded, a desperate whimper slipping from her as he found that bundle of nerves inside with crippling precision and thrust harder. Building her up again, slower this time, and she mumbled incoherent pleas into the bed with each snap of his hips. It made her nerves tingle as he woke her back up, pulled her up from the sated pool he'd put her in until she was squirming under him again.

Releasing her hands he shifted, stroking down her sides, squeezing her hips, before kneading the bruised and welted skin of her ass as he slid from her. She gasped, and felt his weight shift on the bed, confusion clouding her already scattered mind — until the click of the lube bottle opening made her tense.

"That's right. You know you want this." He laughed low, one hand in the small of her back to keep her in place as he settled back between her thighs. Then a slippery thumb rolled around the entrance of her ass, and she whined, clenching her jaw as he pressed in.

Lube is a gift, angel. I don't have to use it.

He had told her that once before, but she was still struggling with him fucking her ass, no matter how much the idea turned her on when he said it to her in that low, rumbling tone. The one that made her wet and turned his tawny eyes dark.

"Relax," he commanded, spanking her with his other hand, which only woke up the welts and made her tense harder. She shook her head as he slid his thumb in and out, his other hand squeezing and pinching the marks he'd delivered with the belt. Then he said the magic words, "Do you think you have a choice here, angel?"

The question sent a shiver through her, woke up the darkness inside, beckoned her closer with sinful promises. His thumb popped free and she pushed forward on the bed on instinct, but he grabbed her hips and jerked her back, *tsk*ing low.

"I said I'm not done," he hissed as he braced one hand between her shoulders and pressed against the tight ring of muscles. A choked cry slipped from her as he leaned forward, letting his weight, his strength, the sheer power of him, force his cock inside. It was an impossible stretch, a burn, a pain that spread with each inch. She locked up, and he groaned behind her, the sound devolving into a

273

guttural growl. His hand moved to the back of her neck, pinning her down as he twitched his hips forward, driving in deeper.

She whined, voice cracking as he slid back and thrust harder. When she reached back to stop the next, he caught her wrist and pinned it to her back, crushing her to the bed.

"Take it," he snarled, and then he started to fuck her in deep, brutal strokes. Tears came to her eyes, pinned under him, only able to snag shallow breaths with the weight of him holding her wrist to her back. And yet, the darkness swelled, purred deep inside her, rewarded her as the pain faded and she gave in to the power of him. The predator taking his prey, pure animal instinct taking over as he filled her again and again.

Her body buzzed with the after effects of the pain, the delirious hum in her nerves as he growled behind her, releasing his grip on her to brace himself on the bed. When the first quiet moan slipped from her, he groaned in response, her body tightening around him.

"You like it when I make it hurt, don't you?" he asked, driving deep again, and she cried out, gasped, but found herself nodding. "Say it!"

"I like it!" she shouted, screaming when he fisted her hair and bent her back, forcing her onto her knees to handle it, which only give him a better angle. Let him fuck her more fiercely, as the tingles started to build between her legs.

"You like it when I fuck your tight little asshole? Make you scream, and beg, and come for me?"

"YES!" Her scream echoed back on the walls as he

released her hair and buried his hand between her thighs, finding her clit, and it was what she needed. It turned the ache and the strain into something so much better, something dark and tempting and dangerous.

Just like him.

"Please! *Please!*" she begged, and he groaned behind her, filling her ass as he teased that bundle of nerves until she panted and whimpered and the world narrowed down to sparkling lights and the sensation of his cock swelling inside her. Then she crashed, shattering into fragments of gasping moans and shaking muscles and exhausted bliss.

David collapsed against her back, pressing deeper for a moment as he breathed hard, and she tried to come down from the high, but she was floating. Body tingling, and surfing along an overdose of dopamine and endorphins and every other chemical her body had been capable of providing.

When he dropped to her side, his hand stroking her ribs, she let go completely.

David

His heart was trying to burrow out of his chest one beat at a time, still dizzy from the powerful orgasm that had almost left him too disoriented to avoid crushing her to the bed. As he worked to slow his breathing, he found himself grinning, laughter sneaking out with each heavy exhale. When he turned to check on Lianna he found her eyes closed, ass still draped over the pillows, arm tucked close to her side, with her hand near her chin.

Fucking beautiful.

Her reddened lips were parted. Even, shallow breaths passing over them like a whisper. Dark smears of eyeliner and mascara swept under her eyes from the tears, and he couldn't help but shake his head as he lay back on the bed again. She'd passed out, and she'd earned it.

She was fucking perfect.

Fearless. Strong. Brave, and impossibly sexy.

How the fuck had he ended up with her? Here? In this place where she let him do these things?

For the millionth time, the billionth time he felt the never-ending war inside him between guilt and regret. There was no doubt in his mind that if he could do it all over, go back to the night when he'd turned off the alarm system and broken into the apartment — that he would still take her. Still kidnap her. Still rip her out of that false life, away from the bastard who may have fathered her, but had never really earned the title.

No, he didn't regret that at all.

Didn't even completely regret the things he had done to her in the cell, the things that had put his darkness inside her, the things that made her come like she had just now.

But the fucking guilt was still there. Like a sharp thing he'd swallowed that was slowly tearing its way through his insides, impossible to remove as it tangled in his organs and blood vessels.

He'd felt it when he'd come back with the groceries. Seeing the tension in her face, the strain of her voice as she'd struggled to maintain her controlled corporate voice with the lawyer — but he could sense her fear when she'd asked if they would press charges against her. Of all things, he knew her fear best of all.

And it was all because of him.

He *could* have left her there. He *could* have left it alone like Harry had begged him to, and he *could* have moved on with his life. Abandoned his father's crusade, his crusade, and let the world keep turning. None of this shit would be happening if he'd just left it alone.

But then Mercier would have killed more people, would have eventually roped Lianna into the nightmare and corrupted her, and he wouldn't be with her now. Would never have known there was someone on this fucked up planet that was his match. The other half of his coin.

All of her light, and all of his darkness.

Just as much as he'd tainted her, ruined her life like he'd promised, fed her darkness until she was someone who came while he fucked her ass, after he'd belted her, after he'd pinned her down and taken her like an animal... she was affecting him too.

You're being domestic again.

It was true, and the fact that he liked it, that he enjoyed making her meals, watching her eat, tucking her into bed, and being there for her while she dealt with the shitstorm he'd created — it meant he was changing too.

Lianna liked to describe it as a coin, that they were two sides of the same one. Except he'd spent his whole life face down, in the dark, and she'd only ever had the light. But the same history shaped them both, they had the same story, the same world, it was just they'd only had half of it.

And now they were knitting them together. Building a new future out of the wreckage he'd caused, with some of the light, and some of the dark.

And the two of them.

Leaning over, he pressed a kiss to her temple, careful not to wake her, and then he slid off the bed. Pulling the pillows free, and tugging the covers up over her shoulders so he could grab a shower. As he stripped in the bathroom he thought about his last call with Harry, about the word moving through the underbelly of the world that Lianna had never even touched.

Her hands were still so clean. Everything about her still so innocent, even with all of the knowledge she had now, even with the hint of darkness he'd put inside her. She was still so fucking *good*, and he wanted to keep her that way.

Had sworn to Harry that he'd protect her, that he'd die before anything happened to her.

His angel was fighting her battles in courtrooms and boardrooms, and he would fight the battles she couldn't see. The ones in the streets, and the gutters, and the darkness.

Because the last thing he would allow was for the Faure family to have her.

No matter how much they wanted her.

THE END

End Notes

I really hope you all enjoyed this dark romance as much as I enjoyed writing it. Lianna and David have such a fun dynamic to explore, and I'm not done with them yet! There is plenty more drama to come, and Lianna's trouble is only just beginning.

Their next book, tentatively titled 'Inheritance', will come out in 2018. Depending on what these crazy characters do it may be a duet, or possibly a trilogy. Either way, you'll get to dive back into the dark and twisted fun of these two again!

Keep reading for an EXCLUSIVE sneak peek at the unedited Chapter One of the next book!

I'm so grateful for all of you, lovelies! Make sure to tell me if you're looking forward to the rest of their story.

<3 Jennifer Bene

A sneak peek at Chapter One of 'Inheritance'!

Eight Months Later

Pulling another page of the newspaper free, Lianna folded it around a coffee cup, tucking the excess paper inside, before she nestled it in the box with its brothers. One more cup and that shelf was empty. Which meant she was possibly five percent of the way there. Staring at all the open cabinets, she sighed and grabbed her wine glass.

There were boxes everywhere. Most of them still open, because she couldn't figure out how much to put in a box, or *what* to put in each box.

It's not like she'd ever packed herself before.

David had rolled his eyes when she'd told him. *Time to learn, angel,* he'd said, before handing her the packing tape. He had showed her how to tape off the bottom of the box *before* she put shit in it, and then he'd gone to work.

She was supposed to have one room finished by the time he got home, but there was no way in hell that was going to happen. It felt impossible. Too overwhelming to pack her whole life into boxes.

Especially the ones marked *sell* and *donate*.

Going through her closet had added a few things to each, but on top of everything else going on... it was more tempting to empty the last bit of wine in the bottle and open another one to keep drinking. Getting drunk before six o'clock in the evening was normal, right?

"Fuck," she muttered under her breath and walked out of the kitchen. Moving past the scattered boxes, she paused before the floor to ceiling windows, watching the sun drooping low in the sky, peeking between two skyscrapers as it painted the world orange.

Only a week and she'd never see this view again.

Her twenty-fourth floor, corner apartment had a panoramic view of the city. It had been what sold her on the place the moment she'd walked inside. Not the custom cabinets, or marble countertops, or high-end appliances… it was *this*. The wide view of the city that wrapped behind the fake fireplace, high enough that the noise of the city faded, suspended like a bird flying high in the sky. As she stepped closer to the edge, planting her toes on the metal window sill, she looked down at the street far below and for a moment it *felt* like she was up in the air. Hovering on the wind so high above the cars and people that the world faded away which was a stupid thought. She wasn't flying anywhere, wasn't escaping. This was her new reality.

Pulling herself away from the window, she swallowed a mouthful of wine. The apartment wasn't huge, but it was hers. She had paid for it out of her own money, her own paychecks from Mercier Systems. Back then, it had mattered to have something that *she* could claim instead of something her father handed her. Even if the job that supplied the paychecks had been, even if every dollar was tainted. She had still *earned* it.

Not like that mattered anymore.

Groaning, Lianna walked back into the kitchen to pour the rest of the wine in her glass, tossing the bottle in the recycling. She had just opened a drawer of kitchen utensils to continue packing when she heard a series of knocks on the door. Laughing under her breath, she shut the drawer.

"Did you get more groceries? I told you that we needed to do take out for" Ripping open the door she saw a tall man with light brown hair, and he smiled at her as she reminded herself to speak. "Um, hi. I think you have the wrong apartment. This is 2402."

"I don't have the wrong apartment, Lianna." The use of her name in that subtle French accent sent a chill down her spine, and she tried to slam the door but he nudged his foot into the gap.

"Move," she demanded, wishing she'd agreed to keep a gun in the apartment.

"I am only here to talk, *mon oisillon*. My name is Jean-Luc Faure."

Lianna's world spun, her grip on the door easing, and she parted it just enough to look into his face as he stepped backwards, hands lifted by his shoulders.

"I am alone, and I just want to speak with you."

"Why?"

"Because I was never able to meet you while your father was alive, and you are my niece. May I come inside?"

Everything about him seemed designed to make her feel comfortable. He wore a light peacoat, a simple button-down shirt, and dark jeans. No high-end suit, no intimidating expression or tone to his voice. Opening the door a little more she looked down the hall and saw no one else.

"I assure you, I am alone as I said."

"What do you want?" she asked, still bracing one foot behind the door.

"I just want to know you, and for you to know us. That is all." Jean-Luc sighed, and then pulled off his coat to offer it through the gap in the door. "Here, search my coat."

As she took it in her hands, he pulled out the pockets of his jeans to show they were empty, and then turned around to slowly lift out a cellphone and wallet from his back pockets. Lianna didn't pull her eyes from him as she blindly slid her hands into the pockets of the coat, before searching along the inside for any hidden ones. "I'm keeping this, and those, until you leave."

"Of course." He held out the phone and wallet and she snatched them.

"Lift the back of your shirt."

"Ah, you are intelligent." Jean-Luc Faure turned around again and pulled his shirt free of his pants, showing only his back, and as he turned to face her again she saw his stomach. No gun. He dropped the fabric and held his arms out. "I am not here to hurt you, Lianna. I just want to talk, to get to know you. Can we sit down inside?"

"Show me your ankles too."

He nodded and leaned down to lift one side of his jeans up his calf, and then the other. "Shall we?" he asked as he stood tall again.

"Fine," she mumbled as she finally stepped back from the door, letting it fall open. Lianna backed up towards the kitchen as he walked inside, hands relaxed at his sides, looking around the apartment until his eyes landed on the windows.

"What a lovely view," he mused as he strode towards the

windows, deftly avoiding the boxes haphazardly placed across the tile.

She dropped his things on the bar, and moved to close the front door, an uncomfortable realization closing in as she faced him. "How exactly did you get up here?"

"You mean how did I get past your doorman?" The man turned back to the windows, bracing his hands on his hips as he stared into the setting sun. "It really was not complicated, which is a concern. I simply told the man that I was your uncle, and was here to surprise you for your birthday... which is in three weeks, if I recall correctly."

October 4th. He was right, and she almost gave him the date, but instead she just stared at his back, mulling over the fact that her building security had let him inside. "And he just believed you?"

"I had photographs of you and your father, photographs of him and I, but they are downstairs with my men in the lobby." He shrugged slightly and turned around, back to the warm, red-gold of the setting sun. "I only want to speak with you, Lianna."

"You've said that. But I know who you are, *Jean-Luc Faure.* You're the head of the Faure family, and I'm not stupid enough to think you're here just to talk."

"So your father *did* tell you about us before he died?"

"I want to know why you're really here," she replied, avoiding the question as she took a few steps forward, trying to hide the trembling in her limbs by crossing her arms.

"Would you believe that I have been asking Alain I apologize *Robert* to let you meet us for years? Decades, actually. I flew to the US when I heard you were born, but he only let me inside his flat for a moment." Jean-Luc paused, smiling slightly as he seemed to reminisce. "I heard you crying, looked around to see where you were, but your father told me to leave."

"Why would you do that? Why would you want to see me when I was an infant, or now for that matter?"

He laughed softly and spread his arms. "Lianna, you are my niece. My family. Why would I *not* want to know you? My own children want to know you. My wife. Your cousins, your uncle Marc. Everyone wants to meet Alain's daughter."

"Why?" she hissed, even though she felt like a broken record.

"Because family is very important to us, and you have been a missing piece for too long," he answered smoothly, the hint of his French accent making the words into a teasing offer.

"*Right*," Lianna huffed, turning to grab her wine from the kitchen. When she stepped back out, he was sitting on the couch, arms braced on his knees as he looked up at her.

"Wine? You are definitely a Faure." He smiled broadly and sat up. "May I join you?"

"No."

Jean-Luc shook his head a little, still smiling, before resting his hands in his lap. "That's fine. I understand why you may have reservations, which makes it even more important that we speak. Will you sit?"

"I don't know what you expect to happen here, but I'll give

you ten minutes to tell me whatever it is." Moving to the chair, she sat down and crossed her legs, suddenly remembering she was in yoga pants and a t-shirt with no bra. *Not a great outfit to meet the leader of your evil family.*

"Alright, then I'll be blunt. We have a family estate in Provence that I would like you to visit, at my expense of course." He laughed quietly. "I may have accidentally told my children that I was going to visit their cousin in the US and invite you back, so of course everyone knows now. The last text message I received was from my youngest daughter, Emilie, asking what day the party would be, and"

"I'm not going to France with you!" she cut him off, raising her voice. "Are you insane? Did you not hear me before? *I know who you are.* You run all of it, the whole damn Faure family. Why on earth would I want to get involved with you?"

"I understand that my arrival came as a shock. I had planned to come earlier, but I knew that you had enough to deal with and that this could wait."

"Exactly! I have enough shit going on without being connected to you." Standing, she gestured to the door. Feeling foolish for ever letting him in the door. "I think it's time for you to go."

"Lianna," Jean-Luc said her name with a smile, and didn't move an inch. "Things are not going well for you here. Let me help. Let me introduce you to the family your father kept you from. There is nothing like having family to lean on in times of trouble."

"I'm not interested."

He sighed, the smile finally fading from his face as he seemed to debate over his next words. "I know this was a surprise, and I apologize for that. My wife, Cécile, wanted me to call first, but I thought it was better to be face to face. Honestly, I should have brought her with me. She is so much better than I am at talking to people…" Shrugging, he brought his hands together with a quiet clap. "But I thought it would be less overwhelming if it were just me. My mistake, *mon oisillon.* I will go for now."

"You should just go home," Lianna replied, watching as he stood.

"I have other business to attend to in the city. Perhaps we can have lunch before I leave?"

"I don't think so."

"Alright, Lianna, perhaps next time." He offered his hand as he approached her, but she didn't take it, and he nodded as he let it fall to his side. "I do wish you had taken the job with Sotheby's in Lyon. I think you would have really enjoyed it."

"How" Lianna started to ask how he knew about the job, but the sound of the door unlocking and opening made her turn. Flat boxes came through the door first, and then David with a plastic bag on one arm.

"Hey, angel! How is packing going?" he asked loudly as he set the boxes against the bar, and then he froze when he turned around. It only took a second before he had his gun out and pointed at Jean-Luc. "What the fuck is"

Raising her hand to stop him, she spoke quickly. "It's okay. I'm fine and he's leaving."

"I am leaving. Sorry to disturb you both, I simply wanted

to meet Lianna." Jean-Luc Faure had his hands up again, stepping away from her toward the door, while David tracked him with the gun. "I would appreciate if you could lower the gun. I am unarmed. Ask Lianna."

"It's true, I checked. He doesn't have a weapon, and those are his things behind you." Approaching David, she squeezed his arm before she gathered the man's coat and items. "He hasn't done anything, I promise," she whispered.

"You need to go," David growled, lowering the weapon, but he kept both hands on it and a finger on the trigger. "Now."

Handing everything to Jean-Luc, Lianna nodded. "I agree, it's time for you to leave."

"Of course. Let me just leave you my card." Flipping open his wallet, her uncle pulled out a business card and held it towards her. "Please, call me if you're willing to meet this week. Both of you are invited."

"Out," David snapped.

Jean-Luc smiled, reminding her too much of her father for a moment as she took the card from his fingers. "I am glad to know Lianna has someone watching out for her. I wish you both a good night." He opened the door and then held it to look back at her. "You deserve to know your family, Lianna. That's all I want for you."

"Good night," she answered and he stepped into the hall.

As soon as the door shut, David moved to it with the gun at his side, locking the deadbolt and then peering through the peephole for a moment. Finally, he turned around and tucked the gun into the back of his pants as he approached, tension etched into the lines of his face. "Did he touch you?" he asked, cupping her cheeks in his hands.

"No, I'm fine. I promise."

"Fuck," he muttered as he pulled her against his chest, arms wrapped around her back as he hugged her tight. "Do you have any idea who that was?"

Hugging him back, she nodded. "Jean-Luc Faure, he introduced himself."

"Then why the hell did you let him in?" David asked, holding her by the shoulders as he pulled back.

"I don't know. He surprised me, and he *was* alone and unarmed. I just *dammit.* I guess I wanted to know what he had to say, what he wanted. And just before you got here he mentioned a job in Lyon that I'd been looking at last year, and I still have so many questions." She sighed heavily, touching his arm as she met the tawny brown of his eyes. "I promise I was smart."

"That was *not* smart," he growled, and then he kissed her, tongue teasing at her lips until they were tangled in each other. One strong arm behind her back, a hand in her messy ponytail, as she clung to him with Jean-Luc's business card crushed against her palm. David nipped her lip one more time before leaning his forehead against hers. "Swear to me you won't go anywhere near him."

"David…"

"No." His fist tightened in her hair until she hissed air between her teeth, forced to look into his eyes. "Promise."

"Fine. I promise." Before she'd even finished the word he

was kissing her again, turning them until he could press her against the wall.

"I would lose my mind if something happened to you, angel." His hands roamed her curves, lifting her shirt to skate his fingers over her waist. Pressing kisses to her throat, he moved his touch higher until he could cup her breasts and tease her nipples into hard points. "I would kill them all."

"Talk about not smart," she mumbled breathily as arousal blurred her thoughts. "There's no need to make an enemy of him. He just wanted me to meet his family."

"Right." David scoffed before he moved his hands upward to rip her shirt over her head. "You don't want to get involved with them, angel. Trust me."

"I know," she answered, but her thumb brushed over the card in her hand, and she could feel the raised text on it. His number.

"How about I help you get your mind off of it?" Grinning, he grabbed the top of her yoga pants and tugged her closer. "I can help you relax."

"Oh, really..." Humming heat was steadily replacing the nervous energy inside her, and she practically purred when he slid his hand lower to brush her clit. "You going to play nice?"

David chuckled softly. "That depends, angel."

"On what?"

He increased the pressure of those sinfully swirling fingers, and she grabbed onto him as her hips twisted, seeking more and trying to escape at the same time. David leaned closer to whisper against her ear. "On how much packing you got done today."

Shit. Lianna blushed, but couldn't hold back the smile. "Well, about that…"

That's all for the sneak peek, lovelies! Can't wait for more? Tell me, I want to hear from you!

Acknowledgments

There are so many people I want to thank for their support on this book. First, I have to thank my incredible PA, Michelle Brown, for putting up with me and not murdering me when I surprised her with this release. (Sorry, lady!) Honestly, without her you guys wouldn't have it right now because I'd never have had the time to write it as quickly as I did if she didn't help keep my life organized.

Along the same lines, I have to thank Niki Roge who helps me and Michelle out, and always has my back. You two ladies make all the gears turn behind the scenes, and I love you both! CIRCLE OF TRUST!

And then there's Myra Danvers and Addison Cain. I'd be an idiot not to thank you guys for encouraging me and supporting me, and reading this book over to make sure I wasn't crazy. Not sure what I'd do without my chaos demon and my dark soul sister.

Oh, I should *probably* thank my Dom for always supporting my writing, loving my anti-heroes, and encouraging me to keep going. He's pretty fantastic, and provides some excellent inspiration.

Huge thanks to Laura Hidalgo of Beyond DEF Lit for coming in at the 11th hour with the most gorgeous cover. Your skill is beyond impressive, lovely, and you are a dream to work with!

To my ARC team, I just have to say that I hope you lovelies forgive me for springing this new release on you! I adore each and every one of your dark and twisty hearts.

Finally, all of the lovely individuals on the *Dirty Subs* street team, those in the Dark Haven, and those in the Dark and Dirty Romance Book Club thank you guys for helping me to spread the word, helping new readers find me, and for supporting me through all the insanity this year!

You all make this adventure worth every minute.

About the Author

Jennifer Bene is a USA Today bestselling author of erotic romance. She's been in the Amazon Top 50, and had #1 top-selling books in BDSM, Suspense, Thrillers, Action & Adventure, Fantasy, Science Fiction, and Horror. While she's been writing for years, it's always been the dark stuff that makes her tingly, so her books are full of aggressive alpha males, feisty women who may or may not have a submissive streak, and intense, psychological story lines. Don't worry though, she always insists on having a nice little happily-ever-after, because without the dark we'd never appreciate the light.

Want to get a FREE book, news about upcoming releases, giveaways, appearances, and more? Sign up for her mailing list!

Website - https://jenniferbene.com/

Facebook - https://www.facebook.com/jbeneauthor

Author Facebook Page - https://www.facebook.com/jenniferbeneauthor/

Twitter - https://twitter.com/jbeneauthor

Books by Jennifer Bene

Dark / BDSM Erotic Romance:

Security Binds Her (Thalia Book 1)

Striking a Balance (Thalia Book 2)

Salvaged by Love (Thalia Book 3)

Of Fog and Fire (Parts I & II)

Taken by the Enemy

Lethal Sin (Dangerous Games Book 1)

Early Sins (Dangerous Games Book 0)

Black Light: Exposed (Black Light Series Book 2)

Tying the Knot (Thalia Book 4)

Destruction

Dark / Paranormal Romance:

Fae (Daughters of Eltera Book 1)

Tara (Daughters of Eltera Book 2)

BDSM Erotic Romance Novellas:

The Invitation

The Rite

Christmas at Purgatory (Thalia Extra #1)

<u>Reunited</u>

Anthology Appearances:

<u>The Dark Forest: A Collection of Erotic Fairytales</u>

<u>Black Light: Valentine Roulette (Black Light Series Book 3)</u>

<u>Royally Mine</u>

78603794R00182

Made in the USA
Middletown, DE
04 July 2018